The Natanleods
Book 17

Prodigals

By
Sunbow Pendragon

"2023"

To Teresa

Love & Light B

Sunbow Pendragon

Acknowledgements

To the Divine Universe and the beings who run it, I say thank you for the gift you have granted to me. I hope how I am using it pleases You, and that the gift will continue to be granted. So be it.

Table of Contents

Chapter 1

"Once more my friends, and let us have at them!" the High Lord called out, motioning for them to go through. Erinn wore a look of fierce determination as he walked through the portal, closing and locking it behind him.

"My dear," he called out to his wife upon their arrival. "Perhaps we should allow the *bait* to go first," he grinned.

"I would be honored to lead," Deborah answered, her voice strong and fierce. "Shall we go to it, Dames and Knights? I feel as if the day will be a hot one before too long. I should like to be done with all of this before then. Forward then, and May the Goddess be with us! Daughters, if ye would please accompany me?" she called out in a ringing tone before turning and approaching the edge of the Crevasse. Reaching out with her senses, Deborah searched for anything out of the ordinary, finding only deadly quiet. No birds sang, the wind was silent, and even the murmuring of the Army around them seemed muted. Finally she felt the presence of steel, a huge thick chunk, and focused her attention on it. It was a door, she soon discovered, and it was locked tightly. A cold smile passed over her face as she probed the lock, finding it very complicated, making it a difficult task. A half-grin quirked at the corner of her mouth as the most practical solution presented itself to her, and with a simple gesture the door flew off its hinges with a loud explosion, landing close to where the raiding party stood waiting.

"What was that?" they heard a scream from within the huge chamber behind the door.

"Yer death," Deborah answered back, and the two guards at the door found themselves confronted by skilled, fierce warriors, not the common folk they were expecting. The raiding party moved in after her, spreading out through the chamber, which was a huge gas pocket formed by some past volcanic activity, and the sound of an alarm began to echo throughout the entire facility.

"Hunters and Huntresses, deal with those clerics on the upper level!" Deborah ordered, seeing the skilled mages entering the fray. "Scouts, take care of those guards over there! The rest of ye, deal with that mob!" she continued on, and Erinn grinned to hear her issue commands so easily. She was a natural leader, and those in the raiding party simply acknowledged her as such, following her orders as if they were Erinn's.

Chaos ensued as the two parties engaged in battle, screams of pain and death filled the chamber, blood ran on the floor and people ran here and there looking for an escape, finding none. Only those who gave no resistance, and picked up no weapons were spared, allowing themselves to be herded into a side chamber and requiring no guard to hold them there.

The noise level continued to rise as Drake transformed into a huge black dragon and took flight, heading up to where the star portal hung. With a huge burst of dragonfire he set it alight before continuing on, setting each of the large star ships ablaze, laughing deep in his throat to see them destroyed.

At length, a huge door opened somewhere within the cavern, they could feel the current of the air increase, and into the death chamber strode a tall, Elven-looking man. His long silver hair was braided elaborately, he wore the clothing of a king, and he looked a little bit like Athaniar. His voice was thunderous as he spoke his objections to the raid.

"What is going on here?" he shouted out angrily. "Who are ye, what do ye want?" he went on, screaming at the top of his voice as he scanned the room. His eyes finally lit upon Deborah, and recognition flared at once. "YE!" he screamed out, moving towards her. "YE ARE MINE!!!"

"I think not, worm!" she called back merrily. "Ye are too late, I have chosen my mate."

"I AM YER MATE!" he called back. "I am Abbadon, King of all the Naga. Ye were created for me, and me alone! Come to me!"

Deborah laughed loud and long, a fierce note to it. "May I present him to ye?" she asked, and her voice changed a bit, taking on a cold, almost cruel note as she motioned for Erinn, and he approached, kneeling at her feet before standing at her side. "My husband, Erinn Natanleod, the High Lord of the Land!"

"*ERINN?*" Abbadon screeched.

"Aye, Erinn Natanleod, son of Drake Natanleod," Erinn reinforced, a huge grin on his face at seeing the Naga's consternation. "Ye have not been paying very close attention for the last twenty years or so, have ye?" he asked casually.

"Why should I?" Abbadon asked haughtily. "I left trusted agents to do my will."

"O, ye mean all of those I have slain over the last twenty years?" Erinn asked. "Raad is dead, Secundus too, and so many of yer trusted allies, including Nateri. I watched my wife burn her from the inside out, a very satisfying experience, I must say," he went on, producing a sikar and lighting it casually.

"Nateri... is dead?"

"Aye, along with all of her minions. If ye scan the Land, ye will find ye are missing most of yer allies, if not all," Erinn laughed. While Erinn continued to engage the Naga Lord, Deborah was being ignored completely, and she used that to her advantage. With Calla and Lillith beside her, she worked her way around to the other side of Abbadon, and prepared to take action, warning her daughters to stay back.

"He is mine, for all of the harm he has done to the Land!" they heard her say in a hoarse whisper, noting that her voice sounded just a little different. Glancing at her, they noticed her eyes were amber, and that her hair was completely red, the heat of her aura shimmering around her in waves.

Meanwhile Abbadon had lost patience with the conversation he was having with Erinn.

"I am done talking to ye, I shall have what is mine!" he screamed out, beginning to change into his full Naga form. Had he looked before doing so, he might have been spared, but his arrogance was on full display. As the change began, Deborah's sword whistled out, catching him just before the seven heads of his natural form appeared. The sword sang, and Abbadon's head parted from his neck neatly, leaving the Naga body writhing but intact.

"A Masterstroke!" she heard Drake's voice behind her.

"I agree," Erinn's voice joined in as they stood behind her. "My dear, are ye well?" he asked softly as she stood there, holding the sword and breathing heavily. Her eyes were still amber, her hair still fiery red, and waves of heat continued to radiate out from where she stood, watching the last of the death throes.

"He is dead, at last!" Deborah said in an exulted tone. "Abbadon, the evil one is dead. Perhaps now, the Land will be at peace!" she laughed low in her throat as her hair began to return to its usual raven black. "I am very thirsty, are we done here?" bringing a smile to Erinn's face.

"What say ye, War Duke? Are we done here?"

"We have captives, My Lord!" Karpon called out in response. "And we have dead to dispose of. We have lost no one of our group, bless the Goddess!"

"Very well!" Erinn returned. "Ishmael ben Cain!" he called out, summoning the huge Moorish man.

"Aye, My Lord!" he responded.

"I have a task for yer skills. I want the entire skin," Erinn ordered. "And please prepare it for boots. I want my daughters and my wife to have matching sets. Also, I want the head for my trophy room, and I would like ye to use yer skills in Taxidermy in the cause. Be sure ye preserve the look of fear and confusion 'tis wearing right now, aye?"

"Very well, My Lord," Ishmael nodded, understanding what Erinn wanted. It did not take the experienced man very long to strip the hide from the flaccid body of the Naga Lord, and once it and the head were properly rolled and bundled for transport, he announced he was ready to go.

By that time, the dead had been gathered into a pile, and Erinn made ready to set the rude pyre alight, until a shouting could be heard.

"Please, let us out, let us out! We are trapped in here!"

"Follow that shouting! We must discover what is happening!" Erinn ordered. Zameera and her group ran to do his bidding, and once the situation was uncovered, she sent a runner back to Erinn with a report.

"My Lord, the kitchen staff has barricaded themselves into the kitchen, and because of the battle, they cannot escape. The doors will not operate."

"I shall attend to that," Erinn nodded, walking to the pair of swinging doors that led into the kitchen. Putting his hands on the handles, he pulled sharply, using his magickal abilities to clear the obstruction blocking it. The doors fell off their hinges revealing a group of about thirty people huddled at the back of the room. All of them were armed with knives or spears, and they looked ready to defend themselves.

"Stand down," Erinn ordered softly. "I am the High Lord, Erinn Natanleod. Ye are safe, if ye are not Nagas."

"I did everything in my power to keep my people from being implanted with one of those... *things*," one of them said, standing and extending his hand for the Grip. "I am the Kitchen Master here. My name is Geoffrey."

"Master Geoffrey," Erinn smiled, taking his arm and sharing the exchange between them. "Are ye and yer people ready to leave this place?"

"Most assuredly, My Lord," the man grinned wide. "I am glad not to have to serve them any longer. Ye see, these people are all my family; wife, sons, daughters, cousins and I even have my two uncles working with me. 'Twas the only way I could watch out for them properly, and keep them safe from the Naga's deviousness."

"Ye have certainly earned a reward for doing so," Erinn replied.

"I wish no other reward than to be allowed to serve yer House, My Lord," Geoffery said at once.

"We also!" his family chimed in. Erinn's eyebrows rose a bit, and a warm expression appeared on his face for the first time that day. "Very well," he said. "I am certain that the Lady has plans for all of ye then. Black Dragons, escort these people out of the battle zone!" he called out and several of the burly Knights stepped forward and surrounded the group. As Erinn watched, Geoffery and his family were summarily marched out of the place, then taken across the Crevasse to where the rest of the captives were waiting.

"Are all of our people out?" Deborah asked tersely, her hair now fully aflame again.

"Indeed, My Lady, we are all ready to go now," Karpon answered respectfully, mindful of the waves of heat emanating from the High Lady.

"Good, then take our people and go, My Lord. I still have work to do before I cease my labors today. The Naga's handiwork must be destroyed utterly, and I intend to do just that."

"I shall take great pleasure in watching ye work, My Lady," Erinn replied formally, kissing the palm of her hand when she answered his touch. She waited until the entire scouting party were across the Crevasse before she began her work, seeking the pockets of hot gas and molten rock lurking behind the thick walls of the canyon. Finally, she found what she needed, and with a thought, she opened the way for it to flow into the vast cavern in which she stood. Once the molten rock began to flow, it was unstoppable, tearing through the rock that had long restrained it and melting the metals of the Naga's mechanical devices, returning them to the Goddess from whom they had been stolen. Deborah could hear the Elementals singing as the cavern filled with hot rock, and just as it reached her feet, she rose on flaming wings and soared out of the gaping hole. Hovering there for just a bit, she waited for the molten flood to flow out of the hole, and then she began her work once more, slowing the flood and cooling the rock so that it sealed the entrance entirely. Once it cooled, it would blend in with the rest of the landscape, so that no one would ever know it had been there at all. Up she flew, until she was high over the Crevasse, so that her view would be the best in order to spot anything else that might be amiss. She saw and felt naught, and so allowed herself to land a few yards away from where the scouting party stood watching her, all of them silent with shock and wonder. The flames around her died back nearly at once, and then Erinn was there nearly at once to greet her, reaching around her with a steadying arm.

"Are ye well, My Lady?" he asked softly.

"I am, but I am mightily thirsty, My Lord," she answered with a grin. "As well, I am covered with sweat, and Naga blood, which I would like to wash off. Perhaps we should return to the Capitol City, so that the victory can be celebrated by all?" she suggested.

"Very well," Erinn smiled. "Are ye well enough to travel quickly?"

"As long as I do not have to provide the portal," she laughed a bit. "I can stand by myself for a bit," she added in a whisper.

"Black Dragons, Hunters and Huntresses, Scouts, prepare for our return to the Capitol City!" Erinn called out, a huge smile on his face. "Ye were promised beef and ale, and I am longing for both! Come on now, step closer, so we can all travel together."

Geoffery and his group had no idea what Erinn was talking about, nonetheless, they allowed themselves to be gathered up with the rest of those around them. Standing expectantly, they were shocked to see the whirling circle of light appear, and even more shocked to see the Capitol City on the other side of it. Encouraged by their companions, they all walked through the gate, leaving behind little trace of their presence at the Crevasse. The empty houses and inns remained, awaiting the arrival of new owners and operators, now that the way would be safe once more.

Upon arriving just outside the Barracks entrance to the High Lord's House, the group entered the building after observing the proper protocols.

"Who wishes to enter the Army Barracks?" they were challenged, as anyone would be.

"I am the High Lord, Erinn Natanleod, with my wife the High Lady, and we have returned from a very successful scouting mission up at the Crevasse. If ye will allow us to enter, I have promised a meal of ale and beef to those who participated."

"But Sir!" the young man responded. "Master Klietos already has beef cooking outside!"

"Does he now?" Erinn grinned, glad for the man's foresight. "Well then, I should go and thank him. May we enter?"

"O! Of course!" the young man stammered a bit, having strayed a bit from his duties. "Come in and be welcome, My Lord and My Lady! Congratulations on a successful scouting mission!"

They entered the Barracks to a roar of acclaim, their feat underscored by the blood and sweat on their uniforms. It did not take long for those of the Army to escort the soldiers away, allowing Erinn and Deborah to retreat upstairs to their room for some peace and quiet.

"Today was a great victory," Erinn said quietly to his wife. Deborah's hair was still bright red, but he could see small streaks of black beginning to appear. "Are ye ready for some wine?"

"Whiskey please," she answered, walking to the bath and turning the spigot to allow it to fill. "And a sikar. I need to get the taste of dealing with Abbadon out of my mouth. Disgusting pig, to think that... that I would mate with... *that*! Ugh!" she spat. Erinn brought her a cup of mellow, aged whiskey, as well as a pair of small sikars, then sat with her while she bathed.

"Aren't ye going to clean up?" she asked.

"I did not work nearly as hard as ye did, my dear," Erinn smiled thinly. "Are ye well?"

"I am, and today's events have turned out spectacularly well," Deborah answered in a satisfied tone. "Our daughters were fearless today, they both entered the enemy's lair and remained who they are."

"Of course they did," Erinn smiled. "They are our daughters now, what they were before has naught to do with it."

Her hair was indeed almost completely back to its usual raven-wing black, but her eyes glittered gold for most of that night. She had been obliged to tap into greater reserves of abilities in order to accomplish her work today, she thought as she used the cloth and soft soap liberally. Once she felt clean enough, Erinn brought her a towel and helped her from the bath, a pleasant experience for both. Deborah took her time dressing, choosing a light silk shift and slippers, along with a light robe, for the night was a bit humid and hot.

"It feels like a thunderstorm out there," she commented a bit later as they snacked on the antipasto brought for them.

"It does indeed, the air is heavy, and I can feel occasional cold drafts," Erinn agreed as he stood by the window. Sending his thoughts to Master Klietos on the party grounds, he made the suggestion that they might start moving their celebration inside.

"Aye, I can feel it," the man agreed as he spoke mentally with Erinn. "We will round them up and get them inside, hopefully before the storm breaks," he laughed a bit.

Almost immediately, Erinn could hear laughing calls go out among the celebrants.

"Heya all, Master Klietos can feel a thunderstorm coming! We best all get inside, unless ye want to be drenched!"

Erinn watched from the window of their room as the feast was gathered up, the tables moved back inside, and the dance floor put away. They were just moving the meat inside when the first peal of thunder rolled over the party grounds. It shook the House a bit due to the force of it, and once it's echoes faded, everyone breathed a thanks to the Goddess. More rumbles continued throughout the night, but nothing like that first one, which kept conversations going all night long about what it might mean.

Erinn and Deborah slept very late the next morning, and woke with the need for privacy. It did not take long to arrange it, and soon they were at the family house in the valley, the nip of Autumn's cold just starting to suggest frost was coming soon.

"I love it here during this season!" Deborah exclaimed upon their arrival. "Feel that? It might frost here tonight!"

"Indeed it might!" Drake's voice was heard, and his head peaked out of the kitchen area. "Hullo ye two. I should have expected ye to arrive today, I suppose."

"Are ye slipping, Father?" Deborah asked with a grin.

"Ye should know better than to ask me that," Drake answered, a serious tone in his humor. "As it so happens, I have just finished cleaning the entire house from top to bottom, feeling as if I should for some reason. I see now the reason, ye two are here for privacy's sake, is it not so?"

"Aye, Father 'tis indeed."

"I see," he grinned knowingly. "Very well, is there aught I can do for ye before I go?"

"And where will ye sleep, Father?" Deborah asked.

"O, in the new cabin I just finished," he replied airily.

"New cabin?"

"Aye, just a small little place up the river a bit, close to the fishing hole," Drake replied grinning widely. "I split all the logs myself, and the house has a "snow peak" to help keep the roof from being compromised. I and Jovita will be quite comfortable there, once I finish furnishing it. At least the bed is done," he grinned mischievously, chuckling low in his throat.

"It sounds very remote, and very private," Deborah smiled warmly. "I am glad that ye and Jovita have such a place. I shall have to make a quilt for yer cabin, something nice and thick and warm."

"I would like that very much!" Drake grinned, kissing her forehead in a fatherly gesture.

"I shall begin as soon as I return to the city," Deborah promised him. "We would not want yer aged bones to feel the cold of full Winter, now would we?"

"Hmph! Aged bones indeed!" Drake grumped good-naturedly before taking his leave.

Once he was gone, the two of them attended to the necessary chores; lighting the boiler for the bath, lighting the hearths throughout the house, and then descending into the cold room to choose their supper.

"I have been eating a great deal of red meat lately," Erinn said as they looked through the larder.

"Chicken or turkey?" Deborah asked at once.

"Turkey, a long, slow meal that leaves us a great deal of leisure time," Erinn answered. "Such a meal is good with either red or white wine, and so will suit whatever appetite we might have later," he grinned.

"Here is a small bird," Deborah suggested, pointing at one that looked to be less than twenty pounds. "Such a bird will make tonight's meal, as well as good slices for an antipasto and a hearty soup."

"Very well then, let us get it upstairs, thawed, seasoned and in the oven, woman!" Erinn urged, wanting to relax as long as possible. It did not take them long to attend to the matter, and soon the bird had been dry rubbed with sage, thyme, *joy of the mountain* and parsley, inside and out. Deborah slipped in two large lemons, both cut in half to provide proper moisture, and then the entire pan was covered with its lid and slipped into the oven. A batch of bread stood rising, and the vegetables for roasting had been washed pared, cut and panned before they left the kitchen, wine carafes in hand.

That night was spent in quiet conversation, Erinn being very attentive to Deborah's moods as he watched the last of the amber disappear at last from her eyes. Finally, after they had feasted on the roasted turkey, vegetables and light cream sauce made from the drippings, they sat back with a final cup of red wine, just watching the flames in the hearth. After what seemed a long time, Erinn glanced over to see her asleep, wine cup cradled carefully to keep the few drops remaining from being spilled. He carefully magicked the cup from her hands, glanced out at the kitchen to assure all was well, and then magickally took them both upstairs for a good night's sleep.

Deborah woke to find herself in bed, snuggled under several quilts, Erinn tending the small stove in the room.

"Ye were right to suspect frost," Erinn chuckled, pulling open the heavy curtains to reveal the growing light of dawn. Deborah gasped to see the snowflakes fluttering here and there, and when she rose, wrapping her thick robe around her, she went right to the window.

"O my! It looks as if it has been snowing all night!" she said with a grin.

"Looks like we are snowed in," Erinn rumbled a bit as he answered, coming to slip an arm around her waist. He was not displeased at this turn of events. "Are ye ready for caffe, or for more sleep?"

"Caffe," Deborah answered emphatically. "And I am going to add Cacao syrup to mine. I feel as if we are on holiday."

Erinn stood there, counting the days, and he suddenly realized that their anniversary was two days hence.

"We *are* on holiday," he grinned. "Our wedding anniversary is two days from today."

"What?"

"Ye are the record keeper, my love," Erinn answered, a note of triumph in his tone at remembering the day. "Ye of all people in the Land should remember such an important day," he went on, teasing her just a bit.

"O my," she said, sitting down heavily on the end of the bed. "I let the date slip my mind, entirely. What is amiss with me?"

"Naught, except that ye vanquished a great enemy of the Land yesterday," Erinn answered softly. "And ye were beautiful while doing so, may I add? 'Twas hard to keep my hands to myself, even in front of all of them," he chuckled.

"O Erinn," she scoffed lightly. "We have been married all this time…"

"And I still feel the same way about ye as I did the first day I saw ye," Erinn answered honestly, coming to sit beside ye. "I thought then ye were the most beautiful woman I had ever seen, and I still think so. We have been through a great deal in the last twenty years, but more awaits us as we continue our rule, *together*. I would have it no other way, but to have you ruling at my side equally."

"As it should be, my love," she answered.

Appearing later in the kitchen, the two of them set about making a quick meal; sausage patties, eggs, toast, and cheese, then Erinn sent a quick message to Gwendolyn at the Capitol House.

"Madam Gwendolyn?"

"Aye, My Lord," he heard her answer in strained tones.

"What is amiss?"

"The slaughter has begun, 'tis a good thing ye and yer lady are at the family house," the Kitchen Mistress answered succinctly. "Happy Anniversary to the both of ye," she added quickly.

"Thank ye, my dear," Erinn replied. "Then ye know why I am contacting ye."

"I do, and ye should just stay up there for a few days," Gwendolyn advised. "The barns are very busy right now, as is the kitchen. And I have the pre-cleaning in preparation for Winter in progress as well."

"We would be in yer way then?"

"Most assuredly. However, ye should have someone assigned to sort yer mail," she reminded.

"Indeed I should," Erinn agreed. "Thank ye Madam."

"Enjoy yer time off," she answered with a giggle, and Erinn caught a mental picture of her stepping aside as buckets of organ meats were delivered to the kitchen. "Ye see, we are swimming in it right now!" Gwendolyn laughed aloud as her crew came to deal with the load of fresh meat.

"Go to it, Madam," Erinn replied, and with a thought, sent her a bit of a reward. Later when she took a break, her hand went automatically to her pocket, finding the silk pouch and the sikar with its beautiful black wrapper. She grinned to see an *Imperial*, a sikar treated liberally with the Lady's oil, and tucked it back into her pocket to wait until her shift was over that day. With a cup of wine or two, she thought gratefully, I can drift off to sleep quickly, and sleep without so much pain. The thought gave her a burst of energy, which she used to finish the supper preparations, turning service over to her closest apprentices.

"Now look sharp, all of ye," she said tiredly. "Tonight is an easy service, just hand pies, soup and salad. The outside tables are set up, and I have kegs of wine and ale in the Elan cooling. 'Tis hotter than ever out there, and humid to boot. Make sure to make up plenty of lemon-ginger water for tonight's service. Hmmm…am I forgetting anything?" she queried of herself. Her apprentices could not help but laugh a bit at her worrying, until Selena came to her side.

"Madam, would ye please go and rest?" she said quietly. "Ye have been at it since early this morning, and the slaughter will continue tomorrow. Ye should just go and leave this to us. We have been training a long time, do ye not trust us?"

Gwendolyn made to answer, then stopped herself, for the words would have been grouchy and unkind. Instead, she saw the Lady's hand at work, and a rueful smile appeared as she answered.

"Ye are correct, all of ye are well-trained enough to take on a meal completely without my supervision. I could send any of ye to any of the noble houses, or to the Temples or to a Shrine, and ye would perform well. I am going to take a nice cool bath, drink some of that bubbly wine and enjoy the rest of the evening. If ye have any questions, ye know where to find me," she smiled, hugging each of them in turn to show her trust.

"Good night," she finished and left the kitchen, forcing herself to do so. It was not until she was almost to her room that the feeling of guilt left her, and it was when she remembered just how old some of her closest apprentices were. Some of them had been with her since the Amazon Fortress, some from even before that, many of them were in their forties and were more than capable of running the kitchen among themselves.

"And 'tis more than likely they will work all the harder to prove that very fact to me," Gwendolyn laughed softly to herself. "I should be more open with my praise. Lady Goddess, help me to remember."

Opening the door to her room, she entered and the bolt slammed home sharply. Gwendolyn was not seen until early the next morning as she returned to the kitchen, finding all in order. Her apprentices were there as well, eating their morning meal, so she sat with them for her caffe and pastry.

"Ye all did well last night, I can tell," Gwendolyn began. "The kitchen is perfectly clean, this morning's service is proceeding apace, and I see that second meal prep is in progress. We could do none of that if the kitchen had not been left in good condition last night. Thank ye all. I feel muchly restored," she grinned.

"Ye are most welcome, Madam!" Selene answered for all of them, since her mouth was empty. Gwendolyn smiled and sighed, wishing she had a reward for all of them as they all finished their food and stood to clear the table. Later on that day, she sat for a break and her hand brushed her apron pocket. Reaching into what felt like a bundle of parchment paper, she withdrew it and set it in her lap to unwrap it. A gasp could be heard as she revealed the bundle of twenty-five medium sized sikars, enough for her to pass around to her apprentices. There was also a side package of five more short Imperials, and the entire thing was marked with the Natanleod sign. Her employer was a grateful one, she thought with a grin, glad she had taken the chance and followed her instincts to the High Lord's service.

The Natanleods took the time to properly celebrate their victory and the anniversary of their marriage day, and five days later Erinn was back in his office looking through the mail. Calla and Lillith had volunteered their time without being asked to attend to the chore, saving him an immense amount of work. As he looked through the missives, one caught his eye, as it was addressed directly to him.

"My Lord Erinn," the note began. "I hope this missive finds you quickly. Your actions at the Crevasse have been observed, and there are those who do not approve. If ye will return to the area, ye will find a walled compound hidden some five miles above the Crevasse. 'Tis well hidden, perhaps a dragon might more easily find it? Come quickly, before they solidify what plans are being made, and bring yer Army. 'Twill be needed."

The note was not signed in any way that Erinn could see, and he read it several times to be certain he understood exactly what was being said. It was obvious to him that someone within the compound had written this note, a loyalist among the enemy. Time to revisit the area, Erinn thought quickly, standing and summoning his martial gear, watching it appear it place.

"Black Dragons!" he called out, and they appeared, led by Sir Mittra, as it was Karpon's two day.

"At yer command, My Lord," he acknowledged Erinn's higher rank.

"We were not completely thorough on our last trip up to the Crevasse," Erinn began quickly, picking up the note and reading it to them. "Let us go now, and arrive unexpectantly. Someone needs our help up there."

One moment they were in the office, the next they were outside, where Erinn assumed his dragon form. His personal guard took up their seats, many with quiet delight at the opportunity to be a'dragonback, settled in for the short ride. Once Erinn lifted off, he circled and then made straight for the Crevasse, flying there without stopping. Once the area came into sight about an hour later, Erinn proceeded on, following the old road that led further up into the Iron Mountains. Almost exactly five miles from the Crevasse, Erinn spotted a glint of golden stone, and wheeled sharply after warning his passengers of his intent.

"Look there!" Mittra called out. "I see it, a huge compound with extremely thick and tall walls of stone. The Naga's work, most likely," he growled.

All of them followed Mittra's finger, and gasped to see what looked like a fortressed enclosure, the walls rising thirty feet up and guarded by four guard towers at the corners.

"Someone has put a great deal of thought into the building of this," Mittra heard Erinn's voice in his mind."

"Indeed so, My Lord. The building style reminds me a bit of old Sumer."

"Does it?" Erinn answered sharply. "What would be the best way to assault it?"

"From above, of course, My Lord. I daresay they will not be expecting a dragon to simply drop in on them," Mittra laughed a bit. They all felt the rumble beneath them as Erinn laughed with him as they turned to make another approach. The dragon dove sharply, and then screaming could be heard as people noticed the huge shadow above them.

"DRAGON!!! DRAGON!!!" the men of the Black Dragons heard as they fell out of the sky right into the midst of the compound, and chaos ensued. Erinn transformed back into himself, turning to answer the challenge being roared out by the commander of the place.

"Who are ye, and what do ye want?"

"I am the High Lord, Erinn Natanleod, and I have come to put an end to the Naga's time here in the Land!" Erinn called back, walking purposefully towards him. "Surrender, or die!"

"I surrender to no one!" he called back, and it was then that Erinn noted his half-Elven features.

"Who are ye?"

"My name is Lord Raj! I rule here! What is yer business here?" he demanded.

"I have come to reclaim this place in the name of the Goddess," Erinn responded at once.

"She has no place here," Raj laughed harshly. "We are not part of the Land."

"Ye are within the borders of the Goddess' realm," Erinn pointed out. "Even Oberon lives under Her law, and so will ye, or ye will not be here."

"Ye cannot remove me!" Raj laughed merrily. "I am the ally of Abbadon, he will protect me!"

"He would have a difficult time protecting ye since he is dead, and his skin is even now being tanned by a master of the craft," Erinn responded, laughing loudly. "His compound is no more, and the star portal he managed is destroyed utterly. Ye are alone, and at my mercy."

The being in front of him screamed out his rage and hate as he attempted to shift into his full Naga self. He had not done so for a long time, and so the process was not practiced, it took longer than it should have, much to his dismay. Erinn was upon him and his head was off his shoulders before he could take two breaths.

"And the Goddess' Will is done," he said softly, watching the body writhe. "Take anyone who surrenders into custody, slay everyone else!" he called out loudly, reminding his troopers of his orders. They put his orders into practice, and soon a small knot of people were gathered off to the side, where they remained with only a single guard. Erinn noted the ages of those who had surrendered, and many of them were young, still in their tweens. He wondered if one of them had authored the note, and made a mental note to speak with each one of them in turn.

Meanwhile, those who refused to accept the High Lord's mercy were quickly dealt with, their bodies carried outside of the compound and piled neatly. Once the dead were all gathered, Erinn set the pyre alight with a few bursts of dragonfire, leaving a small group to watch over it.

"I shall have people up here tomorrow to clean and take inventory," he told them. "Take no unnecessary chances during the night, and I shall return at dawn with reinforcements."

"Aye, My Lord," Mittra nodded, taking command as was expected. "We will see ye on the morrow. This place would make a perfect garrison, is it not so?"

"My thoughts exactly," Erinn grinned, handing him a pack of sikars to hand around later. "Keep alert. I shall want a report in the morning."

"Aye, My Lord."

"Come my friends, 'tis time to return home," he called.

"My Lord, we would all like to stay, if we might?" the rest of the troopers standing there said in near unison.

"Very well, all but two shall remain," Erinn decided quickly. "Those two will assist me with these younglings while we return to the Capitol City. Ye and ye," he pointed at random and the two men nodded before walking to the group who had surrendered. "Good night to the rest of ye," he said, opening a portal back to the Capitol and waving the group through. He was the last through, and so they had a sight of his face that few ever saw. It was satisfaction they saw reflected in his expression, and they took that as a sign of a job well done. Nothing more was necessary for them as they began to make ready for their overnight stay. It pleased them all to take quarters in the most ornate of the houses, which had clearly belonged to the former Lord, Raj. There was plenty to eat and drink, but they partook only of the food they had brought, mindful that the Nagas often laced food with their intoxicating, enslaving potion. They slept well, but lightly, the guard changing every two hours according to Mittra's orders, and the night passed without incident.

Chapter 2

Arriving back at the Capitol house with their new "guests" Erinn ordered for them to be taken at once to holding cells, even the youngest of them. He wanted to speak to each one, hoping the author of the note would come forward.

"Take them to the workroom holding cells, but do not frighten them," he added quietly at the end of his orders. "Some of them are very young, and we may be able to re-educate them. As for the older ones, we will see what the Lady's will is for them. Bring me the eldest to start."

"Aye, My Lord," Tristan nodded. "Come along all of ye, the High Lord would like a word or two with each of ye. Ye are not going to be harmed if ye cooperate, and food is being prepared for ye."

"And 'tis about time 'twas too!" they heard a belligerent voice answer. A tall, slightly Elven looking young man stepped forward, his face wearing a sneer.

"And who might ye be to be so demanding?" Tristan growled. "Ye will show respect to the High Lord, yer host."

"Or what?" the youngling challenged. The Knight Commander did not hesitate, and the young man was on the ground wearing restraints, before he could react.

"Shall I continue, My Lord?" Tristan asked, hiding a grin, for despite the young man's obvious warrior build, he was weak and completely untrained.

"I think not," Erinn answered coolly. "Unless he would like to continue resisting?"

"I shall go with him without trouble," the youngling managed through his shock. No one had ever treated him thusly, he was used to being able to bully and threaten to get his way. To know now that someone was vastly stronger, and better trained was a sobering experience for him. Erinn watched them trail away, the younger children exchanging glances of surprise because of the oldest one's sudden change of attitude.

Erinn took it all in, learning quickly from their actions, and reckoning that some of them had been bullied and abused for a long time. Giving Tristan plenty of time to get their new guests installed in their temporary quarters, Erinn called for Deborah to join him.

"I shall need yer help with the younger ones," he explained. "And ye should be there when I take on the older ones. Some of them are very belligerent."

"I would imagine they are, having lived privileged lives," Deborah answered. "I shall be there shortly."

Meeting him at the door, Deborah walked with Erinn through the massively thick, steel bound oak door and confronted the younglings retrieved from the fortress above the Crevasse. Deborah took the lead, approaching them and walking the length of the cells, starting with those holding the eldest.

"This one has been trouble?" she asked, seeing the bruises forming on the Elven one's face.

"A small matter of imposing proper respect, Madam," Tristan interjected in a growling tone.

"I see," she smiled thinly, turning to face the young man. "Come here," she commanded subtly.

"No," he refused and she could not miss the arrogant tone.

"I said, come **here**, *boy*!" she repeated, and even Erinn felt the compulsion in her voice. He could not resist, and walked to her, somewhat unwillingly as she watched, her face set into stone. "Now, tell me who ye are," she went on in the commanding tone. Drake heard it, and a half-smile appeared on his face at her use of the *Voice of Command*.

"I am Tarsyll, I am the son of Abbadon, his *first* son," the boy declared.

"Thank ye Tarsyll," Deborah smiled, her tone cold and without humor. "How old are ye?"

"I have gained seventeen years," he proclaimed. "All of the other children answer to me."

"Not anymore," Deborah reminded. "Ye are now under the rule of the High Lord, Erinn Natanleod. Ye will do as he says from now on, am I understood, *boy*?"

He wavered a bit as he stood there, feeling the loss of power as she stripped it from him in front of the others.

"But..."

"What?" she questioned sharply, and he gasped sharply as her eyes turned amber as he watched. "Ye are not protected by yer father's power anymore, Tarsyll. Ye live now by the High Lord's grace, as all of ye do. Yer parents were enemies, traitors to the Lady and the Land, and they were executed for their crimes. Ye are all suspected of carrying an infant Naga within ye, and we will be watching. Now, attend, and answer the High Lord's questions honestly."

"Aye Madam," he answered, watching her hair streak with scarlet, and wondering just who she was. He retook his seat meekly, and made no more trouble as Erinn began his questions.

"Tell me, son of Abbadon," he began carefully. "What do ye know of yer father's plans?"

"Naught," Tarsyll answered simply. "My father trusted no one and kept all of his plans to himself."

"I see," Erinn nodded, hearing truth in the boy's words. "What were yer duties?"

"I was in charge of the others," the youngling answered, again keeping his responses succinct. "My father did not wish to be bothered when he was here, but he still wanted to see his creations."

"Creations, not children?"

"Call them what ye wish," Tarsyll shrugged negligently, as if they did not matter. "They are younglings, destined to carry Naga implants to carry on the work of overtaking the Land."

"And 'tis all they are to ye? Ye feel naught for them?"

"Why should I?" Tarsyll answered, his arrogant tone unmistakable. "I am the natural son, they are all just creations."

"Ye are wrong, Tarsyll!" an insistent voice countered from a two cells down. "Ye are just like us, and I can prove it!"

"Shut up, Darius!" Tarsyll responded heatedly, his short temper appearing again. "Ye will do as I say."

"So, ye have been dancing around the truth then," Erinn smiled coldly. "Very well. I do not have time to light the forge and begin a proper interrogation, I shall simply take the truth from ye. What I do now is for the defense of the Land," he declared.

Disappearing suddenly in front of the youngling, Erinn reappeared right beside him, within the cell and restrained him magickally. Laying his hand atop the young man's head, Erinn used his abilities to see his memories, all of them. When he was finished, there was no doubt in his mind that Tarsyll was not a natural born anything.

"I am sorry, youngling," he said quietly. "But ye have been made to be as ye are by Abbadon's meddling. All of ye are of the Naga's creation, and therefore all of ye will be watched. I shall choose a place for ye to spend yer time of proving, and when I send ye there, I expect that ye will apply yerselves to learning how to be citizens of the Land."

Tarsyll was now crying, both from the shock of his memories being read and from anger. He had been told all of his life he was the only natural born one, and now to find out all of it had been lies devastated his world. He could do naught but sit there and rock himself while hugging his knees, trying to ease the pain of the truth as it hit him. Erinn paid him no mind as he continued his questioning, finding the other younglings much more cooperative. Finally, he reached Darius, and the young man knelt as soon as Erinn entered the cell he shared with three others.

"My Lord, please accept my service to ye and yer House," the young man asked earnestly, while the others looked on in shock.

"Do ye know what ye are asking for, young man?"

"I do, My Lord Natanleod. I only have one request," Darius answered, his voice unwavering despite his young age. "I only ask that ye allow me to explain."

"We will talk more later of this," Erinn decided after thinking for a moment or two.

"I am at yer disposal, My Lord."

Such nice manners, Erinn thought for a moment before remembering who these children were. Steeling himself once more, he continued on in his questions, keeping them simple for the younger ones. At length, the questions were done, and Erinn stood facing the wall as he thought quickly.

"Very well, my curiosity is satisfied for the moment," he declared. "I shall have these troopers take ye to the baths upstairs, where ye might bathe privately. When ye are done, food will be served, and then we will get ye housed at least for the time being. I expect ye all to act on yer best manners, as ye are all guests here."

"We will, My Lord!" he heard the general response from most of them, noting who said nothing. With a nod, he and Deborah simply disappeared from the locked room, leaving the younglings in the care of their trooper guards. Stopping first at the kitchen for a snack, Erinn and Deborah were surrounded by chatter as the news of the latest raid was passed among the house staff. Clearly, the troopers involved were spreading the tale quickly, Deborah noted with a grin.

"As well they should," Erinn's thoughts whispered into her mind. "I need to wash up, and then a short rest might be in order. I have thinking to do, and I need to speak with Father."

"Do ye want to be alone?"

"Most certainly not," Erinn grinned roguishly. "I think ye should come and join me. Ye look as if ye could stand a bit of relaxation."

"Is my hair still red?"

"Nay, but yer eyes are tinged with amber notes," Erinn pointed out softly. "Calm yerself, Madam. We have naught to worry over at the moment."

"Ye mean naught but a group of spoiled, entitled children," Deborah reminded after a moment.

"We will deal with them as well, in time," Erinn answered, producing a filled pipe from a pocket. "Here, ye get started on this. I am going to go clean up. I am ready for comfortable clothing, a sikar and all of the other comforts we enjoy. I believe 'tis about to get very noisy outside."

"The Barracks has won a great victory today," Deborah replied. "They should feel like celebrating, and today may be the last time in a while that they can do so outside. Feel that chill?" she said, standing at the open window. Erinn came to stand next to her, and felt the touch of icy wind, smelling the distinct scent of snow in the forecast.

"I do not sense any snow," Erinn answered, embracing her from behind. "But ye are right, that wind is blowing right off a mountaintop. Brrr, shall we close the window, madam?" he asked plaintively.

"I think so," she replied, making a subtle gesture. The window closed quietly and latched itself, then the curtains drew across the windows. The two of them spent the rest of that night just sitting quietly and talking, while the rest of the Barracks celebrated. The tale was passed from person to person, so that by morning, it was circulating through the city. Everyone who heard it understood what it meant, that the Naga threat had been reduced once more, which was a reason for great celebration.

While the rest of the Barracks, indeed the entire City celebrated the victory and gave thanks, while down in the holding cells the group of rescued younglings sat in silence. All of them were now feeling the effects of the enslavement potion being withheld, and it was an unpleasant experience for all of them. It was good that there was an elder child or two in with all of the younger ones, to help to keep them calm as the pain level within them rose. When their guards arrived with their supper, one of them ran for the healers, seeing their miserable conditions and soon they were feeling better. Their food was reheated and served once more, and all of the children found their appetites to be ravenous. Finally, they were allowed to bathe and don clean clothing in preparation for sleeping that night, which made them all feel even a little bit better. The room grew quiet as the children wound down and soon all that could be heard was their soft breathing. Darius lay there awake for quite a while, thinking of how his life had suddenly improved. He would find a way, he thought, to be of service to the High Lord. It was almost as if he were being compelled to do so, and he did not understand exactly why. It seemed very important to him, and he determined to accomplish his goal before closing his eyes and allowing himself to fall deeply asleep.

The next morning, he woke very early, hearing low, murmuring voices around him. He laid there quietly listening, recognizing his older brother's usual treachery.

"We will cooperate for now, 'till they relax their guard," the eldest one was saying in a whisper. "We will have our revenge, and then we will be gone before they can do aught."

The other four whispered their approval and agreement with the plan, while Darius lay their burning with anger. How dare they, he thought, when the High Lord has been so very generous with all of us. He decided to simply wait for his opportunity to do something about it, which presented itself later that morning when Erinn returned to continue his discussions with the older boys. Tarsyll took the lead, as usual, spinning a tale of half-truths and falsehoods as he attempted to convince Erinn that the group of them were no threat. Erinn listened with hidden amusement as he heard the lies clearly in Tarsyll's words. Deciding it was best to play along with the young man for the moment, Erinn turned them all over to a group of Black Dragons and told them to work hard before leaving.

"I am not working!" Tarsyll declared hotly. "Such things are for peasants and commoners, not nobles."

"Aye, aye," some of the others muttered in agreement, following Tarsyll's lead as always. Darius held back, and suddenly he spoke out with strength and courage.

"I am going to work!" he said. "I do not like being in this cell all day long, trapped here with the rest of ye. I have never liked any of ye, and ye have not liked me either. Ye are all fat, lazy and believe ye are above everyone else. But ye are not, ye are some of the worst people I know. Ye are not my family, and never have been!"

"O, so finally waking up to reality are we?" Tarsyll laughed cruelly. "Ye were never my brother, nor brother to any of us! Ye were always meant for the sacrifice pit, and ye will never amount to anything!"

Darius said nothing as he felt a power inside him he had never felt before, he felt heat within him, a burning, consuming heat of rage and frustration. His hand swung as if on its own accord and connected with Tarsyll's middle section, causing him to bend over sharply. Darius heard the hiss of his breath escaping his lungs, and knew he had hit a vital spot. Darius had absolutely no training in martial skills, but he had spent hours secretly watching and imitating the warriors in Abbadon's barracks. He was strong and lithe due to it, and he exhibited a natural ability for fighting. Now he stood there before Tarsyll, balanced on his toes and brandishing his fists, ready for anything his older *brother* might do. However, Tarsyll remained on the floor, fully prone and unconscious, his middle section aching painfully. The guards entered the cell at once to tend to the young man, helping him to start breathing again and regain consciousness.

"Take him to the infirmary," one of them ordered before turning to Darius. "Ye, come with me. I want to talk to ye."

Darius nodded and followed the huge black man out of the cells, out of the workroom and into the common area of the Barracks under the High Lord's House. The two of them sat on a sofa, and the huge black man introduced himself.

"I am Ishmael be Cain," he said. "I am a warrior of peculiar abilities, and I can see that ye have very little training in martial ways. Still, ye were able to put that older boy down with one punch, something I find quite remarkable," he went on in his oddly accented voice.

"I didn't mean to hit him so hard," Darius answered quietly. "I just wanted him to know I was not going to help him with his scheming."

"And what is he scheming about?"

"How to escape this place, and hurt as many people in the process as possible. Tarsyll is mean spirited and cruel, he cares for no one or nothing other than himself."

"I see," Ishmael nodded. "Then the Goddess has arranged for him to receive a lesson about being that way," he grinned. "Would ye like to learn?"

"O aye!" Darius exclaimed. "I have always wanted to learn martial ways, but I was prevented. Is it true what he said, that I was nothing more than Naga bait?"

"Possibly," Ishmael acknowledged truthfully. "Such practices are not unknown among the Naga Lords. I recall them in feeding pits, tossing their daughters to the huge snakes in order to be granted extra powers and privileges. Their daughters were *married* to the beasts, only to simply disappear after giving birth a few times. In all, beings like Abbadon are horrible, worthless creatures, who only wish to sit on their fat asses and be fed.

Ye are better off with us, I think," he finished. "Now, come along. I am on my way to the training arena for my scheduled time of work. If ye want to see what martial training is all about, why not come along with me?"

"I would like that!" Darius exclaimed earnestly, his face taking on a curious expression. "Sir, what is that tattoo on yer shoulder?" he asked, seeing the edges of it trailing over to the front.

"Ah, that," Ishmael grinned a bit. "I shall explain as we walk, youngling." Darius fell into step beside him, trying his best to match the Moorish man's long strides, while Ishmael enlightened him about the tattoo he wore. "I was an Outlander," he began, wanting to be honest with the lad. "The Lady arranged for me to come into the Land, which saved my life. Unfortunately, I fell in with the wrong crowd at the first, for 'twas

Raad and Secundus who found me on the beach that day. I was led to believe that things were exactly the opposite of the truth, and when I found out I had been deceived, I decided to declare a private war on the Nagas and their allies. The Lady arranged for me to meet Drake Natanleod in the lowest levels of their dungeons, and together, we escaped. I was wounded in the process, and Drake got me to a healer who restored my health and I swore a life service to him for it. The tattoo is my clan sign from the Outland, 'tis the sign of the Hashashin."

"I have heard that word," the young one said in wonder. "Abbadon used to use it, but it was not in a nice way at all. He used to curse ye all the time."

"Good!" Ishmael grinned widely. "I am glad he finally learned my name before he died. Ah, here we are!" he finished as they turned into the approach of the training arena. The session was just about to start as they entered, but Darius hung back, feeling as if he should not follow the Moor. "What is amiss?"

"I do not know," Darius answered softly. "I just feel as if I should not enter. 'Twould be *wrong*, somehow."

"Very well, the view is just as good from here," Ishmael grinned. Walking away quickly, he took his place in the formation, just as the exercises began. Darius watched, fascinated and entranced, and as he stood there, his body began to move as he attempted to learn the routine. His efforts attracted the attention of the Knight Commander and the War Duke nearly the same time, both of them watching as the young man watched and learned, very quickly.

"His movements look vaguely familiar, My Lord," Tristan pointed out after a short length of time had passed.

"Indeed so," Karpon grinned. The two men watched for a bit longer before turning to each other, their faces wreathed in an expression of realization.

"*DRAKE!*"

Both men laughed merrily as they returned their attention to the youngling at the entrance of the arena, now becoming more and more proficient as he worked. It was not long before the warriors themselves noticed Darius, who was now completely absorbed in perfecting what he had learned. So absorbed was he, he did not feel the presence of the High Lord as Erinn stood there, cloaked with invisibility. He had simply wanted to follow the young man throughout his first day of freedom within the House, without Darius' knowing. Erinn wanted to know if his desire to serve was an earnest one, and so the Lady had granted him the ability to walk unseen. He continued to follow Darius after the exercise broke up, and the young man followed the crowd to first meal, now being served in the Barracks dining hall. Darius was very observant, Erinn noted as he watched the young man's eyes glance around the room, taking in everything without much reaction. Darius watched the man in front of him take a plate and roll of flatware before he approached the service line, and so the young man emulated him.

"What's on the line this mornin'?" he heard the man in front of him ask in a jovial tone, as if he anticipated the meal. Such a thing would be rare in Darius' experience, as the men in the fortress barracks ate a plain diet.

"Well, I've made beef stew from last night's roast, and if ye want, we can fry a pair of eggs to go atop yer bowl," the man behind the counter replied with a grin, as if he knew the answer already.

"Make it three eggs," the man in front of Darius replied, grinning wide. "I worked hard this morning, and I have a full day ahead. The War Duke has called for volunteers to go and open the Scout Camp for next Spring, and I want to be part of that. The quiet of the woods during the Winter season appeals to me," he grinned.

The man behind the counter grinned with him as he turned to fill the large, flat-bottomed bowl with a rich, meaty stew. Darius' stomach rumbled as he caught the scent of it and saw the chunks of meat and vegetables. He could hardly wait for his portion as he watched the man behind the counter lay three perfectly fried eggs atop the stew, then return to the counter, handing it over to the man in front of him.

"There ye go my friend," the kitchen man said.

"Thank ye, Kitchen Master," he replied, bowing a bit to show respect before walking away to join his fellows at a table. Darius felt comfortable now as he walked up to where the huge man stood waiting, and the young man spoke up, making sure to be polite.

"Excuse me Sir, I am sorry, I am new here. I do not know yer name."

"I am Klietos, the Kitchen Master of the Barracks," the older man introduced himself. "And ye are?"

"I am called Darius," the young man answered.

"Ah, ye are one of those the High Lord saved from that fortress up above the Crevasse," Klietos answered in a friendly manner. "Welcome to my kitchen, are ye ready for yer meal?"

"I am, Sir, but I shall take just two eggs please?" he requested with great respect.

"And how do ye like yer eggs cooked?"

"Just like ye served them for the last man," Darius answered.

"Good, that makes it simple," Klietos chuckled, turning to the griddle behind him. Finishing off two *over easy* eggs, he laid them out on top of Darius' stew and handed it over, explaining where he could find bread and cheese to go with it.

"Ye will find green salad, sliced cheeses and warm biscuits over there," he pointed with his egg-turner. "I hope ye enjoy yer meal."

"It smells wonderful, my stomach is growling so hard!" Darius exclaimed as he felt the rumble. He went to the table, took what bread and cheese he wanted, then found an empty seat at a small table next to the wall. Sitting, he offer a sincere thanks to the Lady, the first time he had actually done so aloud, then took up his spoon and dug in deeply.

In the shadows, Erinn watched still completely unseen, until he felt a whisper of wind behind him.

"Father?"

"What are ye doing?" Drake's voice answered.

"Observing," Erinn answered. "He seems very earnest so far, but we will see how the day goes."

"He was Naga born," Drake responded within Erinn's mind. "Ye are right to watch him."

Darius ate his meal with gusto, enjoying every bite of the simple fare, his eyes watching and observing the happenings in the dining hall. He watched as the men and women finished their plates, some returning to the line for a second, smaller portion, while the others walked back into a screened area close to the kitchen. They had plates and flatware in hand when they entered, but their hands were empty upon their emergence. Darius grinned as he discerned that when he was finished with his plate, he was to deliver it there. After eating every bite, then wiping his plate clean with the last crust of biscuit, Darius rose from his seat, wiped the crumbs of his meal into his plate with his napkin, then followed the others as they deposited their plates into the soaking sink behind the service line. Darius noted there were many plates, and no one washing them while the meal proceeded. Surely, he thought, something is amiss and he went to stand at the end of the line until Klietos noticed him.

"What is it boyo?"

"Sir, ye have a lot of dishes back there, and no one is washing them. May I be of service?"

"Have ye ever washed dishes before?"

"Nay, but I can learn!" Darius spoke up, as if he were impelled to do so. "I am not afraid of learning to work! I am not like my former brothers downstairs."

"Ah, I see!" Klietos grinned. "Come then, while I have a short break. I shall show ye the task."

Klietos took him back to the sinks and demonstrated the procedure, cautioning him to watch for sharp knives.

"I have asked them over and over, but it still happens occasionally. I have this hooked wire here to reach down and loosen the stopper, so ye do not have to risk a cut," he showed Darius, who was watching and observing with great focus.

"I see," he nodded. Klietos quickly demonstrated the most efficient technique for the job, washing three of each item slowly, explaining the process and the reasoning behind it.

"Go on then, and show me what ye've learned," Klietos encouraged. Darius did so, repeating the sequence exactly in order as Klietos had demonstrated, impressing the Kitchen Master entirely.

"I can do it, Sir!" Darius said when he had finished an entire sink full of dishes to Klietos' satisfaction.

"So ye can," the man grinned, clapping him on the back. "Go to it then. I should have another person coming on duty in three hours. Just do the essential dishes; cups, plates and flatware. Leave the big pots and pans 'till the end."

"Aye Sir," Darius nodded earnestly, tying on the apron Klietos handed to him.

For the next three hours, the youngling concentrated entirely on emptying the many bins of used dishes, alternating between plates, flatware and cups, until he began to catch up a bit. Klietos looked into the back about half way through the three hours, and there was Darius up to his elbows in the dishpan, now scrubbing the soaked pots and pans. What a worker, the Kitchen Master thought as he finished the first meal service, then turned to coordinating the second meal. Just as he did so, the next man scheduled in the dish area appeared, an hour before he was scheduled.

"Good morning, Kitchen Master!" he called out. "I shall get started right away! I bet 'tis a mess back there!"

"Go on and look for yerself," Klietos grinned, going with him. There was Darius, just finishing the mop up after service, his face drawn with weariness as he took the last few swipes with the mop before putting it in the bucket and taking a seat.

"Boyo!" Klietos exclaimed, going to sit next to him. "Ye have done a miracle's working today. Bruno can now begin his shift without cleaning up, and the work here in the kitchen will go forward without difficulty. How are ye doing?"

"Master," Darius replied after a moment, his voice reflecting weariness. "I do not think I can even rise. My legs are all shaky."

"I do not doubt that, boyo," Klietos chuckled warmly. "Come on then, let me help ye to the infirmary. Ye have worked yerself into near exhaustion!"

Darius could not resist as Klietos simply gathered him into his arms, then carried him to the place where the healers of the House waited to be of service. Walking in, he saw Lyla and went to her at once, knowing her skills well.

"Madam, I have a patient for ye," he called out softly, seeing that Darius was nearly asleep. "He has worked himself to the limit, having never done so before. He is one of the Naga younglings the High Lord brought down from that fortress, and I do not believe he has ever worked so hard before."

"I think not," Lyla answered sharply, looking at the sleeping young man. As she probed his knotted muscles, he woke suddenly, glancing about him in a bit of panic. "Calm yerself, youngling. Ye are in the Infirmary of the Barracks. Master Klietos has brought ye to us for healing, and ye are in sore need of it. Relax, no one will harm ye here."

"I am in the High Lord's House?" Darius asked, looking for reassurance.

"Indeed so young one," Lyla smiled warmly. "Now, if ye will allow, I shall attend to yer healing. But first, ye should drink this tonic, which will assist ye to sleep. 'Twill be better if ye do, as I have a great deal of work to do unknotting those muscles of yers," she crooned a bit.

"O," he replied, as his legs suddenly cramped, and he could feel them knot under his skin. "I would like the tonic, if it means the pain will be less!"

"Yer body is not used to hard work, but ye took it on anyway," Lyla's voice soothed him as he drank down the potion, which was both slightly bitter and mostly sweet. Almost at once, he felt the pain begin to recede, leaving him slightly drowsy and dizzy.

"I feel sleepy," he yawned.

"Then go to sleep," Lyla's voice soothed him and he simply let himself slip off. The healers began their work then, undressing him completely and using a special oil designed for such work, they began to slowly knead the knots out of his over-used muscles. It took them three hours to finish, and when they did, they simply covered his oily body with several warm blankets and left him to sleep the night away.

He started awake in the morning, and when his eyes flew open, it took him a moment to realize where he was. The next thing he noted was that he was completely naked under the blankets, which alarmed him. Being in such a state in his father's house would have indicated something major had occurred, like the implantation of an immature Naga. He pushed the covers back, and felt his abdomen for the scar, finding no evidence of surgery, and a sigh of relief escaped him. Next, he tried wiggling his toes and fingers, finding the pain was not terrible, and gained a bit of courage to push himself up into a sitting position. Again, the pain was not as bad as he had anticipated, but he could feel his muscles were stiff as well as sore. Panic ensued as he tried to push himself to his feet, finding himself unable to do so, even impelled by the urge to find the necessity as soon as possible. Fortunately, the Goddess intervened and the door opened, just as he tried to push himself to his feet again.

"O my goodness!" Lyla exclaimed, rushing to his side to help steady him. "I would imagine yer need for the necessity is quite urgent," she said softly.

"I need to go now," he replied. Lyla nodded her understanding, and making a simple gesture, Darius found himself off his feet, hovering above the floor. Lyla moved her finger again, and he found himself floating to the necessity door. It opened for him, and he went through, watching it close behind him. It did not take him long to attend to his business, and he called to Lyla when he was done.

"Madam, I have finished, thank ye."

The door opened of its own accord and he floated through, finding himself back on his bed in short order and wrapping one of the blankets around himself. Just as he did so, a group of younger healers arrived, bearing clothing and a small pot of a steaming liquid.

"Now, we have some clothing here for ye, and a bit of hot soup to waken yer appetite after such a long sleep. How are ye feeling?" Lyla asked.

"I am surprised I can move around at all," he replied ruefully. "I thank ye all for working on me, as well as for the clothing."

"I shall leave ye to get dressed, unless ye think ye might need a bit of help?" Lyla offered.

"I might need a bit of assistance, after all," he replied shortly after trying to put on the unders. He managed to get that done finally, but only after Lyla sent the rest of the women out. He noted they were giggling as they left, and his curiosity was roused.

"What are they laughing about?" he asked innocently. Lyla paused for a moment to frame her answer in the best light possible.

"Young man, as professional healers, we see more of a man than most women do," she began. "The Goddess has gifted ye well, as ye have more than most men," she went on. Darius' face took on a puzzled expression as he thought about her words, slowly getting dressed as he did so. Finally, he gasped a bit and turned to Lyla, a bit of panic on his face.

"I…"

"Ye need say naught," Lyla told him in a motherly tone, having two tween-aged sons of her own. "What amused them was that ye apparently had no idea of the gift given ye, which would be rare for most young men yer age in the Land. Ye have never been to the Temple?"

"Nay," Darius confirmed as his cheeks reddened a bit, although he did not understand why. Lyla smiled gently, patting his arm comfortingly.

"As I said, ye need say naught. But ye should get used to women looking at ye that way, now that ye are starting to mature. Here, put these on," she said, handing him his trous. "First meal is in progress downstairs, and I see no reason ye should not be able to walk there. I shall walk with ye, to assure ye make it all the way," she offered.

It did not take him long to finish dressing, and after Darius donned a warm pair of slippers, they were off. Walking through the many corridors, he observed and counted the twisting and turning of their path. It seemed deliberately designed to confuse and delay one's progress, he noted, having the mind for strategy. Finally, they arrived at the main staircase that led from the upstairs to the main level, and Darius's stomach growled loudly at the first scent of hot food. He waited his turn patiently, and accepted the plate given him with a hearty thanks, unlike his fellows below. He heard muttered complaints about his former relatives while he ate and he was glad not to be among them anymore. His life had taken a decidedly happy turn, he thought as he munched the contents of his plate. Five griddlecakes, three eggs and a mound of mixed sausage and smoked pork belly later, he burped carefully into his napkin, set his utensils at the proper angle on the plate, and sat back, completely contented. Seeing that the routine was the same upstairs as it was downstairs, he followed the line of people into the back of the kitchen, where the dishwashers stood processing the plates, flatware and cups. All was in good order, he saw, and so he simply deposited the contents of his hands into the proper bins and sinks.

"Thank ye, young man!" he heard them say, and the earnestness of their tone was clear to him.

"Ye are most welcome. May I be of service?"

"We have all heard the miracle ye accomplished in Master Klietos' kitchen," the woman in charge answered, her tone very sincere. "We have all the help we need at the moment, but are ye not supposed to be resting?"

"I suppose I should," Darius answered, and suddenly, it was if a weight had fallen upon him. He was suddenly beset with weariness, and after depositing his armload, he took a seat at the first available table, just to recover a bit.

"Are ye well, young man?" he heard. Looking up, he saw a tall, gaunt woman, whose face could best be described as handsome.

"I am, Madam."

"I am Dame Zameera," she offered her name, as well as a helping hand. "Ye need to rest, 'tis clear enough. Do ye have quarters?"

"I do not," he answered truthfully. "I was brought down from the Crevasse with the others, and last night, I slept in the infirmary."

"Come on with me, let us consult the High Lady. I am certain she will have the perfect solution to yer dilemma."

"O! I do not wish to be a bother!"

"My dear young man, the High Lady will not look upon this as a bother. Many of us have heard the story of how you assisted Master Klietos in the kitchen. What ye did was legendary, as is clear by the popular appeal of the story," the Dame chuckled.

"I do not wish to offend," Darius responded after thinking for a short bit. The Dame turned and gestured, being a woman of few words, and he followed her into the depths of the House kitchen, where the High Lady was working in her test kitchen.

"Excuse me, My Lady," the Dame spoke up after a short wait.

"O! What is it Dame?"

"This young man needs a room, Madam. And I think it should be in short order."

Just as she said so, Darius felt another wave of dizziness, and a bit of nausea, and he leaned against Zameera for support.

"O my," Deborah exclaimed softly, coming to his side. "Come with me, young man. We will find quarters for ye, and then ye will rest," she finished, the words sounding like an order to him. Once they were out of the kitchen, he swayed against Zameera again, and the wiry woman simply took him up in her arms, sparing him further effort. Deborah led them to the family wing, stopping in front of a door and producing a key, she pushed the door open and stepped inside. Zameera saw the flare of lamps and sconces, and then the window curtains snapped open, all while Deborah stood in the center of the small room.

"Ye may bring him in now, Dame."

Zameera did so, stepping inside the door and finding a tidy room waiting. The bed was made up already, and so she stepped up to it and laid him gently upon the mattress, pulling the sheet and the first light blanket over him.

"Ye should sleep now, young one," she whispered to him, patting the top of his head in an affectionate manner.

"Mmmm…" was all he could manage before fading away into sleep, glad for the ease of it.

"The poor lad, he has worked himself into near exhaustion, and on his first effort," Deborah murmured as she came to his side. As Zameera stood there, Deborah's hair suddenly took on streaks of red, and the temperature of her aura increased a bit. "Dame if ye would please guard the door, I must do something for him."

"Aye Madam," Zameera agreed at once, going to the portal, locking the key and then standing there, sword drawn. Once she was set, Deborah put her hand on the head of the young man and whispered to the Goddess.

"Let him be healed, My Lady, if it be Thy will."

A tidy flame emerged from Deborah's left palm, and she put her right on the young man's chest, her eyes closed, allowing the Goddess to work as She would. It seemed to take a long time to Zameera, but finally Deborah's hair returned to its usual raven-black color, and the waves of heat ceased to course from her. While she did so, something else was revealed to her that she could not speak to Zameera about, knowing she must first speak to Erinn.

"I shall summon a healer to sit with him, but all he needs to do now is sleep," Deborah whispered. As she spoke, Lyla appeared in the room, her bag with her, and she came at once to the High Lady's side.

"Are ye well, Madam?"

"I shall be," Deborah replied, a small smile appearing. "I just need to get to my quarters, if ye would help me a bit?"

"Of course!" Lyla smiled, making a gesture, and a short portal appeared. They could all see the common area of the High Lord and Lady's quarters, and it was clean and tidy.

"Thank ye Sister," Deborah smiled, walking through, Zameera accompanying her, because she felt impelled to do so. "I am well, Sister," Deborah said as soon as the portal closed. "Unless 'tis something ye need to speak with me about?"

"Actually My Lady, I do have a concern. As ye know, when I spent my time at Secundus' fortress, he insisted that I be one of those to pleasure him daily. As with all of us, he performed a surgery on me, so I could not conceive, as he was not interested in being a father," Zameera spoke slowly, the pain of if clear. "As such, I was led to believe I was sterile, at least 'till three weeks ago."

"And?" Deborah asked, pouring wine for both of them, and waving Zameera onto the sofa.

"My Lady, I did not have courses for many years," Zameera began. "At least'till I and Ishmael moved in together."

"O?"

"Aye, I was as shocked as anyone," Zameera replied with a sigh. "However, within the last four months, they have become spotty, and now have ceased completely. I am gaining weight in places I should not, if I am sterile."

"What are ye saying?"

"I think I am with child," Zameera said in a whisper. "Can ye help me find out?"

"I can, but not right now," Deborah told her honestly. "If ye can wait 'till tomorrow, I shall divine the truth for ye."

"Thank ye Madam," Zameera smiled, holding out her cup for more wine. "I need to know quickly, so I can adopt the right diet. I shall need a midwife as well. I do not wish to do this alone, and Ishmael will be no help," she chuckled. Deborah could only join into her mirth, knowing that Ishmael's reaction to the news would be complete shock. Zameera left her then, and Deborah retired for the day after summoning Gwendolyn to explain the need of it.

"Ye should rest, if ye have done such a healing," she agreed, eyeing Deborah critically. "I shall send down some bone broth, to help ye recuperate. A warm bath and a change of clothing might also be in order, My Lady, if I might be so bold. Ye work as hard as or harder than anyone, and ye must learn to take better care of yerself. We all worry about ye," she finished quietly.

Deborah smiled warmly, grateful to be with such earnest and honest folk. "Ye are all kind to worry about me, but ye need not," she said. "I shall be just fine in the morning, after a good night's rest."

Gwendolyn nodded, curtsied and took her leave, returning to the kitchen and pulling out a very specific jar of half-glaze. They made many jars of this mix, which was used throughout the year to help those with upset stomachs, or a case of the sniffles. It was heavy with herbs and lemon peel, the color was dark golden and clear, and the scent always roused even the sickest man to take a sip or two. Now the Kitchen Mistress took a few cubes and put them into a pot of hot water, allowing them to slowly dissolve into a beautiful pot of simple broth. Heating a teapot, she poured the broth into it, wrapping the quilted covering around it to keep it warm. Taking it up on a tray, and adding a cup, she walked it down to the High Lady's room and knocked, receiving no answer.

"She must be in the bath," Gwendolyn thought, making a gesture and then trying the door again. It swung open and the older woman stepped through, closing it behind her and locking it. There was Deborah, asleep on the sofa, a small smile on her face. Gwendolyn simply straightened her out carefully, brought out her pillow from the bed and covered her lightly, leaving her to sleep. Turning to the tray holding the heated broth, the older woman put a hand on the teapot cover and whispered a few words.

"Please keep this hot 'till the High Lady can drink it?"

She felt a rightness within her after she said it, and after patting the top of the cover affectionately, she took her leave quietly. As she emerged from the room, Erinn was just approaching the door.

"Is she within?"

"Aye, and I think her work today has caught up with her a bit, My Lord," Gwendolyn answered.

"I would imagine so, since she has done a healing for Darius," Erinn agreed. "I shall take over her tending now. If ye would send supper when 'tis ready, I am certain she will be ravenous later."

"I have some bone broth in there keeping hot," Gwendolyn told him. "She should have that first."

"I shall assure that she does," Erinn smiled warmly.

"Enjoy yer day, My Lord," Gwendolyn smiled back, truly glad to be in the employ of such people. She continued on her way, her heart light, and when she arrived back in the kitchen she found the first round of berry hand pies just emerging from the ovens.

"They look wonderful!" she complimented, waiting until one cooled enough to try. "And they taste just as good as they look! Thank ye everyone!"

Chapter 3

Zameera returned to her room and said nothing to Ishmael about her health concerns. If she was not with child, there was no sense in raising his hopes, she thought to herself as she prepared a simple supper of saffron rice, roasted chicken and a green salad. Ishmael had always hoped to become a father, she knew, as he believed he was the last of his family. He had no son or daughter to pass on his skills and knowledge to, which would be a shame to lose, Zameera thought on. Just as she was ready to lay supper on the table, Ishmael came through the door of their new home, a bouquet of fresh flowers in hand.

"Good evening my love," he called out in a good natured tone.

"Thank ye for the flowers, Ishmael!" she returned, coming to kiss his cheek. "Supper is nearly ready to serve, but it can wait a bit if ye wish to relax first."

"I would like to sit with ye, my lady," he smiled gently, still finding it difficult to believe he was now living with her openly. They sat and talked about Ishmael's day, and then he asked about hers.

"I spent the most of the day in the company of the High Lady, accompanying her as she performed a healing on the young lad Darius, then making certain she got back to her room without difficulty."

"What a marvelous day ye had!" Ishmael grinned.

"I enjoy being in her presence," Zameera shrugged, rising to serve their plates. The rest of their evening went as it usually did and they retired early when Zameera's weariness caught up with her after supper. She was gone when he rose in the morning, but that was a usual thing and Ishmael thought nothing of it. He rose, dressed and consumed the portion of oat porridge she had left for him on the stove, then cleaned up the kitchen, a thoughtful gesture. Only then did he depart to take up his usual duties, completely unaware of what Zameera was doing.

The tall, gaunt woman was now sitting with Deborah in a darkened room. She answered the few questions put forth by the High Lady, then allowed herself to be examined by the knowledgeable woman. Deborah was certain of the results by the time the appointment was over, and she answered Zameera's anxious question.

"Ye are with child, in fact, ye are carrying twins," Deborah told the stunned Amazon warrior.

"WHAT? But how can that be after what Secundus did to me?"

"Apparently, the Goddess has decided to intervene in that regard," Deborah smiled warmly, pouring a cup of wine for the Amazon woman and handing it to her. "I have heard of other such surgeries reversing themselves, what Secundus did to so many of ye was done to other women in the Land as well, especially those of great magickal abilities. The Nagas wanted to keep all of the magick for themselves, after all," she finished with an almost feral note in her voice. Pouring herself some wine, she sat with Zameera for another hour, going over what foods she should be eating, and what she should be avoiding.

"Ye may have one cup of the brown ale per day, and a cup of wine at night to help ye sleep if ye need it," Deborah recited professionally. "I shall give ye a tincture to help ye with the nausea, I remember with Artos I was sick all the time and this tincture was the only thing that helped. How is that part going?"

"My stomach has been upset from time to time, but I am not vomiting," Zameera told her. "I am not anticipating that part of the pregnancy."

Deborah grinned, went to her pharmacopeia cabinet and pulled out a small bottle with a dropper. "One or two drops in water any time ye feel the nausea," she advised as Zameera tucked it away. "When are ye going to tell Ishmael?"

"Tonight, of course," she answered. "He should know right away."

"He should indeed," Deborah smiled, embracing the Amazon. "I am so happy for ye both. May the Lady's blessing be with ye throughout this pregnancy. Is there aught else I might help with?"

Zameera stood there for a moment considering, and then her eyes lit as an idea hit her.

"Madam would it be possible to take home a lamb?" she asked.

"An entire one?"

"A small one," Zameera chuckled. "Ishmael loves lamb, and I have learned how to spice it properly for him."

"Ah, the *Father's Feast* then," Deborah nodded. "Most appropriate, since ye are an Amazon. Come along, and let us see what is available, and if I do not have what ye need, we will go down to the lamb pens. Shall we go the quick way?"

Zameera nodded and seconds later, they stepped forth from the icy emptiness into the burgeoning cold room. Deborah went at once to the huge ice room, where entire carcasses hung in the salt-lined aging room. There were several lamb carcasses there, perfectly frozen and properly aged, but Zameera purposefully picked the smallest one.

"After all, 'twill only be the two of us," she reasoned as Deborah made a gesture and the frozen meat magickally lifted off the hook and floated down to a metal cart.

"Do ye need wine?"

"I have plenty at home, Madam," Zameera assured her, laughing a bit as she did so. "Ishmael is going to be so surprised, I can hardly wait to see his face! Madam, could ye indulge one more request?"

"Consider it done," Deborah agreed, knowing what the older woman was about to ask. She opened the traveling portal, so that they could see Zameera's kitchen on the other side. "Take the cart, 'twill make it easier for ye. Ye should not be lifting large weights," the High Lady cautioned.

"Aye Madam," Zameera nodded. Standing behind the cart, she pushed it through the whirling aperture, appearing in her kitchen. The portal closed behind her, leaving her there and the gaunt woman went to work at once. First, she washed up and put her hair back, being certain to wash her hands again afterwards. Donning an apron, she pulled the required spices and herbs from the cabinet, being certain to put the mortar and pestle beside it. A glass of wine appealed to her, and so she helped herself to the cold carafe in the small basin of trickling water. Washing her hands once more, she went to work on the rub mix, mixing and grinding until she had enough to cover the entire carcass. Quickly, she tended to the trimming of it, removing all of the excess fat and silverskin, trimming away things she knew would flavor the basting broth, and setting all of that to cook in salted, herbed water on the medium heat of the stove. Now, she took up the spice rub and began to work it all over the inside and outside of the carcass, making certain to coat every surface several times, and using her strong fingers to rub it in a bit. Once that was done, she rinsed her hands, dried them and attended to the oven, adding in just enough fuel to bring up the temperature a bit. She intended to slow roast the meat, giving it time to soak up all of the spice rub, and granting her the extra time she would need to discuss the situation with Ishmael. Turning to the side dishes, she prepared a batch of saffron rice and set that to slowly cook, then chopped and diced a green salad together, setting it in the cold room to keep until supper. Now that all of the preparations were done, all she had to do was get the lamb into the oven, and that was easily enough done. She simply chose the largest roasting pan she had and laid the carcass within it, using the rack to keep it from sticking to the bottom. Deciding that roasted vegetables would be good, she pared and cut carrots, onions, papas and cabbage, salting and peppering them before setting them aside in the cold room under a cloth. Now, she thought as she closed the oven door and let the meat do its work, I have time for a bath before Ishmael arrives. Taking her carafe with her, leaving several still within the basin, she retreated to their tub to soak for a bit, using the time to consider the best way to tell Ishmael the good news. Perhaps the direct approach would be best, she thought to herself with a grin, thinking of the expression such news would bring to the dark-skinned man.

While she made her preparations, Ishmael went through his day as he always did. As he walked by the market, he saw beautiful blossoms and stopped at the flower booth to pick up a fresh bunch of flowers. The woman had his usual order ready, three dozen assorted colored roses, and he marveled at their scent and intense shades. Paying the fee, he took them with him and hurried back to his horse, mounting easily despite his burdens. Setting the horse's pace at a slow canter, he proceeded to the new house along the Elan, enjoying the ride as he went. The new ostler was waiting to take his horse and care for him, earning Ishmael's gratitude.

"Thank ye, boyo. Take good care of him."

"I shall Sir!"

A grin appeared on his face at the earnest tone of the lad as Ishmael walked away, headed for the first flight of stairs that led to the kitchen and living quarters. As he hit the bottom of the second flight, the scent of spices and herbs hit his nose, and he stopped to enjoy the fragrance.

"Mmmm, Zameera is cooking!" he thought with glee. "I should get up there quickly and offer my assistance, if necessary."

He increased his pace, *walked on the wind* the rest of the way, just for the practice. When he opened the door to the kitchen and walked in, the odor of the roasting lamb surrounded him, and a wide smiled appeared when he saw Zameera tending the meat. She was wearing one of the twisted dresses, her hair back, and a cold cup of wine in her hand as she basted the meat in the oven.

"Are ye cooking lamb?" he asked, approaching the cooking area to get a better scent.

"I am, and I used the spice rub ye like best," she answered simply. "Also, we are having saffron rice, roasted vegetables and a green salad. I suggest ye get into the bath waiting for ye, so we can sit and talk for a bit. I have something to tell ye."

"What?"

"Bath first, and then a pipe of Herb and a sikar," she answered evasively, putting a cup of cold wine into his hand. "Go on, while the water is still warm."

The bath water steamed pleasantly when he entered, and he washed himself quickly, enjoying the wine while he did so. A set of light house clothing waited for him, along with his slippers, and he wondered how long she had been home as he donned the outfit. Taking his empty cup with him, he returned to the kitchen, where she waved him over to the trickling basin, and the many carafes of wine waiting there.

"Are we expecting company?"

"Nay, but I have something very, very important and joyous to tell ye. Now, take that pipe I loaded for ye, and light those sikars if ye would please."

He did as she asked, exercising patience despite his excess curiosity about what was going on. Finally, she sat across from him, leaning back against the sofa's comfort, trying to compose her words.

"Ishmael, ye are going to be a father," she finally and simple stated.

"We are adopting?" he asked with a smile. "When may I meet the child?"

"In about seven months," Zameera smiled, rising to come sit next to him. "Ishmael, I am with child. Twins, actually. Ye will not be the last of yer line."

Ishmael's shock was complete, he sat there holding his wine cup to his lips, unable to move as his mind processed what Zameera had just told him. Finally, whispered words emerged over the cup as he managed to finally break through his shock.

"Ye…but…what about what Secundus did to ye?"

"Apparently, the Goddess has reversed that, in answer to a prayer of mine," Zameera responded, her voice soft and emotion-laden. "Ye are a Hero of the Land, ye have earned this reward, and I am honored to be the one to have children with ye."

"I…I am to be a…father???" he said with difficulty. "A FATHER!!! May the God…Goddess be praised!" he said, quickly amending the usual prayer offered on such an occasion by his people. "Wait… did ye say *twins*???"

"Aye," Zameera confirmed with a grin. "The High Lady suspects a girl and a boy."

"O...O my," Ishmael responded, leaning back heavily against the sofa. "I am astonished, awed and very grateful. Is there aught I might do for ye, my lady?" he asked, slipping an arm around her.

"I have everything I need right now," she smiled, kissing him gently. "But perhaps ye might take over basting the lamb? Ye have the ken of when 'tis perfectly done. All else is ready to cook, and the rice is done."

"I am in no hurry, but I am going to check the meat and slide those vegetables into the oven. I want to enjoy the night with ye, but have supper ready when we are," he rumbled a bit as he rose to accomplish the task.

When he returned, he had two fresh carafes with him, which they shared as they spoke about what preparations needed to be made.

"Ye will need a good midwife to help with twins," Ishmael thought out loud.

"We may need a wet nurse too," Zameera pointed out quietly. "At my age…"

"If we need to find such a woman, then we will. Ye need not be concerned, my dear. I have all the wealth I need to assure ye have good care."

"Of course ye do," she smiled warmly. Their night went forward after that as they discussed the new situation in their home. If they had known the Goddess' plans, they would have simply waited a few days.

As Ishmael and Zameera discussed their new family, out beyond the fog barrier of the Land floated a small raft. The raft had only one occupant, a large dark-skinned man carrying a huge scimitar, and very little else. His clothing was torn, his turban nearly gone after being torn into bandages, fire-starters, and a sun shield to protect him from the intense heat of day. It was night now, for which he was grateful, for even his dark skin did not protect him completely from being burned, and his skin felt dry, tight and stretched now. When he saw the thick curtain of fog, he drew his weapon and went through it armed, arriving on the other side into the warmth and light of early Summer.

"Where am I?" he asked himself, a twinge of fear hitting him. "Have I fallen into the land of the Djinn?"

Such a place was rumored to be filled with mythical, terrible beasts, as well as the powerful, trickster Djinn. He walked carefully as he went, keeping his blade in hand and keeping his eyes on the path before him. He saw fresh melons growing and helped himself to a few as he walked, making sure to discard the husks and innards off the path a few steps each time.

Thusly refreshed, he continued on, eventually sighting the Causeway and the Port City beyond. As he entered the bustling port, he was challenged at once by the alert sentries at the guard post guarding this access point.

"Heya! Who are ye, and what business do ye have in the Port City?"

"My name is Azeem ben Cain. I am the survivor of a shipwreck many days past. I washed up down the beach several miles that way, and I have seen no one until now. I am a peaceful man by nature, however I am a poor man who needs to work for his living. Is there employment to be had?"

"Azeem ben Cain?" the man questioned, and suddenly Azeem realized they were speaking the same language. He was momentarily stunned by the revelation, and took his time answering.

"Aye," he responded warily. The man in front of him laughed heartily and opened the gate to the guardhouse.

"Interesting, I have only heard of one other in the Land with such a name," the man in front of him grinned. "Come along, I need to take ye to see Lord Triton. He runs the city, and everyone who enters must be taken to him."

"I shall go willingly," Azeem agreed. The man reported his errand to the commander, who nodded in agreement with whatever suggestion was being made.

"Would ye surrender yer weapons?" he was asked by the man in command, who had hard eyes, and an expression to match.

"Sir, to surrender my weapons would be to put myself at yer mercy. I am unaccustomed to placing myself in such situations."

"So 'twould," the man agreed. "My name is Bartholomew, I am the Captain of this guardhouse," he introduced. "I swear upon my oath to the Lady that yer weapons will be returned to ye, if Lord Triton agrees. Will that suffice?"

Azeem looked about him, seeing over fifty men standing about and knowing that even his prodigious skills would be insufficient.

"I shall allow that to suffice, Captain. But if I find ye false, ye will be one of the first to fall to my sword."

"Come, let me take ye to Lord Triton," Bartholomew invited, ignoring the threat. He had expected to hear it, after all, he would have done the same he thought. Turning, he led the way, Azeem behind him, and two burly Marines behind him. Azeem studied the way they went, marking the way mentally, just in case he had to make a quick escape. They walked up the long ramp and through the massive gates of the City Manager's house, where Bartholomew announced he had a guest to present to Lord Triton.

"Bring him in," came the word in return and they continued on their way through the large but very circumspect house. Finally, they came to a door and the Captain knocked three times. The door opened presently and they were told to come in.

"Captain Bartholomew!" they heard a boisterous voice call out, and Azeem had his first sight of Lord Triton. He had slightly blue-ish skin, the huge black man noted. "And who is our guest?"

"My Lord Triton, this man has introduced himself as Azeem ben Cain," the Captain revealed. Triton sat back, his face taking on a look of astonishment and awe.

"I had no idea Master Ishmael had a brother," Lord Triton began.

"We have been separated by circumstances for many years now, My Lord," Azeem revealed. "I find myself surprised to be here, and to know I might have a living brother."

"Yer brother is a muchly honored man here," Triton pointed out. "Ye should learn about his exploits during our recent civil difficulties here."

"And how would I do that, My Lord?"

"I can help!" Bartholomew spoke up. "As can nearly every man in the Marines! Ishmael's skills with all manner of weaponry is legendary among those in the Martial services."

"I would like to hear these tales!" Azeem grinned, starting to feel comfortable in his situation.

"Captain, do ye have room for our guest at yer table?" Triton asked, understanding instinctively that fighting men would make good company for each other.

"We do, My Lord, and he is most welcome to come and stay with us! The brother of the Land's Hero would be good company, I think!"

"Very well then, so be it," Triton spoke, and the scribe wrote it down. "I suggest ye start at the Sea Spray, with a few cups of the Port's specialty."

"I think ye might be right, My Lord!" the Captain grinned. "Master Azeem, if ye would join us?"

"I would be honored," the Moorish man intoned gravely.

"Step lively then," the Captain motioned for him to follow. "We should get down there before the shift change at the wharf. Would ye mind a bar seat?"

"I like sitting at the bar," Azeem nodded. "But my friend, would ye ask me to go into a bar without a weapon?"

"Of course not," Bartholomew nodded. Reaching into a pocket, he withdrew a few of Azeem's smaller weapons, along with his belt knife and boot knives.

"Ye had those on yer person all this time?"

"I did," the Captain grinned, and Azeem detected a bit of mischievousness in his tone. Azeem secured the weapons quickly out of long practice, and just as they approached the entrance to the Inn, he felt more confident due to their presence.

They walked into the Inn, which was not busy at the moment. The owner, Valentina, saw them and motioned them over to the bar, her area of service.

"Barty!" she greeted warmly, throwing her arms around him and hugging him like a son. "Who is this? He looks a bit familiar to me."

"He should," the Captain laughed merrily. "Madam I wish to present Azeem ben Cain, newly arrived in the Land due to the Lady's favor."

"Ye are Ishmael's *BROTHER*?" Valentina questioned, looking him up and down in an assessing manner.

"I have that honor, if 'tis the same Ishmael ben Cain I remember."

"If he is a huge man of epic proportions, then 'tis the same man," Valentina laughed. "Tell me, Azeem, do ye like spiced rhum?"

"I do!" he grinned, accepting the cup of delicious liquor, poured over chunks of ice with a generous piece of lime squeezed into it. After taking the first sip, a long and thirsty one, Azeem put the cup down with a gentle thump, then turned to the older woman behind the bar. "Truly, I must be drinking ambrosia out of this cup, Madam!" he complimented extravagantly after a few swallows. "I am enjoying this very much!"

"I am glad," Valentina responded, looking up to see the first large group of men entering. She knew then it was time for the shift change, and called to her servers to come tend the crowd. Azeem watched the service floor fill rapidly, reckoning that everyone serving would make a generous pocketful of tips tonight. He continued to simply observe as the crowd increased, until finally Bartholomew touched his arm to get his attention.

"I think 'tis time for us to go," he said quietly. "Besides, the guardhouse is quieter, and more comfortable."

"I am willing to go if ye are," Azeem agreed.

From that point on, Azeem was treated as an honored guest. When they arrived back at the guardhouse, the shift change was done, and the day shift was ready to relax. Rhum and brown ale flowed freely, there were snacks to ease the appetite set out on the table, and one of the squires was strumming a gitar, a quiet and pleasant sound. He drank, smoked and ate with the Marines until his eyes drooped, and then they escorted him to a comfortable room with a warm, not too soft bed.

"I hope the room suits ye?"

"I thank ye for the use of it," he told the Captain, his voice reflecting gratitude. "I hope ye sleep well too."

Shutting the door, Azeem turned the lock, surprised they would leave it functional. Looking about the room, he saw that the rest of his weapons were there, laying on the bed. It did not take him long to carefully put them aside, clearing the bed for sleeping. Turning to the small necessity area, he found hot water running from a tap after turning it experimentally. A grin of delight crossed his face as he tried the paste in the small jar on the sink, as it smelled of lavender and thyme. He felt refreshed after rinsing off, remaining naked as he climbed into the bed, noting the sheets were clean. The last thing he did was tuck his blade under the mattress, and whisper a prayer to the Divine that he was not in the land of the Djinn.

A soft knocking roused him from sleep, and he noted the position of the sun stood at mid-morning. It had been many months since he had indulged such a late rising, he thought to himself, wondering what to do. Finally, he called out.

"I am awake!"

"Good!" Bartholomew's voice called back. "Yer clothes are being mended, so I put a few sets of our casual clothing in the closet for ye. I hope they fit."

"Thank ye, Captain for yer thoughtfulness," Azeem called back gratefully, slipping from the bed and walking to the small clothespress against the wall. Opening it he withdrew a set of plain grey, slightly napped, trous and shirt, holding them up to see if they were of the correct size. He marveled to see that indeed, they might fit his enormous dimensions, and when he had them on, they felt warm and comforting. There were slippers in the bottom of the press, which also fit well and provided a bit of luxury for his well-worn and sometimes abused feet. "I am dressed now," he called, walking to open the door.

"Ye look well in the clothing of the Land," Bartholomew noted as he walked in, carrying a steaming carafe and two mugs. "Caffe?"

"Ye have that here?" Azeem exclaimed with delight. "I would enjoy sharing a cup with ye. I have not enjoyed caffe for a long, long time."

"Have ye looked outside yet?" Bartholomew asked as he served the beverage with practiced grace.

"I can see the sun is approaching mid-day," Azeem answered. "I am unused to sleeping so late."

"Ye are a guest here, yer schedule is more lax," Bartholomew pointed out. "However, we hold a group exercise in the mornings for everyone who can attend, and ye are welcome to join us if ye would like to. We are going to work outside in the sun, which I enjoy a great deal. I always feel as if I have more energy instead of less after such a session," the captain explained conversationally. Inwardly, he was watching Azeem carefully, looking for any hint that his nature might be other than benign. "Of course, first meal will be served after that. I cannot work hard on a full belly."

"I agree," Azeem nodded, sipping the delicious beverage and enjoying it a great deal. It was strong, but not too muchly so, and it held an overtone of cacao which only accentuated the robust flavors. With the little bit of honey he added, it was an enjoyable cupful, and he drank every drop. He spent that day simply wandering about the place, offering to be of help where he saw the need, all of which got back to the Captain quickly. They spent a friendly night again, and when Azeem woke in the morning, he felt much more comfortable with his new surroundings. The word *home* began to surface in his mind, which puzzled him in every way, as he had been a virtual nomad for two decades. As he slept that night, his muscles tired from the group exercise, as well as all of the volunteered labor, he thought of his brother. The longing to see Ishmael was a keen one, that night he barely slept as he prepared to take his leave in search of his brother. In the morning, Bartholomew noted the dark circles under his eyes and came to sit at his table to share the first meal.

"What is amiss?"

"Do ye know where my brother is?" Azeem asked in return.

"Ye will find either him, or news of his whereabouts in the Barracks of the Army, below the High Lord's house in the Capitol city."

"How would one get there?"

"As it so happens, Master Azeem, the time for our rotation has come. A group of troopers who have been here a bit longer than usual will be departing for the Capitol this morning, and they are impatient to leave. Ye may ride along with them, if ye wish, and ye will have company and guidance along yer way. 'Twill give ye a chance to see some of the most beautiful parts of the Land, I highly recommend the trip."

"Thank ye, Captain. Ye have been most gracious and welcoming to a visitor. I am grateful to find good manners exist here, as they are often missing from interactions in the outer world."

"The Outlands," Bartholomew snorted a bit. "A place of rudeness and greed, as I understand it. I would not wish to visit there, except to help the Lady better establish Her rule there. I think the Outlanders would benefit from such a hierarchy."

"Indeed," Azeem nodded. "As things are now, one can barely trust a merchant, or an innkeeper in most ports. With all of the trouble in the Holy Land, as well as other places in the world, I find it comforting to find a place of refuge and safety."

"We have certain dangers here ye will not find anywhere else in the world," Bartholomew responded. "Yer brother will have many stories to tell of his exploits in that regard. I wish ye well, Azeem ben Cain, and I bid ye welcome to the Land in the Lady's name. Ye are home, if ye wish to be."

"Strange ye should say that," Azeem responded as Bartholomew offered the Grip. "I feel as if I *am* home, something I have not felt for almost two decades. I thank ye for yer kind welcome, and for the company of the guardhouse."

"Ye are most welcome," Bartholomew smiled, releasing his arm. "Come, let us find ye a horse big enough to accommodate yer frame."

Leading the way, the Captain took his guest out to the stables, where the departing troopers were now assembling. The Stablemaster took one look at Azeem, grinned a bit and asked only one question.

"How experienced of a rider are ye?"

"I have tamed wild horses in the desert to carry me without bridle or saddle," Azeem answered calmly, for it was truth.

"Very well, come along. I think I might have the perfect horse for ye," the man grinned wider. Azeem began to suspect a good-natured prank of some sort, which would be usual in a guardhouse filled with warriors. They led him out to the farthest field, where a huge, piebald stallion stood calmly grazing.

"That horse is named Pyrite," the Stablemaster said quietly. "He is at rest right now, so ye would never suspect his wild nature. He is the only horse born to our mares I cannot even get close to, and I am considered to be a *horse whisperer*. I was thinking of just turning him out to be free, since no one can ride him. However, ye may have the skill and if ye do, he is yers to keep."

"I accept this challenge!" Azeem grinned widely. "However, such a thing is thirsty work."

"Ye will find plenty to slake yer thirst at the next guardhouse," the Stablemaster countered. "Sharing the tale of taming such a horse would guarantee yer cup would be full for many hours."

Azeem said nothing, simply accepting the sturdy halter and lead rope handed to him. Seeing the baskets of fresh apples and carrots at hand, Azeem stopped and quickly filled his pockets with the treats, knowing most horses craved them. Finally, he took a few deep breaths, summoned up all of the knowledge he carried concerning horses and entered the enclosure, walking slowly up to the huge horse. Keeping the halter in hand in a non-threatening manner, Azeem stopped just out of the horse's easy reach, offering a quarter apple as a temptation. Pyrite simply eyed him speculatively, as if this had been tried before, and Azeem nodded.

"So ye are not stupid, nor uncautious," he commented quietly, and the horse's head rose a bit, as if he understood the words. "Good, I do not want a stupid horse as my working partner. I have ridden the swift ones of the desert and the small ones of the steppes, I ask only that ye be a partner with me and if ye will allow me to ride ye, I shall be a grateful man. I take good care of my partners, they eat before I do and we share the load of work. What say ye, Pyrite?" he asked, reverting to a mental plea.

"I hate that name," he heard plainly in his mind and stifled a gasp. Talking to the horse had been more of a calming exercise in the past, and Azeem had not expected to share conversation with a horse. "I shall not answer to it anymore."

"What is yer name?" he continued on, adapting quickly to the new ability.

"My name is Jaspa!" the horse exclaimed. "It means piebald, but I didn't like that name either."

"Very well, Jaspa ye will be as long as ye are with me," Azeem answered easily, offering the apple piece again on a flattened palm. Every man now watching held their breath, knowing that the last man to try this had been savagely bitten and was still recovering at the Main Temple as they watched to see if he would keep two fingers. The horse lipped the piece of fruit off his palm neatly, chewing with delight as Azeem slipped the halter over his head and fastened it into place. "Now, may I ride ye?"

"Do ye have more apple?"

Azeem grinned and offered two more pieces in succession until the horse's thoughts indicated he could mount. The huge black man vaulted up onto his broad back, looping the long lead rope up and around to use as a set of reins. As the astonished troopers watched and passed silver coins back and forth among one another, Azeem put the horse through his basic paces without a single refusal. Afterward he slipped off and offered more fruit, which was gladly accepted by the horse.

"Thank ye."

"Ye are most welcome, Jaspa. Now, would ye go with this man without fighting him please? Ye need a nice bath and rubdown before we depart."

"I would like a bath and a rubdown. I am tired, but I feel good," the horse responded, and Azeem could hear his weariness. Jaspa went with the ostler, walking beside him as if his wild nature was a thing long past. The bath was endured, as well as the drying rubdown, especially since the ostlers made certain he was completely dry before dressing him for the ride. Finally, the horse made his reappearance and everyone was shocked to see him simply accept Azeem on his back once more.

"Come, let us take our place in the line. I am ready to see more of the Land," Azeem whispered into the horse's mind.

"I only know this place, and the stables at the High Lord's House," the horse replied. "I look forward to visiting there again."

"We are going there now, so ye will have yer wish fulfilled in short order," Azeem answered with humor as the horse simply traveled with the rest of the trooper's horses, making no trouble for the entire day. When he heard the troop captain give the order to move out, he swung out in line with the rest, trotting along at a comfortable traveling pace.

Jaspa simply behaved as the rest of the horses did, at least until the sun hung over them all afternoon. All of them were sweating and overheated, but they rode on, trying to travel as many leagues as possible before nightfall. Jaspa's exchange with his new rider became irritable and sarcastic, the horse wanted to stop and swim in the river that ran alongside the road.

"We cannot stop now, my friend, not until we are ready to camp for the night, or until we find the next guardhouse. I am hot and sweating too under my armor and clothing, but we must endure."

"O very well," the horse replied in an exasperated tone. "I hope we will have a chance to swim later then."

"I hope so too," Azeem agreed, wistfully thinking of a cool river and a cold mug. The day wore on as they stopped a few times to help citizens in need, and finally as the sun sank behind the trees, the next guardhouse came into view. It sat right beside the river, Azeem noted as they crossed the bridge to the gates and called up for entry.

"Hullo!" they heard, and a man wearing chain mail peeked over the ramparts. "Ye are a bit late, but not to worry. We are cooking and eating outside tonight! Just smell that pig cooking!" he said enthusiastically.

"Pig?" several of the men echoed, and Azeem grinned to see the look of longing on their faces. Like most men of his race, Azeem followed the Path of the Prophet, which forbade the eating of pork. However, if it was the only thing available, he simply ate enough to satisfy his hunger, then apologized to Allah in the morning.

"Aye! But the cook also is roasting chickens, for those who do not like pig meat. I shall open the gate for ye in a moment. Welcome to the guardhouse!"

It took a short time, but at length the massive steel-bound oak gate rolled up and open, allowing them to enter. Once they were inside it closed after them, sealing the gate. Ostlers came to take their tired, sweaty horses, and Azeem took a moment to speak with Jaspa.

"Please just go with the ostlers, my friend. They will take care of ye, and see that ye eat well. Ye will have a warm stall to sleep in tonight. I thank ye for the comfort of the ride, I think we will be good partners."

"Good night," Jaspa replied wearily, his head dragging a bit as the ostler led him away. Every man in the stable stared with shock, knowing the stallion's reputation well enough to know that his current behavior was out of character. Azeem grinned widely, for it brought the huge man a vast amount of humor when his sharp ears caught the sounds of silver coins exchanging hands, he simply accepted it as part of barracks life. Troopers would habitually bet on almost anything, he knew from his vast experience, having served in more than a few barracks. He gave them a discreet moment or two, so they would have plenty of time to complete their transactions under the cover of not being seen. It was easy for a smart man to keep plenty of coins in his pocket that way, Azeem grinned to himself as he joined them.

"Well now, my friends. Where can we clean up and change before supper?" he asked with a wide smile.

"I am going swimming!" he heard many of them exclaim, grabbing the small bags hanging on the rumps of their steeds. Azeem understood their extra clothing was within the bags, and glanced at Jaspa quickly. There was a similar bag on his horse, and Azeem called to the ostler to toss it to him, which he did so that the bag landed precisely in Azeem's hands.

"Thank ye, my friend!" the huge man called to the ostler, making a mental note to hand the man a coin when next they met.

"Come in come in!" they heard, and turned to see a woman wearing Captain's rank bars approaching. The rest of the troopers saluted her respectfully, then greeted her with a grip to the forearm. When she saw Azeem, her expression changed at once to one of interest and speculation. "And who might ye be?" she asked, noticing his resemblance to the Hero of the Land.

"I am called Azeem," he answered cautiously, noting her trim and athletic build.

"He is not just Azeem," the captain of their traveling troop put in. "He is Azeem ben Cain."

"I know yer brother," the woman answered. "My name is Iniri, I am in command here. I once served a short time at the same facility as Master Ishmael. He is a unique warrior of amazing skill, and the Land is better for his presence here."

Azeem's eyes opened a bit at the tone of respect her words held. "I am looking forward to catching up with him. We have not seen each other for a little over twenty years now."

"Ye have a great deal to catch up on then. Now, we will find a place for ye to sleep, Azeem. Just leave yer bag here with the rest of them and follow the others to the river. Ye will find cold ale and wine there, as well as cold water to cool yerself. I shall be down in a short while, a swim sounds like an excellent idea on such a hot day." Iniri said in an instructing tone, pointing out the open door. Azeem could see those he had travelled with, now running for the ribbon of blue water in the distance. Her suggestion there would be cold drink there motivated his movements, at least until Iniri's voice halted him.

"If ye would wait, I shall walk with ye."

"I would be honored... Madam?" he questioned the use of the title.

"Commander is my title," she corrected him. "But since we are in a casual atmosphere, *Madam* will be appropriate," she went on. "Ye must understand, I command here. I cannot be seen as weak or indecisive among the troopers," she went on in a halting tone. He stopped and turned to her, his face composed in a gentle expression.

"Madam, I would do naught to upset the balance here," he said quietly. "All I am doing is walking beside ye to the swimming hole, surely 'twould be seen as innocent enough?" he asked quietly.

"Indeed," she nodded. "It has been a long time since a man caught my interest," she went on honestly. "I would not mind if we could not find the extra bed space for ye among the troopers."

"I can make myself comfortable just about anywhere," Azeem told her. "One of those sofas over there looks good enough to me."

"If ye accept the offer I am making, ye will not have to sleep there all night," Iniri replied boldly. Azeem simply took her hand and turned it, kissing the palm despite never having done so before to any woman of his acquaintance. It just seemed *right* to do so, and he heard her gasp of response.

"I think some cold water would benefit both of us, aye?"

"We had best be on our way, Madam, before I find a dark corner to pull ye into," he answered, being just as honest about his interest in her. A smile crossed her face, one that held anticipation and he released her hand, returning to his casual, jovial self.

"Very well, let us walk the short distance to the river," Iniri answered. They said naught until they reached the swimming hole, where Azeem simply disrobed to the skin and ran for the water. Once he reached the bank, he launched himself up into the air as high as possible, trying to reach the middle of the river. Once he reached the full height, he rolled himself into a ball, and let himself drop into the water like a large stone. The sound, a deep *K'thunk* could be heard clearly, the ripples from the impact lapped against each bank, and Azeem rose from the water, laughing merrily.

"Good one!" Iniri called out, bringing him a cup, not minding his nakedness. They were all naked, and such was usual for the Land, where the people were not prudish, but practical in every way. Azeem was treated to a full view of her lithe figure, as well as the various tattoos and scars that decorated it. He could see bite marks and scars from many lashings, his blood boiled to see such abuse heaped on the fairer sex, as he liked to think of women. It was a short time later when he returned to the river for a quick dip in the slow running waters, and he felt something brush by his foot. His face reflected surprise as Iniri watched from close by, and she whispered her question to him.

"What is amiss?"

"Something brushed by my right ankle," Azeem whispered back. "Are there large fish in this river?"

"Aye, huge catfish!" Iniri replied, her excitement obvious. "They nest in the bottom of the river, deep in the mud. 'Tis considered quite a test of skill to catch them by hand. I have done it, 'tis not as easy as it sounds," she finished, and he heard the note of challenge within her words.

"I have tickled trout from a river, but never a catfish," Azeem confessed with a grin, wondering how it was done. "However, catfish are usually very large in rivers such as this, and I would imagine their teeth are quite sharp as well."

"As I said, 'tis a test of skill," Iniri laughed. "Come, I shall help ye find one, then coach ye through it. I love grilled fish, and catfish is good like that, if ye prepare it right."

"I accept the challenge!" Azeem stated, following her into the deeper part of the river, where the water ran slowly, and the temperature was a bit warmer. Azeem noted the differences at once and nodded, he would be more likely to find such a bottom-feeding fish in such an environment. He watched as Iniri knelt in the water, feeling the bottom mud carefully, and he joined her, kneeling beside her and emulating her. It did not take long for something to try and swallow his hand, and with a grin, Azeem grasped onto the bottom of the mouth firmly. The fish thrashed and bucked, trying to get loose from Azeem's iron grip, and as Iniri watched with admiration, the huge man pulled a huge fish from the water, brandishing it so they all could see it. "Look Commander Iniri! I have caught one!"

"And 'tis a big one too! Look, 'tis nearly as long as I am tall!" Iniri laughed as Azeem hauled the struggling fish to the shore of the river. One of the troopers brought him a stout stick, but Azeem waved it off.

"I would not dispatch this fish with such a cudgel," he said, his tone deep with respect and gratitude. Instead, asked for his trous to be brought, and withdrew a small sharp blade from a pocket, using it to quickly and mercifully dispatch the fish. He simply took the tip of the blade and thrust it into the fish's brain. It stopped struggling almost at once, and he whispered a thanks for the nourishment it would provide. "My thanks to ye, monster fish. May ye pass into yer next incarnation quickly, and may it be a better one."

A pair of squires was summoned to help bear the fish to the cooking area, where those preparing the meal grinned with delight. They descended upon it with sharp knives, and soon it was grilling on a separate grill than the rest of the meat. They continued drinking from the ale cask until the meal was declared ready to be served, and he sat beside Iniri to enjoy the food. The tastes and textures of all of the foods delighted his palate after such a long time aboard ship, he thought as he filled his plate once more. The second plate was eaten more slowly than the first, but enjoyed just as much, and finally he wiped the plate with a crust of bread then pushed it away, laying the fork upon it.

"I must compliment the cooks!" he said loudly, over the buzz of conversation. "In my country, one does so with a loud belch, but I can see that would be considered rude here. I offer my thanks to those who prepared the meal, the flavors were remarkably good, and the service was also excellent throughout."

"Ye are most welcome, Master ben Cain!" the Kitchen Master of the guardhouse responded, speaking for his entire tired crew. "We are honored to serve!"

Everyone stood then and began to clear the tables in short order, Azeem joining in. He even did several sink loads of dishes to make the work go faster, and the kitchen crew thanked him with warm smiles. Once the meal was put away, tables wiped down and dishes done, it was time for the shift change. Iniri yawned wide and said her goodnights, ordering that Azeem be made comfortable on a sofa for the night.

"Aye Commander," her Second in Command answered seriously. "Good night, and sleep well."

"Thank ye," she yawned a bit. "Make sure ye get yer fair share of sleep as well."

"I shall, Commander," the man replied, his voice heavy with respect. Azeem could hear another note as well, one of longing, and he wondered why it was unrequited. His curiosity was soon appeased, for as soon as Iniri was out of earshot, the Second in Command explained his reactions.

"Master Azeem, 'twould be entirely inappropriate for her to take any one of us to her bed. Such things lead to a breakdown in the order of things, which none of us would want. All is as it should be, at least for the moment, and if I must look upon her from afar, I shall. If I can arrange for her happiness, I am glad to do so out of respect and love for her. If ye follow her now, ye need not worry. I shall muss up the covers enough to provide the proper cover. Every trooper here approves of yer relationship with her, ye need not fear any reprisals. Good night."

"Good night," Azeem returned. "I am sorry, I did not get yer name?"

"Ah, my name is Atlas, after the Titan who carries the world upon his shoulders," the man grinned. "I hope someday to earn a command of my own, but for how, serving with Iniri is a great honor."

"Good night, Sir Atlas," Azeem bid him, then followed his discreet finger pointing to the door Iniri used to leave the common room.

In nearly every guardhouse, the Commander's room was somewhat isolated, on purpose. Such a thing provided the proper space in between herself and the troopers, as well as assuring her privacy. Iniri had an entire wing to herself, there were no other troopers there, only the massive armory of the guardhouse. Azeem walked on silent feet down the long hallway lined with swords, pikes, lances, shields, axes and assorted other small weaponry, admiring the quality of their making. He wondered if every warrior here in the Land carried such excellent weapons, and if they did, it meant this was a rich kingdom, the richest he had ever visited. He saw an open door at the end of the long hallway and made for it, seeing that Iniri was within when he walked through. She had changed clothing into something sheer and gauzy, due to the heat of the evening. It covered everything, but showed everything as well, and Azeem found himself even more interested in her than before.

"Would ye shut the door please?" she asked quietly. "I have a balcony just outside my window, if ye would care to join me for a sikar and a sip of good whiskey."

"I would enjoy both, Madam."

It was not a long time afterward that the lights dimmed in Iniri's room, and the entire guardhouse grew quiet except for the faint sound of boots walking on the stone floors as the night guard patrolled and protected.

Chapter 4

In the morning, Azeem woke first, attended to his morning needs then sponged himself free of the night sweat. Once he was clean, he returned to the bedroom to don his clothing, finding it had been washed and dried, as well as being mended completely. A grateful smile passed over his face as he began to dress, trying to be as quiet as possible so as not to wake Iniri, who he thought was still sleeping. He was very surprised a few minutes later when Iniri opened the door to her room and entered, carrying a large tray covered with a clean, white cloth.

"Good morning," she greeted with a warm smile. "I went downstairs and found this waiting," she explained, flipping back the cover to reveal a carafe of caffe and a plate of treats. "Apparently, the guardhouse approves of ye being here. I know I do," she chuckled softly.

"Good morning," he replied, a bit overwhelmed by her words. "I hoped that the troopers would not be resentful."

"Taste those pastries, and tell me if they taste of disapproval," she laughed.

Azeem picked up the closest one and sniffed with caution, his eyes widening at the rich, sweet scent. He could not discern, however, what provided such an odor, and so he bit cautiously and sampled. His eyes widened when he tasted the cacao, worked into a custard-ish filling, hit his tongue. He chewed with delight, finding that an occasional sip of the caffe provided an additional layer of texture and taste. With a swallow and a final sip of the hot beverage in his cup, Azeem smiled at Iniri, feeling contented, but ready for another sample of the pastries.

"They are marvelous, I have never tasted anything quite like them!" he said with enthusiasm. "What is that filling made from?"

"Cacao, a gift from across the wide ocean. We have established trading relationships with the Natives who dwell in the *Land of Mist and Frogs*," she told him. "I enjoy it too, and a little spoonful of the powder in my morning caffe is always welcome," she went on. "I thank the Goddess for yer arrival," she added softly. "I thought I might go mad if I did not have male company of the intimate kind," she told him. "I can think clearly now, a boon to any lonely Amazon."

"I would stay, if I thought 'twould benefit either of us," Azeem answered after a moment or two. "But I must find my brother, and catch up on twenty years of news before I can think of remaining," he replied, and she detected evasion in his words for the first time. What is he hiding, she wondered to herself as she sat there with the huge, handsome man.

"I can certainly understand such a need," she answered at length. "Perhaps we shall see each other at the Summer Tournament. I would enjoy that."

"Summer Tournament?"

"Aye, a testing of yer endurance, stamina and skills. The High Lord simply wishes to see what we can do, what we have and are learning, and how we put it to the best use. Also, 'tis a very festive occasion where ale flows and the Herb is passed about freely every night. Live music and dancing are encouraged, 'tis a time to socialize and renew friendships, as well as make new friends. Ye will learn more about it when ye get to the main Barracks, under the High Lord's House. I wish ye well, Azeem ben Cain, and I look forward to seeing ye this Summer."

"Ye will be there?"

"I shall, as I am resigning this commission. My term of service is ended, I can choose to return to the isolation of the Amazon Fortress if I wish. I do not know yet, what I want to do, but attending the Tournament is something ye should not miss."

"And where will ye be staying if ye attend?"

"I can beg a room in the city, I have friends with homes there," she grinned. "Otherwise, ye will see me in the Barracks' common room."

"I look forward to that," Azeem smiled warmly, truly enjoying her company. They finished their caffe and treats slowly, letting silence reign in comfort as they both began to consider a longer term relationship between them. Finally, she rose and put everything back onto the tray, covering with the cloth and setting it outside for the squires to pick up. "Come 'tis time for first meal."

"Ye do not mind if they see us together so early in the morning?"

"Ye are dressed for travel, I am dressed for duty. They may think whatever they please," she answered with a grin.

The first meal was sumptuous; griddlecakes, sausages and fried eggs, all neatly piled onto a plate, ready to be consumed. Iniri showed him the compotes available, then suggested the dark amber liquid in a small pitcher at hand.

"What is it?" Azeem questioned, taking a sniff and liking the scent.

"Syrup made from the sap of sugar maple trees," Iniri answered. "I like it a great deal because of its rich, wholesome taste. I like it on frozen custard too, as well as in my morning oat porridge and on fresh biscuits."

Azeem grinned and poured a bit on a section of his griddlecakes, then cut a small bite to sample. His face lit in delight when the taste of the syrup hit his tongue, and he could imagine many other uses for such a flavor.

"My goodness, what a stupendous taste!" he complimented, never having experienced anything like it before. "I imagine this would be a good thing to use when roasting meat, especially pig."

"Are ye not one of those who follow the teachings of *The Prophet*?" she asked, knowing the outside world well, having come from it herself.

"I and *The Prophet* have an understanding about such things, both of us being practical men," Azeem grinned. "I eat what is on the table, and I make recompense for it later by fasting. 'Tis a good relationship to have with one's religion."

"We only have one faith here in the Land," Iniri told him seriously. "The Lady rules here, and She tolerates no other faith. Ye would be wise to court Her favor, my friend, since She has brought ye here."

"I look forward to learning more of all the Land has to offer," Azeem replied. It did not take him long to consume the plateful, and then it was time for the troop to depart. He said his farewells to Iniri privately, out of sight of the others, respecting her need to keep the distance between her and the troopers.

"As soon as I am in the Barracks, I shall ask about the Tournament, and where I might sign up for it," he told her quietly. "I wish to see ye again, if ye would permit."

"We will see, Azeem ben Cain," Iniri replied mysteriously, kissing him fully and deeply, leaving him wanting much more. "I shall attend the Tournament, if only to see my sister Amazons, whether I participate or not is still under question. In any case, I shall make time for ye, no matter what. May your travels be pleasant, on your way to the Capitol City, and may the Lady watch over ye."

"Thank ye Iniri," he replied, embracing her once more, just to try and keep her memory fresh in his mind. "I hope to see ye soon."

With that, he squared his shoulders and left her standing there, walking the short distance to join the others who were leaving. Iniri appeared just as they mounted up, calling out a traveling blessing for the entire troop.

"May the Lady watch over ye all as ye travel to the Capitol City," she called as they rode away. Those words rang in Azeem's ears throughout the day, even while he marveled at the beauty that surrounded him. The evergreen trees were tall and thick, proving their age, and Azeem marveled to see such huge trees still standing. The roadbed was smooth and well-kept, the verges beside it trimmed and planted with flowering shrubs and plants. Every so often, they would come upon a small farm, and he saw that each one was in good repair, the fields planted with crops, the herd animals grazing on thick green grass, fat and content. He was truly startled to see each farm so well groomed, each village so clean and the people smiling and happy. Surely, he thought again, I must be in the land of the Djinn. No one is this happy, at least no one I have ever met before.

They stopped well before sundown that night to camp beside a river, and once the tents were up, the men were in the water cooling off. The horses joined them to take their ease in the waters, and once everyone had bathed, they went upstream a bit to do some fishing for supper. Two dozen trout later, the fishermen were back in camp, handing their cleaned catch to the person appointed to do the cooking that night. Azeem enjoyed the meal of crispy fried fish and papas, with a wild salad foraged from the surrounding woods. The huge man could not remember enjoying a meal more, he thought as he finished the last of the fish, then followed the example set by the others, taking his dishes to the cooking tent where hot water and soap waited in a deep, wide tub. Azeem bent to the task voluntarily, winning approval and respect from the others for doing so, and soon they were rolling out their beds and making ready for sleep.

"Thank ye for doing that chore for us," the troop captain thanked him. "I was glad to be able to offer some service in return for how well I have been treated here in the Land," Azeem replied truthfully. "What other service can I be?"

"None tonight, nor 'till ye are officially one of us," the captain replied. "Unless ye do not mind washing the dishes more often," he added with a grin.

"I do not mind at all," Azeem told him. "I like clean dishes as much as the next man."

The rest of their journey passed pleasantly as Azeem became more and more familiar with the routine, and as the troopers talked to him about how it was to live in the Land. Most of them had never known anything else, and they were shocked to learn how the outside world truly behaved.

"I am glad to be here now," Azeem put in. "I would not want to leave."

Ten days later, just as the sun sank, the patrol arrived at the Capitol City, and coaxed their weary horses up the hill, then down the pathway to the Barracks' entrance. Their animals were taken by the ostlers to be cared for, Azeem having had a chat with Jaspa beforehand.

"Now, ye will not be any trouble to the ostlers in the stables, will ye?" he asked of the horse as they entered the city.

"I shall not, I am too tired to do anything but sleep," Jaspa answered indignantly. "Besides, 'tis the High Lord's House, and the Barracks below. Such is not a place to be making trouble."

"Good, I am glad ye understand," Azeem nodded. He was just as tired as the horse, and the men had been talking about the hot spring in the Barracks for hours. He wanted to soak, and perhaps have a cold ale or two while doing so. Instead, he was taken at once to Tristan, the Knight Commander where he was introduced.

"Azeem *ben Cain*?" the man grinned widely. "I am happy to meet the brother of such a Hero! Welcome to the Barracks and to the Capitol City. Let us find ye a room, and ye may speak with the War Duke and the High Lord in the morning. We are cooking outside tonight, and I hear 'tis pig or two cooking."

"Indeed? Then I have arrived just in time!" Azeem laughed a great guffaw, the others joining him.

"Ye should all get to the baths and clean up, the ale has been cooling in the Elan for over an hour and should be sufficiently cold. Master Azeem, a moment of your time please?" Lord Tristan requested and Azeem noted the change in his tone of voice.

"I am at yer service, My Lord."

Tristan smiled a bit at the words he used as he motioned for the black man to follow him a short distance away, out of the earshot of others.

"I simply wanted to warn ye of a custom here in the Land," Tristan began, keeping his voice low. "If ye decide to go swimming in the river, remember, ye may look all ye wish, but ye may neither touch nor take anything ye see on the bottom. All of it is considered sacred, no matter how much gold and luxury it may represent in the Outlands. The Lady has been known to punish people severely for touching or taking anything from the River Elan, the most sacred river in the Land. Please keep that in mind as ye enjoy yerself."

"Thank ye for the warning, My Lord," Azeem acknowledged gratefully. "I would not wish to make such an error due to ignorance. Now, can ye tell me where I might find my brother, Ishmael?"

Just as Azeem entered the Barracks, Ishmael was sitting down to supper with Zameera. They ate the sumptuous meal she had prepared slowly, enjoying all of the flavors her hard work had produced, then Ishmael rose to clear the table and put the leftovers away.

"We have so much to put away," he said finally as they made the last trip to the cold room. "Whatever shall we do with all of that lamb?"

"I could make stew, or hand pies, or simply reheat it in the leftover sauce," Zameera told him, yawning wide. "Listen, ye can hear them on the party grounds, even all the way down here," she laughed a bit.

"I do not mind," Ishmael responded, coming to put his arms around her. "I feel safer for knowing they are there."

"As do I. I am tired Ishmael, are ye coming to bed?"

"In a bit, I have thinking to do," Ishmael told her. "Ye have presented me with a gifting I thought I would never receive. 'Twill take some getting used to, the idea I am to be a father," he continued on, being his usual honest self.

"Very well, tonight starts yer two-day," Zameera yawned again. "Ye can sleep a little later than usual, if ye wish. Good night."

"Good night, my dear," he responded, kissing her warmly before releasing her to go. He watched her walk up the stairs, then heard the bedroom door open and close, then sighed, knowing he was alone.

"Great Goddess, I thank ye for this…this gift," he whispered as he poured a large cup of whiskey and picked out a sikar. "I thought I was to be the last, and ye have rescued my bloodline. I am grateful, in every wise, for Yer favor, Great Lady."

"Ye are most welcome, Master ben Cain," he heard a faint and feminine whisper in his mind. "Ye have earned all ye shall receive, and I am happy to assure the gifting of it. Enjoy yer two-day," the voice continued on. He waited a moment or two more, in case She wanted to say more to him, and when only silence reigned, he sighed heavily, returning to his line of thought while he finished his sleep easers. When he finished the drink and the smoke, he stubbed out the sikar thoroughly, assured all was well by testing the entry doors. They were securely locked, to his relief, and so he retired to the bed waiting for him, sleeping easily until morning.

He woke to the scent of caffe brewing, laying there appreciating the rich flavors. He had no idea what was about to occur in his life to further alter it as he rose and dressed, then headed for the kitchen, where he knew Zameera was nearly ready to pour the hot beverage. Resolving to visit the local Temple that day to make an offering to express his gratitude to the Goddess for the gift of such a wife, he walked into the kitchen, offering an embrace to his wife.

Down in the Barracks, Azeem awoke slowly, a tinge of pain in his head due to the amount of drink he had imbibed the night before. Opening his eyes, he found himself lying on a couch in the common room, a group of beautiful women on the chairs and sofas surrounding him. He noted he was fully clothed, always a good sign when waking into such situations, he thought as he carefully sat up, trying to be quiet. Taking a moment, he attempted to recall his memories from the night before, finding it hazy at first, but as he sat there, all of them suddenly surfaced. He had been sorely tempted the night before by each and every one of the women on the furniture around him. It was nearly painful to recall, the touches and kisses they had all heaped upon him, separately and then all together. He had resisted, with great difficulty, he thought with a slight grin as he eased himself off the sofa. Quickly looking himself over, he found all of the laces and buttons intact, and so he knew he had not succumbed to the passionate kisses and touches they had offered. A sigh of relief escaped him as he realized his words to Iniri were intact and true, he quickly and quietly walked away, leaving the women to sleep. Walking into the dining hall, he found the Kitchen Master serving griddle cakes.

"Good morning, Master…Klietos?" he fished for the man's name from his hazy memory.

"Ye have good recall, Master Azeem," the man answered, grinning widely. He turned to a side table, poured a small cup full of what looked like clear water, handing to the huge man in front of him. "Now, if ye want to be rid of that head and body ache from too much drink, sip that down quickly. 'Tis willowbark powder, and though 'tis bitter, 'tis a good pain reliever for such things."

"Thank ye Master Klietos," Azeem nodded slowly, not wanting to aggravate the headache already brewing. Taking the cup in hand, he simply tipped it back and swallowed quickly, having experienced the brew in the past. It did not take long for the pain in his head to fade, and his body felt better too. His hunger returned with ferocity, and he took the plate offered him with anticipation. Klietos watched with a smiling face as the contents on the plate disappeared quickly, but neatly, with several cups of hot caffe. Once he finished, he simply scraped the plate with the fork to get all of the egg yolk off the bottom before standing to take it to the dish area. "As always, the food in the Land is delicious and filling, prepared in clean kitchens with clean hands. I am grateful," he told the Kitchen Master.

"The Knight Commander and the War Duke have eaten already this morning, and asked me give ye a message for them. They would like ye to join the exercise in the arena, when ye feel rested enough," he said with a wide smile.

"Which way would I go to get there?" Azeem asked, being new to the Barracks.

"I think 'twould be better to show ye," Klietos answered. "The hallways twist and turn a bit, ye must pay attention as we walk."

"I shall do so, I assure ye. I learn quickly, and retain what I learn."

"Good, such a thing will serve ye well if ye decide to join the Army," Klietos responded conversationally. Azeem walked beside the man, watching how many lefts and rights they took on their way, until the hallway opened up into the exercise area and the sandy circle where the Knights and Dames practiced their art and kept themselves fit. The second session was just about to start, and when Tristan saw Azeem in the entryway, he motioned for him to join in.

"Come Master Azeem, we are just about to start!"

Azeem nodded, turned and offered his hand to Klietos, who responded with the Grip. Azeem accepted the gesture easily, knowing the honor being done him, and thanked the man for his guidance.

"Have a good day, Master Azeem," Klietos wished him, before walking away. Once he was gone, Azeem turned back to the lines of warriors, all standing their dressed as briefly as possible. The men were stripped to shorts and boots, the women barely dressed at all, which was quite distracting for Azeem. Before his night with Iniri, it had been years between relationships, and his one experience had lit the fire within. However, it burned only for Iniri, he realized as he stripped off his shirt, and tucked up his voluminous trous to make them shorter. He could admire the women's beauty, but it did not distract him from thoughts of Iniri, and so he found it easy to ignore them. He followed along with the others, quickly learning the routine, and finding the set of exercises very challenging to perform correctly. He was intrigued entirely, and worked his hardest to learn quickly and perform perfectly, as was his nature. All the while, he could feel female eyes upon him, and occasionally he could hear them make admiring noises, which made him feel a little uncomfortable. He felt as if he were on display for them, without wanting or intending to be, and he did not like the feeling. When the exercise was over, he put his practice blade away and walked to where he had left his shirt folded neatly. He found the Amazons waiting for him, and steeled himself inwardly, for they were all very, very beautiful.

"So, ye are Azeem ben Cain," one of them said with a grin, her red hair a deep auburn color. "I am Jasmine, and these are my sister Amazons; Tellia, Maral, Fiona, and Nina. Perhaps ye would like to join us for a drink later?" she invited in sonorous tones. Her voice was deeper than most women, he could not help but notice, something that usually appealed to him. However, all he could hear was Iniri's voice whispering in his ear as they circled him admiringly.

"Ye certainly are well built," Tellia noted with a faint smile as her eyes swept up and down admiringly. "Is Ishmael ben Cain truly yer brother?"

"He is indeed," Azeem answered as her hand swiped slowly across his flat, muscled stomach.

"Ye are built very much like him," Fiona noted, and he felt a hand caress his buttocks seductively. "Come and have a drink with us, unless ye are frightened," she challenged good-naturedly.

"Any man should be concerned about being alone with so many beautiful women," Azeem answered carefully, wondering what they were about. "But, I would be honored to have a drink with ye."

"Good!" they all said together, gathering around him and literally pushing him out of the arena, guiding him back to the common room. Tristan and Karpon watched them, and reckoned Azeem was about to be tested as only Amazons could.

"I wonder if he will survive," Karpon mused, fishing a coin out of his pocket.

"One can only hope," Tristan answered, matching the coin with one of his own. The two shared the Grip on the wager, then parted to their daily duties, a grin on their face for the rest of the day.

The next time Tristan saw Azeem, it was early morning in the common room. He was sound asleep on one of the sofas, surrounded by sleeping Dames. He had managed to keep his unders on at least, Tristan grinned as he carefully woke the man, being careful not to wake the women at the same time.

"Brother Azeem, wake up and come with me," he said quietly. Azeem roused a bit, blinked and looked about him, a look of alarm on his face.

"Where am I?"

"In the common room," Tristan told him, helping him to rise so as not to wake the woman beside him. "Come, ye can use the necessity in my quarters to clean up. How do ye feel?"

"Confused," Azeem answered honestly. "What happened last night? What were those women up to?"

"I believe ye have been subjected to the most severe of Amazon testing. Tell me, do ye know one of them?"

"An Amazon?"

"Aye. I do not wish to be indelicate, but if ye have shared a bed with one of the sisters, the rest of them will want to know what ye intentions are. Ye managed to keep yerself dressed, despite that, and I suspect ye have passed their testing," Tristan chuckled, knowing he had won the bet he placed the day before.

"Are all of the women in yer Army also Amazons?" Azeem asked as they walked along.

"Aye," Tristan confirmed, watching Azeem's face. A look of momentary confusion appeared, along with a touch of red to his cheeks and Tristan understood the situation perfectly.

"Then to answer yer 'indelicate' question, I have shared a bed with one of them."

Tristan thought over the current troop assignments along the way from the Port City, and the answer hit him heavily. He said no more about it however, as he considered it a private thing between Azeem and the woman involved.

"And so the rest of them tested yer intent, and yer commitment. Her name is Iniri, is it not?"

"Aye, Commander Iniri," Azeem sighed heavily as they reached Tristan's office and entered. Tristan fetched a set of clean house clothing out of his closet, handing it to the large black man with a bit of a grin.

"I hope these will fit well enough," he commented. "We are the closest in size of those awake at the moment. The necessity is through that door over there. Just turn the left hand tap for hot water."

"Thank ye Sir," Azeem answered gratefully. It did not take him long to use the soft soap and hot water to clean up, then don the fresh clothing, finding it fit well enough. Emerging from the small room, he found Tristan sitting with hot caffe and pastries, just delivered from the main kitchen upstairs.

"Join me?" Tristan asked politely.

"I would be honored, Sir."

"Tell me, Azeem ben Cain. Why are ye here?" Tristan finally asked outright.

"To be truthful, Sir, I am fleeing those who are seeking revenge against me for putting a final ending to the feud between my family and a powerful rival family. Since the other family has been completely eradicated, the feud is over for me. There are those who feel the need to continue it, however, and one of those was aboard the ship I was on was headed for the New World, and the vast empty territory it represents. I could have simply gotten lost in those mountains, and been forgotten in time. When the ship went down, I imagine he went with it, at least I hope so. I find the situation as it has turned out to much more to my liking, and I am glad to be here. Once I reunite with my brother, I wish to find a way to be of service, and use my skills for a good purpose."

"I am certain the Lady has brought ye here for just that," Tristan grinned over his caffe cup. "Commander Iniri is a good friend of mine, as she is for many in the Barracks. Ye may expect that the testing will continue, one way or another, for a few days at least. She is well liked, and well-respected as well, for surviving a horrific confinement by a skilled torturer."

"She told me about Secundus, and the fortress," Azeem responded. "It makes me angry to know she suffered so."

"Which does ye honor," Tristan told him. "The time for the Summer Tournament is upon us. Tell me, have ye any intention of participating?"

"I would like to enter," Azeem replied after clearing his mouth of the delicious berry pastry. "I can think of no better way to exhibit my skills for the High Lord."

"Very well," Tristan nodded turning in his chair to a large scroll behind him. Azeem watched as Tristan added his name to it, then sprinkled sand over the ink to dry it quickly, rolling it and tying it closed.

"I was just about to take this downstairs so as to allow the occupants of the Barracks to add their names freely," Tristan told him. "I am glad we talked, so yer name could be added first. It indicates a certain seriousness of intent, to be among the first fifty to enter. Now, if ye will excuse me, I need to begin my work for the day," he finished abruptly, as was his custom.

"Very well, I should not wish to be in yer way, Commander. Tell me, how may I find my brother?"

"I would wait 'till the morrow, so he might have his two day alone with Zameera, his mate," Tristan advised wisely. "I can take ye to the house, if ye wish."

"I would like someone to take me there," Azeem answered, offering his arm for the Grip. "I find navigating the buildings and roads in the Land a challenging experience. Has anyone ever remarked to ye that the buildings look smaller on the outside than they do inside?" he asked in a puzzled tone.

"The Land is a place of magick and mystery," Tristan quoted Drake's favorite phrase. "Anything is possible here, due to the Lady's presence. Keep that in mind."

"I shall Sir," Azeem nodded, again wondering just where he was, actually. "Good day."

The rest of that day, the newcomer found ways to keep himself busy. After his first meal, he asked if Klietos needed any help at all in the kitchen that day.

"As a matter of fact, I am jerking meat for traveling rations, and I need someone to tend the smoker today," the man answered at once.

"I can do that!" Azeem volunteered. "I have done so many times, preparing meat for my own use!"

"Good, all ye need do is assure a plentiful supply of smoke, and to keep the water dishes filled with water, so that the meat does not dry out too much. Come, let me get ye started!"

And so Azeem sat in the shade that day, tending the meat and receiving a cold cup of ale from time to time for his work. He was hardly alone, however, as Amazons came to visit and test him, making seductive suggestions until he politely but firmly turned them down, one at a time.

"Sisters," he finally said. "Ye are all beautiful, of a certainty, but my heart belongs to another. I cannot consider being with anyone else in that light, but I thank ye for the offers. I am most honored," he finished with a warm and friendly smile.

"She is a fortunate woman, to have captured yer heart so completely," one of them responded, a short, plump woman with a heart-shaped face, answered for all of them. "Still, ye would have yer choice of women, should ye choose to accept the offers. Think on it, we Amazons do not make such offers often."

"I shall indeed consider all of the offers, but if I were to take them all, I would surely be exhausted," he grinned.

"I would certainly hope so!" the shorter woman answered, laughing merrily as she and the other women walked off, laughing with her.

"I *am* in the land of the Djinn, I know it now!" he commented to himself with a grin. "Where else would I be so sorely tempted?"

He kept to himself that night, eating his meal privately in the solace of the small room they gave him upon request. He slept very well that night due to the quiet and the security, rising early the next morning. He looked forward to the day, and what it might bring, then laughed a bit at himself for his optimism. Sponging himself off, then donning clean clothing supplied by the Barracks Quartermaster, he was out of the room with a good attitude and a smile.

Ishmael woke that morning to find Zameera already up and about, he could smell cooking from the kitchen he realized when he sniffed deeply. Dressing himself quickly for his first day back to work, he joined her in the kitchen, finding her making hand pies from the remainder of the roasted lamb.

"Caffe is ready over there, I put yer cup over there," Zameera said after they greeted each other warmly, Ishmael patting her stomach in a protective manner.

"Thank ye, Madam," he replied simply, going to prepare his cup. The oat porridge steamed on the back burner, and she had the accompaniments set out, a clear indication he was to help himself. He did so gladly, wanting to spare her the work, and once back at the table he enjoyed the homey bowl of porridge, eating every bite.

"I am going out to tend the chickens," he told her, taking the egg basket with him. "I shall also stop at the stable, to make certain all is well there. I shall not be overlong to return."

"I should have the first pan of these ready by then," Zameera replied as she worked to fill and seal the pan she was working on.

"Ye are making a large batch of those," he questioned.

"One never knows when company will arrive, and even if we do not have friends to entertain, making these hand pies will make the meat last longer."

"Ye are a practical woman, and I like that," he replied, kissing her cheek before taking his leave. It did not take a long time for him to complete his tasks, and by the time he returned, Zameera was just putting the second pan into the oven. The first pan stood on the counter, cooled enough to be eaten, but Zameera was nowhere to be seen. Ishmael went to the necessity door and knocked, hearing the faint sounds of retching within.

"I am well," he heard her say. "I was hoping the tincture would suppress most of this, but I suppose every woman must go through it," she continued, and then he heard more retching. A look of empathy passed over Ishmael's face, he filled a glass of water, setting a lemon into it and waited for her to appear. When she did, she reached for the water and drank the entire thing all at once.

"Thank ye, I was quite thirsty," she said quietly.

"Perhaps 'twould serve ye well to make a large carafe of lemon water and keep it handy?" he suggested. "It seems to be of help to ye."

"Ye are right of course," she said, remembering the advice of the High Lady. "Thank ye for reminding me. I think I am going to relax on the sofa while these bake, and let myself settle. Have a good day, my love."

"Ye also, and do not work too hard," he said softly, his voice warm and rich. Kissing her deeply, he embraced her once more, then turned to leave despite his desire to remain with her. It was traditional in his family for one of the younger brothers to take up residence with the eldest brother's family in such situations, to provide a personal guard for the woman. It was now that Ishmael missed his family the most, he thought as he went out to the stable for his horse. It was a short trip to the High Lord's house from Zameera's residence, but he did not feel like walking that morning.

The ride was a pleasant one, the sun was warm as it rose behind the mountains, the river made a nice splashing as he rode by, bees buzzed in the field, collecting their nectar and he felt generally good. Upon arriving at the Barracks, he stowed his horse in the stable there, then made his way to the War Duke's office for the morning meeting.

"Good morning, My Lord!" he greeted boisterously, for he was in a good mood. "What is on the agenda this week?"

"Yer regular trainees await ye, and then I shall need yer input on how to construct the brackets for the Tournament. We have a large crowd this year, with mixed skills. I do not want someone with lesser abilities fighting someone with vastly superior ones."

"I agree, no need to make anyone feel shame," Ishmael nodded. "My Lord, I have an announcement to make, one I never thought I would. I am to be a Father!"

"Is that so?" Karpon smiled wide as he stood to fetch the whiskey bottle. "Congratulations, Master Ishmael. It seems as if the Lady wishes to continue yer line. May your wife's pregnancy be an easy one."

"I am honored to share a cup with ye," Ishmael grinned, accepting the cup handed to him. "Zameera is having twins, a girl and a boy, according to the High Lady! I am truly blessed!"

Karpon offered an embrace, one warrior to another, which Ishmael gladly accepted, both men thumping each other on the back enthusiastically. "Join us later in the common room. I shall order a keg from the cellars, whatever ye wish."

"The brown, of course," Ishmael grinned. "Everyone likes that. Perhaps for the Dames, we might include a small cask of white wine or maybe the new wheat ale is called for. I know Zameera likes to squeeze a lemon wedge into that. Perhaps Master Klietos might put out snack plates, so everyone's hunger might be assuaged?"

"I shall ask him," Karpon responded at once. "Come at the fifth hour, we should be ready by then."

"I am not expected at home until the seventh hour after midday," Ishmael nodded. "I would be honored to attend."

They exchanged another Grip, then Ishmael was off to his training sessions. Each person he greeted along the way was informed of his new situation, and he received an enthusiastic congratulations each time. By the time he got to where he conducted his training sessions, the Barracks was abuzz with the news, and he received congratulations throughout the day from everyone.

While Ishmael's day proceeded, so did Azeem's. He had continued to offer his service in whatever way he might, and now was working in the garden, helping to harvest the vegetables that were ripe. He had done such work many times, and bent to it willingly, noting the quality of the produce was superior to most. When the day ended, he was told of the gathering in the common room, but only that a keg was open and everyone was welcome.

"A cup or two of cold ale would be welcome before I bathe," Azeem thought to himself as he carried his last baskets up to the collection area.

"Thank ye, Master Azeem for yer work today," the supervisor said warmly. "We are right on schedule now because of yer skill and knowledge. Are ye going to visit the common room tonight? I hear a keg is available."

"I heard that as well, and I intend to drink a cup or two before I bathe and retire," Azeem grinned.

"I shall see ye there then," she replied with a warm smile, watching him bow a bit before walking away. She thought him a handsome man, and wondered how she might arrange a moment or two of private talk with him about sharing supper with her. Azeem appeared to be ignorant of her interest as he walked away from her, she noted.

"I wonder when I shall be able to speak with my brother," he wondered as he walked tiredly up to the House, finding the path to the Barracks entrance and making use of it. He went without delay to the common room, finding that cups were just being handed out and that his was full when he received it. He sipped that one and enjoyed another before seeking the baths, and the hot spring water that flowed copiously below the House.

While he bathed, the celebration in the common room grew louder and more boisterous as the rest of the residents joined in.

"Congratulations, Master ben Cain," Karpon said loudly, so as to make the announcement. "May yer lady be well throughout the pregnancy, and may yer children be fat and healthy!"

"Congratulations!" he heard many voices call out, and a general atmosphere of gaiety emerged. Ishmael found that his cup never emptied throughout the first part of the gathering, and his shoulder hurt a bit after the many exchangings of the Grip between the warriors. However, his delight at the situation consumed him, and each new person he encountered that day was greeted with the same refrain.

"I am going to be a Father!"

"Congratulations, Master ben Cain!" came the reply each time, along with a sharing of the Grip and an invitation to the common room's ale cask that night.

Azeem never made it to the common room that night as he was feeling quite weary. He made his way to the room had been given, stripped and fell into bed, falling asleep at once. He missed the entire celebration, and the opportunity to meet his brother once more. Hours later, as morning broke he rose, sponged off and dressed in the clothing he found in the room, finding that it all fit perfectly. Even the pair of boots he found in the clothespress proved to fit his feet well, and he grinned with delight to see himself in the mirror, dressed in the clothing of the Land.

"I look very different," he thought to himself, looking at his face and realizing his facial hair needed attention. Using the kit he found in the necessity cabinet, he performed a quick trim, then shaved the rest, returning his face to the neat goatee he favored. Examining himself once more in the mirror, he thought again that while he looked different, he also looked better. His stomach rumbled loudly as he gazed at his reflection, reminding him it had been hours since the last meal. Azeem grinned with anticipation, for all of the food he had tasted so far had been filled with excellent tastes and textures. He was glad they were not afraid of spicing their food with chilies, as he favored their effect on meats and beans. Now dressed for his day, Azeem left the room, instinctively leaving the door ajar to indicate it was ready for cleaning, after taking a moment or two to pick up and put his used clothing and towels in the hamper provided.

The smell of the first meal drew him to the dining hall, where he found griddlecakes being served and gladly took his portion. Looking about the room, he saw no seats available, at least until a group of Dames moved closer to make room for him at their table.

"Master Azeem, over here!" he heard the feminine voices call. Closing his eyes and summoning up his resolve, he accepted their invitation and sat among them.

"Thank ye swordsisters," he said gratefully as they passed the tray of compotes to him, as well as the caffe carafe on their table. These women were just here to eat their first meal, and so their conversation was less intimate than those over the last few days.

"Have ye signed up for the Tournament, Master Azeem?" one of them asked conversationally, and he felt comfortable among them now, knowing they were not planning to tempt him.

"I have, and I am looking forward to participating," he answered with a smile.

"Ye should work in the morning with us, and take advantage of the training facilities here," the young woman spoke up again. Her name was Rhian, and she had been trained by both Zameera and Sylvene. "We even have a trainer, who will help to find yer faults and suggest how to correct them."

"Is that so?" Azeem nodded, hearing the opportunity to improve his skills being presented. "Is he available this morning?"

"Come along with us," Rhian invited. "As soon as we finish our fruit and yogurt, we are headed for the training arena. He will be there, for certain," she went on. Somehow she had not yet made the connection between Ishmael and Azeem, and did not realize they were brothers.

"Why thank ye!" Azeem grinned in between bites of his meal. "I would be honored to walk with ye."

It did not take a long time for their meal to be consumed, and once they finished and dealt with their plates and bowls, they were on their way to the arena.

Ishmael was already there, conducting his first session of the day. One of the younger squires had difficulty switching between his right and left hand during battle, and Ishmael was trying to teach him the correct method to do so.

"Try it again, boyo. Ye've nearly got it!" he encouraged, watching the young man deal with the frustration of failure.

"Are ye certain, or are ye just trying to make me go on?" the young man sighed. His name was Darius, he had recently come to the House as a prisoner, but had gained enough privilege to join the exercise daily. It occurred to Ishmael as he watched the young man's work that it reminded him a great deal of Drake's work, despite the lack of refinement. He wondered if the young Drake had encountered the same difficulties in learning this technique as he shouted encouragements.

"Now ye've got it!" Ishmael complimented when the young man performed the thing correctly, and quickly. "Try again!"

Once learned, Darius was able to adapt the movement to his swordwork with little further difficulties. When his session was complete, he thanked Ishmael sincerely for his help.

"Now that I have learned this, I shall not forget. I am grateful for yer patient instruction, Master Ishmael," Darius said elegantly, again reminding Ishmael of Drake, even in his speech pattern.

"Ye are a quick learner, young man. 'Tis a pleasure to teach such as yerself. Just be certain to practice daily, even if ye must do so on yer own."

"I shall, Master Ishmael!" Darius responded with enthusiasm, and Ishmael shook his head a bit, trying to clear a memory from a long time ago. He had tried to teach the natural son of the High Lord, but the young man had only learned the martial aspects, not the spiritual ones behind it all. Now, he looked at young Darius, seeing similarities between the two young men at the same age. It was uncanny, he thought to himself as he watched Darius put his weapon away and leave the arena.

Azeem entered the training arena, passing Darius on his way. The young man's face took on a look of recognition as they passed each other, but surprise kept Darius from saying anything. Azeem simply did not notice the expression on the young man's face, as his thoughts were consumed with finding Ishmael. Walking into the arena, he headed to where he saw Lord Tristan standing, meaning to ask him about his brother's whereabouts. His route took him right by where Ishmael's training station was, but he only saw his destination due to his fierce determination. Ishmael stood to stretch and begin warming up for the next training session, he saw Azeem walk across the sands and the shout of recognition was loud and joyful.

"*Azeem*!!!! My brother! What are ye doing here?"

Azeem turned at the mention of his name, his eyes met Ishmael's and a feeling of shock came over him. He nearly fell to the sands in astonishment and surprise, Ishmael had to run a few steps to catch him.

"Ishmael?" Azeem whispered, his voice hoarse with joy. "Is it truly thee, my brother?"

"Ye are not seeing things, nor are ye in the land of the Djinn, brother," Ishmael chuckled. "I am alive, and I have been here for over twenty years. What have ye been doing?"

"Trying to find ye for over twenty years, ye great lummox!" Azeem answered with glee, now over his shock and throwing his arms around his brother. "Ye have been here all this time?"

"I have, thanks to the Goddess. We have a great deal to catch up on, my brother. I am to be a father! Our line is not ended!"

"WHAT?"

"I shall tell ye everything later, after my work is over for the day," Ishmael told him, returning the joyful embrace.

"Master Ishmael!" they both heard, and turned to see the High Lord magickally appear within the arena. He had felt the force of their meeting, and decided it was time to make his appearance. "I believe that yer work can be suspended for the day, due to the circumstances. What say ye, My Lord Knight Commander?"

"My Lord has it right," Tristan answered with a grin. "The occasion of such a meeting would be call for a bit of a Mother's Holiday, would it not?"

"I think so," Erinn grinned. "And I think the two of ye should be at home, catching up. If ye will both step closer, I shall provide the transportation," he offered.

"Thank ye, My Lord," Ishmael responded at once, stopping to put away his weapon and don his shirt. "I am ready. Azeem, stand closer to me so 'tis easier for the High Lord," he ordered quietly, and his younger brother simply responded without thinking. The bite of cold struck them for a long moment and then they were just outside the kitchen door of Zameera's house.

Chapter 5

"Will ye come in for a bit, My Lord?" Ishmael asked politely.

"I would be delighted to do so, if only to greet yer lady," Erinn responded. In the three of them went through the first door, walking up the long stairway to the main level, where the kitchen and living quarters were.

"Good morning Zameera!" Ishmael called brightly, and the woman poked her head out of the kitchen, a look of surprise on her face. "We will be having a guest for the foreseeable future, my dear, if ye will permit him to remain. May I present my brother, Azeem?"

Zameera's face took on a look of interest, she wiped her hands free of the ground meat she was working with for that night's supper, then washed them with rose-scented soap before walking to greet their guest.

"In the name of the Goddess, I welcome ye to our home, Azeem ben Cain," she said formally, offering him the Grip. "I shall prepare a room for ye. Ishmael, are ye returning to work? And greetings to ye as well, My Lord Erinn."

"The High Lord has granted me a Mother's Holiday today!" Ishmael announced with a grin. "Would ye allow us to enjoy the day, Madam?"

"Allow?" Zameera laughed, coming to embrace them both one at a time. "I am honored to have yer brother with us now, most especially."

"Indeed!" Ishmael agreed. "I am going to show Azeem to his room, and then we may begin our holiday. I shall take care of anything ye need done, my dear."

"And I shall help!" Azeem offered at once.

As he stood there, he heard a round of feminine laughter from a side room, and some of them were hauntingly familiar. He recognized several as those who were most ardent in their pursuits over the last few days. These women had been in and out of his dreams for three nights, and his reaction was one of both shock and a bit of anger.

"What is that?" he asked, losing his grace in the heat of the moment. He wanted to confront the women, and tell them again to keep away from him, but he felt Ishmael's hand on his shoulder, restraining him.

"That?" Zameera smiled warmly. "Ye are hearing the laughter of my sister Amazons," she explained, sipping her wine.

"Amazons? Sisters?" Azeem stuttered, his composure in shreds.

"Aye, all Amazons are Sisters according to the dictates of our Order," Zameera replied. "As such, we often talk as if we truly are blood sisters, and yer name has recently come into those conversations. We are all beholden to Iniri, those of us who survived Secundus' torture and enslavement. Ye see, as Amazons, we value freedom above almost everything else. We join the Amazons to be free, so we do not have to live under the dictates of a Patriarchal society. To be made a slave, to be used without consent, is the worst thing we can possibly imagine, and Secundus Natanleod was well aware of that. His mother was an Amazon, he knew our ways well enough to use them against us, and Iniri fought him, as many of us older women did. We were not broken, despite his every attempt to do so. He even tried starving me and Athena to death, not realizing how ascetic a path we both follow. We had to watch our Sisters be tortured, blinded, then fed to huge evil snakes, we had to watch our younger Sisters be used by Naga priests over and over again, and all the while, we had to stand fast and not be broken. Such a thing will never happen again in the Land, I and many others would gladly give our lives to prevent it."

Azeem stood there transfixed by her tale, his mind suddenly filled with images of pain and suffering unlike any he had seen before.

"To know ye suffered that way, it makes me angry," Azeem finally said. "I want to find those who did those things to ye, put those marks on ye, and make them suffer equally."

Zameera smiled, turned to the counter she stood in front of and poured cold wine for both men, bringing the cups to them.

"Which explains why ye are here in the Land, Brother Azeem," she said to him with a small smile. "Ye have been assessed by all of us and found to be acceptable to have a relationship with one of our Sisters. With the gift ye have been given, ye suit her well, and she says ye have the stamina she requires. Ye must forgive us for talking so frankly about men, but 'tis the same among men, is it not? Ye compare women for sizes of breasts, and dimensions of body, aye?"

Azeem flushed a bit, knowing it was true and an abashed smile appeared on his face. "Ye are correct, Madam, much to my shame."

"Women discuss the same things," she grinned, "Iniri was most impressed."

Azeem's face took on a look of confusion until Zameera continued. "What ye have between yer legs is considered a Mother's Blessing here in the Land," she explained. "We Amazons are most appreciative of such things, and Iniri said her time with ye was very pleasant. We approve, my brother, for if ye can please someone as discriminating as Iniri, then ye have both skill and sensitivity. We value those things here, unlike in the Outlands. If ye wish to continue yer relationship with Iniri, none of us would object."

"And if ye did object?"

Zameera chuckled, a dark tone to her laughter. "Then my friend, ye would be discouraged by all of us, and if such was not sufficient, 'tis usual for a group of her closest sisters to confront ye with swords. Is it not fortunate ye are well thought of?" she smiled.

"Zameera! Where is that wine?" he heard one of them call out in laughing tones. The woman with the heart-shaped face and curvaceous body appeared in the doorway, saw him and a wide smile appeared on her face. "Sisters, if ye would like to meet the man, he is here!" she called to the women in the room.

Azeem suddenly found himself surrounded by at least a dozen women, all of whom had teased and tested him before.

"We are most sorry to have had to test yer intentions, Brother Azeem," the curvy one explained. "But 'tis our way, to assure that the men are of good heart, and that they will treat our sisters well. Ye are a good man, with a good heart, and we approve of ye."

"She means that we approve of *ALL* of ye!" he heard one of the others put in from the rear of the group. Peals of feminine laughter ensued at the older woman's statement as she stepped forward, her face covered with deep scars. "I can see that our Sister has lost none of her ability to describe a person," she said, looking him up and down in an assessing manner. "I would have recognized him just by her description of him," she went on as she walked around him. He jumped a bit in shock when her hands cupped his buttocks and squeezed a bit, bringing merry laughter to her and her companions. "His ass is rock hard!" she commented brightly.

Azeem found himself both alarmed and amused by their assessment, at least until he was touched, and then the alarmed part started to take over. It struck him suddenly, that men often treated women in such ways, and shame made his cheeks flush pink in embarrassment. He would never again subject a woman to such treatment, he vowed to himself as he stepped away from her and turned.

"So, tell me Elder Sister, would ye like me to demonstrate how I pleased Iniri?" he asked in a deep and resonate voice. "I could do so right now, if ye wish," he continued in a teasing tone. The older woman stopped speaking for a moment as her eyes met his, and he felt a flush of unexpected desire, wondering how that could be considering her age. He was even more surprised to realize that she was truly considering his offer, and he found that even more arousing, much to his shock.

"I am not looking for a lover," the older woman finally responded with a grin. "But if I were, I might challenge Iniri for ye," she finished, kissing his cheek lightly. "Treat our sister well, and ye will have no objections from any of us. Treat her ill, and ye will answer to all of us," she whispered. "Welcome to the Land, Azeem ben Cain."

"Thank ye, Elder Sister," he responded with a respectful nod. "And thank ye to all of ye for yer acceptance."

He shared the Grip with all of them as they left, but once they were gone, he sat heavily at the table, feeling somewhat drained by the experience. He felt a gentle hand on his shoulder, and a cup of wine appeared by his hand as Zameera served him.

"Ye did well, Brother Azeem. They like ye!" she whispered in his ear.

"And if they had not?"

"Ye might not be here right now," Zameera told him. "Ishmael, would ye please see Azeem to his room? I must watch this food carefully now, especially the rice."

"Aye my dear," Ishmael agreed. "Come brother, let us find ye a place to sleep."

And so it went for about a month as the Tournament approached. Azeem made his way to the Barracks the next morning with Ishmael, intending to use his time constructively. He found himself completely occupied with exercises and weapons work for the next three hours, until Ishmael ceased his training sessions.

It was raining that morning, and the rain was heavy. In the Capitol City, the small drains that kept water flowing through the streets and off the walking surface were nearly overflowing due to the amount of water that fell. In the kitchen of the High Lord's House, all was proceeding as usual for the Summer. Foods were being dried and pickled while meals were being prepared, and suddenly the cry went up.

"The drains are backing up again!"

Deborah appeared out of her testing kitchen to see it happen, the first "burp" of water that bubbled forth from one of the sinks and the rush of the staff for buckets, mops and towels to contain the flow. They managed to keep up with that until the second sink overflowed too, and Deborah's frustration peaked.

"Enough is enough," she thought to herself as she used her magick to correct the issue, at least so it could be contained until she summoned Theodosius, the Master of Guilds. The man came running, finding Deborah in the basement, nearly knee-deep in water backing up there. "Master Theodosius, I am at my wit's end with this situation! I want it fixed, at once! I want ye to consult the original plans for the building and find a way to redirect the outflow of the kitchen, so that *this* does not happen again!

Requisition whatever help ye might need, get the supplies ordered and get it done, at once!" she said slowly, enunciating each word as punctuation.

"Aye My Lady," Theodosius simply agreed, knowing she was not to be thwarted at the present moment. "I shall see to it right away."

"See that ye do, or we will be speaking again!" she ordered before wading away, heading for the bottom of the stairs. "I want it done before Tournament time!"

"Aye Madam," Theodosius sighed. He was already heavily into planning the bridge project the High Lord had ordered, wanting to put his plans into action by next Spring. Now he was further burdened, and he sighed heavily as he followed the High Lady out of the cellar, headed for his own quarters. Once inside and the door locked, he went at once to the small altar in his room, lit a candle and knelt in supplication. "My Lady, how can I get this project done as quickly as the High Lady wishes?" he whispered. "I need yer aid."

"And ye will have it, Master Theodosius," he heard Her whisper into his mind, and a wave of relief washed over him to hear it. He would have the help he needed, he thought as he washed himself and dressed in clean clothing, ready to resume his regular duties for the day.

That night, Mittra started awake in the dead of night, his movements rousing Zenobia a bit.

"What is amiss?" she asked sleepily.

"I heard the Goddess call my name," Mittra answered honestly. "I am going to the altar for a bit."

"Would ye like me to wait with ye?"

"Ye need yer sleep," Mittra responded, his voice filled with love for her. "I shall not be long."

They hugged briefly, and then Mittra tenderly tucked her back in, watching until she fell asleep. Then he went to the small altar in the room, lit the candles there, and knelt in supplication.

"What is Yer will, My Lady?"

"I have a task for ye and yer fellow demi-gods at the High Lord's House. I have called a dozen or so, and they will be seeking ye shortly. Ye should be ready to receive them at yer house by morning, and have a hearty meal ready for them," She chuckled as Her presence faded.

He went downstairs to check his provisions, knowing his fellow demi-gods had appetites to match their reputations. He was well provisioned, he saw with a grin, and brought up a huge ham from the cold room, carrying it on his shoulder up the stairs. Laying it out on the counter, he took one of the sharp knives from the holder, rinsed it in hot water, then cut the entire joint into thick slices, setting them on a large oval platter and returning them down the stairs to the cold room to await their disposition. He saw that they had at least four dozen eggs, and nodded in satisfaction, knowing they would have plenty to serve. Returning to the kitchen, he saw three full loaves of beautiful bread made by Zenobia that morning, and his relief was apparent. All he needed to do was put on some barley to provide a perfect side dish for the meal he saw in his mind, and when that was accomplished, he set it on the back burner to slowly cook until morning. All was in readiness when he left the kitchen to return to his bed, snuggling beside Zenobia and falling asleep at once.

All through the night, in small villages and towns throughout the Capitol District, men of renown woke suddenly, hearing the Goddess' Call in their dreams and knowing it was time to offer their service. Taking up their traveling packs at once, they left their beds, hit the road, turning their faces to the Capitol and the High Lord's House. By morning, they met up with each other in ones and twos, until finally they encountered one of their kind, the demi-god Hercules, driving a large wagon pulled by four stout horses.

"Aye, 'tis plenty of room back there," he laughed when he met up with the others. "And I took the moment to put a keg back there for our friend Bacchus, who will be more than happy to share with ye all."

Sometime in the early morning, that wagon rumbled through the back gates of the Capitol City, being waved through by troopers who recognized the lot of them as those who had served the longest in the Army. However, most had no idea these were the legendary heroes of the Age of Wonders. There were Perseus and Theseus, as well as Hercules and Achilles, Amphion and his twin brother Zethus who built the great city of Thebes, Arcas the Hunter, Castor and Pollux, Sarpedon, and in the very back of the wagon was one more. He was not a demi-god of Olympus, he was of the race of Titans however, but he had always loved the human race and tried to help it. The quiet figure sitting there looking out of the back of the wagon was none other than Prometheus, who had been punished heavily by Zeus for bringing fire to the humans and teaching them how to plant seeds to grow food before the Father of the Gods thought his young creations were ready for such things. Now he sat there without speaking, thinking about the task at hand. He had not overly partaken of the cask in the wagon, as the others had, and so when the wagon finally pulled up in front of a beautiful house in the city, he was capable of intelligible speech. He hopped out to help the others get out of the wagon, adding a steadying hand especially to Bacchus, who was showing the usual effects of wine upon him.

"Well brothers, I think we have arrived," Prometheus said quietly. "I shall go and knock to announce our presence."

The others simply stood there nodding, weaving slightly as they stood there, a comical scene in every way. Prometheus came to the door and knocked soundly, but not impatiently, and when the door opened to reveal a gorgeous red-haired woman, he assumed his most genteel manners.

"Madam, is Mittra within? We are his brothers, and we have come to visit."

"Just a moment," she replied in a hushed tone, clearly awed. She closed the door softly and they waited a short time until Mittra opened the door.

"Brothers, come in and please wipe yer feet? First meal is nearly ready, and we have plenty to share. The woman inside is my wife, and I shall ask ye all to be on yer best behavior around her, please?"

"Of course!" he heard them all say in turn. "Brother, congratulations! We did not know ye had married!" Prometheus grinned, offering the Grip.

"We are with each other, and 'tis all that matters to me," Mittra answered, his words speaking volumes. "Now come inside before ye wake my neighbors. 'Tis very early still, ye know."

"Aye," Prometheus grinned in return. Turning to the others, he waved them into the house, instructing them to be sure to wipe their boots on the mat outside. Mittra took the horse and wagon to their small stable and made the animal feel at home with a bucket of grain and one of water too. He loosened the traces so they could eat and drink easily, reckoning he would be out after first meal to see to him properly. Walking quickly back to his kitchen, he found his brothers now inside, with the nearly drained cask. They were sitting in his common room, Zenobia trying to play the good hostess on short notice. He watched critically as his fellow heroes treated her with respect, remembering their manners and using the proper words with her. Good, he thought with satisfaction. I have explained myself properly, so they understand the situation. Pleased that there would be no problems, he relaxed a bit and let himself enjoy their company.

"Brothers, now would be a good time to wash up and get seated," he called out over their quiet roar, an unusual sound in his house. "First meal is ready to go on the boards, and we will be eating in the kitchen. I shall set up a service line, and we will cook yer eggs to order," he continued.

A cheer went up from their guests as they got in line to use the sink for washing their hands and faces, toweling off with the soft cloth handed to them before depositing it into the hamper by the door. Once they were clean, they lined up for their plates, dishing up the ham and barley generously on the large plates. When Zenobia asked how many eggs they wanted, each man asked for three, she gladly complied so that they all had a trio of large brown eggs to accompany the rest of the meal. Once they were all served they ate quietly, taking the time to chew thoroughly, enjoying the delicious food.

"Thank ye, Madam," Hercules said about halfway through his plate. "My eggs are cooked perfectly, the ham is sweet and tender, and the barley well-seasoned. I am enjoying my meal a great deal!"

"Aye, aye!" went around the table in agreement, the others nodding their heads and smiling as they continued to plow through their plates.

"Well, I did not cook the barley, Mittra did," Zenobia answered modestly. "But we are both glad ye are enjoying yer meal."

After they finished, their company gathered up their plates and utensils, two of them volunteering to do the dishes and three more to clean up the kitchen, the rest filed out into the common room. To Zenobia's astonishment, they all sat on the floor, then laid down and stretched a bit before closing their eyes and falling immediately to sleep. The volunteers finished their tasks quickly and joined the rest, leaving Zenobia in a state of wonder.

"We should get a few blankets to cover them," Mittra chuckled a bit as he moved to the cabinet and open it.

"We are just going to leave them there?"

"I think 'twould be best," Mittra smiled warmly

"But…the floor is so hard!"

"They are used to sleeping on the ground," Mittra told her. "They will all sleep well, since they are inside and warm. We should just leave them to it. Come, let us go to the market and resupply our cold room," he chuckled. "We are out of eggs completely, and I think I need to stop at the butcher's shop for a side of beef."

"O goodness!" Zenobia worried aloud. "How will we feed them all?"

The Goddess heard the worry in Zenobia's tone, and Her heart went out to the couple. By the time they returned to their home, their cold room was refilled with fresh supplies, and the ice room where their meat was frozen was nearly bursting. Mittra's gasp of surprise was audible and brought Zenobia rushing down the stairs, only add her gasp to his.

"Wherever did all of this come from?" she asked.

"I believe that the Goddess has taken a hand here," Mittra chuckled. "Ye were worried about how we would feed them all, and look, we have everything we need and more. Come, let us light our outdoor hearth and get that side of beef cooking. 'Tis a large one, and 'twill take hours to cook just right. I have a feeling they will be here until tomorrow morning."

He was correct in his feeling, the heroes remained that night and after supper, the group of them all sat about after Zenobia retired. The subject of their talk was the task at hand, which had been revealed to all of them during their morning nap.

"We must go up there tomorrow, very early," Prometheus was saying. "I want to see the place and understand what the problem is with the plumbing. I have a feeling 'tis a simple matter of redirecting the flow of water going out, rather than slowing the flow of water coming in. We will see in the morning how best to attend to the matter."

"Indeed," Mittra nodded as he passed the pipe to the man beside him.

"Perhaps the High Lady's grapes need to be tended," Bacchus put in. "I shall offer my services, unless ye think I am needed with the water project."

All of them knew that Bacchus was not a skilled laborer, however his expertise with grapes and vines was unmatched. He would be of little use in the digging, or the laying of the pipes, and so all of them nodded their agreement to his proposal.

"Besides, I am the best cook among us," he chuckled. "I can take the burden of preparing our meals upon myself, freeing the High Lady's kitchen from being overly burdened."

"And I can help Bacchus with the cooking!" Orpheus volunteered eagerly.

"Good, ye have a sound idea there, brothers," Mittra nodded. "The Lady Deborah is a very hard working woman, as ye will all see. She reminds me of Artemis a bit, her practicality is something of a marvel," he sighed.

"I miss her," Bacchus sighed heavily, a tear appearing. "Perhaps someday, the Lady will allow us to rejoin our fellows."

"We are all paying for our mistakes," Mittra answered sadly. "I wish I had thought more and done less."

"Aye…" he heard the word run around the room, and the regretful tone was unmistakable. The mood only lasted a short time, and then they were back discussing the project at hand. At length, the visitors took their places on the floor of the common room, while Mittra retired to his bed to sleep a bit, glad for the opportunity.

In the early morning, Bacchus was up and about, wearing just a simple robe and slippers. He was delighted to find caffe in the cabinet, as well as several large pots so he could make enough for everyone. Filling the huge kettle in the sink, he admired the view of the garden, seeing it was very well kept. There were even staff members out there picking the ripe produce, he noted with a gentle smile, remembering the old days when he and the others ruled over ancient Hellas.

Seeing that the kettle was nearly overflowing, he shut off the tap and carried the heavy thing to the stove, a short distance, then set it to heat. He noticed a pot on the back burner, pulled it forward and lifted the lid to find a cooked oat porridge, heavy with squares of apple, huge fat raisins and large brambleberries. He was glad to see the industry represented, knowing how much work it took to gather and process the fruit, for it all had been dried for storage. He took an experimental spoonful, enjoying the cooked grain and fruit without any additional sweetener, chewing thoroughly and finding the balance of flavors to his liking. He stirred it well, added just a bit of water, then replaced the cover and returned it to its former place.

He continued to work in the kitchen, bringing up a rasher of smoked pork belly, as well as the basket of eggs, Zenobia finding him there.

"Good morning, Ma... I should call ye Sister, if 'tis acceptable," Bacchus said when she entered the kitchen.

"Sister will be quite fine," she smiled hesitantly, mindful that she was speaking to the God of Wine and Vines. "Thank ye for beginning my work," she went on, tying on an apron.

"I enjoy cooking," Bacchus replied with a smile. "I do not often have the opportunity to do so. May I be of assistance to ye?"

"I would enjoy that!" she smiled warmly.

They worked together well, she noted, almost dancing around each other as they prepared the meal. Delicious odors roused those in the common room, as well as the occupant of the main bedroom, and soon the kitchen filled with large, hungry men with cups of steaming caffe in hand. They served by the plate, cooking eggs to order and handing the dish off to the man in line before plating the next one, and so it went until all were served. Silence reigned over the table as the legendary men consumed the hearty meal with good manners, finishing quickly while enjoying the simple tastes and textures.

"Thank ye, Madam for hosting us. We are all glad that our brother Mittra has found the right one for him here in the Land. Ye are a good cook, and an excellent hostess, even though we surprised ye by arriving without warning. We will be living up at the High Lord's house from now on as we take on the service the Lady has commanded of us, and so yer burden will be relieved. We are most grateful for yer acceptance of our presence, and apologize for any harm we may have done."

Zenobia smiled brilliantly, honored by his words, which were delivered with humility and grace. "My Lord Prometheus, I was truly honored to meet such legendary men. Not everyone can claim to have met such as yerselves, and my man was happy to see ye. Ye are all welcome here anytime ye wish to come and see yer brother," she replied elegantly. Smiles appeared on their faces, and all of them bowed a bit at the waist to show her respect before they took their leave, Mittra with them. Once they were gone, Zenobia began the process of gathering up the used blankets and pillows, taking them to the laundry area. Once the first batch were soaking in warm, soapy water, she returned upstairs and began on the common area. The staff soon joined her, and between them all, the house returned to its customary tidy state, while Zenobia waited for Mittra's return. He would be staying up at the High Lord's house as well until the plumbing problem was fixed, leaving her to her own devices for a few days. She took advantage of the time to work with her whips, as well as with the *doru*, a weapon she found quite challenging to master.

The heroes all walked to the High Lord's house in the quiet morning, noting that the city had grown since they had all last been there. It did not take them long to gain the bridge, then make the somewhat sharp turn that lead to the Barracks main entrance. Of course, there were sentries on duty, young squires who had distinguished themselves in some way, and they were challenged at once in accordance with proper procedures.

"Who goes there? State yer business!"

"We are here by the Lady's Will, to perform a service for the High Lord's house. May we enter? Surely the problem at hand could use a bit of extra help?" Prometheus asked.

"Well…" the young man stuttered a bit, feeling the power of their presences and suddenly realizing who they might be. "I should summon the War Duke and the Knight Commander. Please wait here."

"Of course."

It did not take a long time for Lord Karpon and Lord Tristan to appear and when they saw the group, smiles appeared, for their faces were well-known to those in the Barracks.

"My Lord Prometheus, all of ye, what are ye doing here?"

"Ye have a plumbing problem, we hear," Prometheus answered with a grin. "We have come to offer our knowledge and strength to assist. The Lady called us to perform this service, and we would like to begin as soon as possible."

"Ah, I see!" Karpon nodded. "Brother Tristan, would ye please find these men a group room in the Barracks for the next few days?"

"I shall do so at once, even if I must open a new room," Tristan nodded. "If ye will excuse me to the task?"

"Go to it," Karpon grinned. Tristan saluted, fist to chest then arm extended, open palm, before striding off to his task. "Now gentlemen, allow me to escort ye to the work site. I believe that Master Theodosius will be right happy to see ye," the War Duke continued. The group followed him through the hallways, then down a broad set of stairs several flights until the unmistakable scent of stale kitchen water hit their noses. Rounding the last turn in the flight, they found themselves at the top of a stairway that led into a basement, where Master Theodosius stood knee-high in grey water.

"Keep bailing it out!" he encouraged as he dipped a bucket full of it and walked to the small drain on the other side of the room, carefully pouring the water into it. "We are starting to make some headway at last!"

All of them could see where the water had been as compared to where it was now, the evidence was the distinct waterline that ran around the room at approximately the same height.

"They do not have enough drainage!" Hercules noted at once. "I can fix that!"

"Do so cautiously, my friend," Prometheus warned. "We do not want to make the situation any worse by our actions. But my senses tell me this room tilts slightly that way," he pointed to where the small drain spout stood. "Why in the world is the outflow over there, on the high side of the room?" he thought out loud, walking down the stairs and wading into the water. "Master of Guilds, may I present our group?"

"Ye have no need to do so, I know ye well enough," Theodosius answered seriously, offering the Grip to the demi-god before him. "Ye are the Heroes of Legend, they who were called by the Lady to live here among us."

"Aye, in order that we might have the opportunity to pay for our mistakes," Prometheus smiled a bit. "She has called us together to perform a task, to help ye with this project."

"Ye do not need my help," Theodosius chuckled wryly. "Ye are all Masters of Engineering, as well as the other Guild Trades."

"Exactly my point," Prometheus continued warmly. "Ye may return to yer regular tasks now, and leave this to us."

"I am dismissed," Theodosius grinned widely, grateful for the Lady's intervention. "I am grateful, as I have bridge plans to continue drawing up. Perhaps the Lady will allow ye to join that work party too? I could use the help of such as yerselves, especially in moving some of the rock."

"Ye have only to ask," Prometheus answered, and Theodosius understood he meant that the Guild Master should ask the Goddess to send them. The Master of Guilds left the cellar, and Prometheus took command at once. "We must first drain out all of this water," he thought out loud.

"I can help with that!" Hercules volunteered at once, wading into the water. He made his way to the opposite wall, feeling the slight decline in the floor as he went, and knew it was a sure sign that the outlet should be relocated to this spot. Putting his hands on the wall before him, he let his fingers run over the dressed stone, looking for any flaw or weak spot that might help him in his task. He had just located just such a flaw and made ready to punch a drain hole right through the stone when the High Lady made her appearance at the top of the stairs.

"Hold there!" she called out, and every man turned at once due to the commanding tone. "Master Hercules, surely ye do not mean to put a random hole in the wall?"

"I see no other way to drain out this water in a timely fashion, My Lady," he called back respectfully. Deborah's face took on an impatient expression and suddenly a glowing feather appeared in her hand, one of the *Flameblades* she was famous for as a Phoenix woman. She whispered a few words to it, then cast it towards the wall, causing Hercules to move aside rapidly. The flaming feather hit the water, making a hissing sound, and they all expected it to go out. Instead, the feather went straight for the wall and began to spin rapidly as it penetrated the stone, creating a smoothly surfaced tunnel through the thick stone until it had created an outlet. The water gushed out in a torrent and soon the floor of the cellar emerged, allowing the work to begin. A smile appeared on the High Lady's face then, and she called out to the heroes.

"Is there aught else I might do to hasten the work?"

"Ye have given us a good start, My Lady," Prometheus called back, mightily impressed.

"Very good then. I shall return in two hours with a snack for all of ye, as well as a ration of brown ale. I hope to see more progress now that ye are all here," she smiled warmly. All of them bowed deeply to show respect and she nodded in acknowledgement before taking her leave, simply disappearing into thin air. All of them stared at the spot for long moments before a collective sigh escaped them and they returned to their work.

"She reminds me of Hera," Hercules spoke out after a long time had passed. "That sudden decision and action, 'tis a bit frightening."

"Hera was a Peacock, the High Lady is a Phoenix. Let us remember which one is higher in rank," Prometheus responded. "The Land requires a woman of power and command, one that can be respected and loved by all. Hera was not that kind of Queen."

"Aye," Bacchus responded as he found a place to set up an eating area for them. "I am going upstairs to start our meal, brothers. I shall see ye shortly. Come along, brother Orpheus!"

The pair took their leave of them then, walking the distance from the cellar to the kitchen in a rapid manner. When they entered, they found the High Lady directing the cooking of the heroes' second meal, a generous feast. Walking to her, they waited for her to finish giving directions to one of the staff before getting her attention.

"Excuse me, My Lady?" Bacchus inquired.

"Aye Master Bacchus, how may I be of assistance?" she answered.

"The two of us have volunteered to prepare the meals for our brothers downstairs, since we are not muscular workers," he grinned a bit. "However, I am a good cook, and I know my brother's tastes well enough to be able to prepare a good meal for them. Orpheus is here to learn and assist me."

"Come along then," Deborah grinned. "I can use all the help I can get right now. The berry pickers are coming in with many buckets of huge berries and we are inundated right now. I have a meal cooking for yer brothers right now, which I would gladly allow ye to take over preparing."

Bacchus smiled wide as she handed him an apron, then brought him to where the huge meal was cooking, introducing him to those tending it.

"I am entrusting this space to Master Bacchus and Master Orpheus, so that he might prepare meals for our rather large working crew downstairs," she introduced him to the others. "Please work with him as ye would with me?"

"Of course, My Lady!" she heard them all agree, then watched for a moment as they greeted Bacchus with warmth and respect. Seeing that all was well, she returned to her task of supervising the jam-making. All of the younger staff were now committed to the duty as part of their over-all training, and she watched over them carefully as they washed, sorted then turned the berries into the large pots according to the recipe posted at each station. All seemed to be progressing well as she watched, glad to be able to sit for a few moments and just supervise. Even the new hires from Nathan, the Master Innkeeper were doing well, despite the fact only two of them had cooked in a kitchen before.

When the time came to serve the mid-day meal, Bacchus came to Deborah, his face wearing a troubled expression.

"Madam, how do ye propose to get all of this feast downstairs before it is cold?" he asked plaintively.

"Such is no difficulty for me, Master Bacchus," she grinned. "Assure that all is in readiness, including flatware, plates and napkins?"

"Of course, Madam," Bacchus agreed, his face now a bit confused. Once they had the food properly assembled, Deborah came to provide transportation, simply snapping her fingers. They appeared in the cellar, the food arranged on a table, finding the heroes in the process of finishing the cleaning work.

"Ah!" Deborah remarked when they arrived. "I see that progress is being made! I shall be sure to pass that along upstairs, 'twill cheer the staff considerably to know the work is proceeding so quickly. Thank ye, Gentlemen."

"Ye…Ye are welcome, Madam," they all replied collectively, all of them slightly unnerved by her sudden appearance, along with a fully prepared meal.

"Now, be sure ye wash up a bit before taking a seat," Deborah instructed warmly. "When ye are finished, all ye need do is pile everything neatly, then call for me. Enjoy yer meal, the next one will arrive in about two hours," she finished before disappearing from their sight.

"Whew!" Bacchus remarked as he began to serve the hungry heroes. "She is truly a force of Nature! One can hardly refuse any request she makes!"

"Is that not how it should be?" Prometheus asked, biting into the delicious, tender meat. "Bacchus, did ye season this?"

"I did not," he admitted as he continued to serve the meal. "The High Lady and her staff had the meal started when I went upstairs. All I did was simply finish it. The pork is quite delicious, I shall have to learn what rub mix she used!"

The food disappeared quickly, leaving only a few crumbs as they carefully scraped those all onto one dish, then stacked plates carefully into two stacks, the flatware between them. The cups were carefully turned upside down for stability, then the entire thing was covered with the cloth. They had just finished that when Deborah arrived, Bacchus having summoned her quietly while the clean-up was in progress.

"Ah! Ye enjoyed the meal!" she remarked with a smile.

"We did, and we would ask that ye teach our brother Bacchus the rub mix ye used for the meat," Hercules spoke out with respect. "All of us thought 'twas delicious!"

"I would be honored to teach the Master whatever I might," Deborah smiled, using her words carefully. "Thank ye for the neat job of stacking the plates and such, 'twill make it much easier for me to deal with now," she went on, turning to the dishes and snapping her fingers. They disappeared, reappearing upstairs in the dish station, where they quickly sorted themselves into the proper piles and tubs. Deborah remained a moment or two, letting them take her on a brief tour of the work site and listening as they described their next steps.

"Does all of that meet with yer approval, My Lady?" Prometheus asked at length.

"Of course it does," she smiled. "Ye are here to do the Goddess' work, and so far, all is well. Yer next meal will be in about three hours, and 'twill be supper. Surely, ye will cease yer labors afterward?"

"I think not, Madam, if we are to get this done quickly. We will work late tonight, so that we will not interrupt yer work too much tomorrow. Ye may wish to make alternate kitchen arrangements though, as we may have to shut off all of the water for a few hours."

"I see," Deborah nodded. "I shall make proper arrangements then," she went on. "Thank ye Gentlemen."

Disappearing, she arrived in the Barracks Kitchen, finding Klietos and his brothers discussing that night's meal. The kitchen was very warm, even with the new circulation installed, as the temperature outside was humid and hot.

"Good afternoon, Master Klietos, and all of ye," she greeted warmly, using a softer voice so as not to startle the men.

"Good afternoon, My Lady. How may we be of service?"

"What are yer feelings on cooking outside tonight?" she asked simply.

"I think the Barracks would enjoy that, especially since we have so many guests for the Tournament already," Klietos answered at once, knowing the mood of the Barracks well.

"Make it so then, I think we will all want to eat outside tonight. Ye may wish to draw water for cooking though, it may be that the water in the House will be turned off for a few hours to accommodate the work in the cellar."

"Whatever must be done will be done, Madam," Klietos assured her. "Having the flooding problem fixed will be a blessing for all."

"Indeed so, Master Klietos," she smiled gratefully. "I shall leave it to ye then, to make the announcement here, while I do so upstairs. The sooner we start cooking outside, the better, aye?"

"Aye!"

It was not long after their conversation that Deborah looked out the windows to see the occupants of the Barracks hauling out the pavilions, setting up the cooking stations, laughing all the while. A fond smile passed over her face to see them enjoying themselves, for such things were usually rare for the warriors of the Land. Later that night, she sent down supper for the heroes, asking Calla and Lillith to attend to the service.

"Of course! We would be honored to help out!" Lillith proclaimed happily, for she wanted to meet the group of famed individuals. Calla was not in a hurry to do so, she was still recovering from her run in with a marriage minded, Naga-possessed Elf lord, who was even now paying off his crime as a bondsman.

"If ye need us to do this for ye, I would be happy to help out," the older daughter said. Deborah heard the tone in her voice, and a fierce expression crossed her face.

"If they make one move that makes either of ye uncomfortable for any reason, call for me and I shall deal with them," she said, and Calla was comforted at once.

"Thank ye Mother," she said quietly. "I am not ready to be alone with anyone again."

"Nor should ye have to be," Deborah answered. The two young women clustered around the table, while Deborah snapped her fingers. The entire supper service disappeared from the kitchen, reappearing downstairs, where the heroes were working.

"Gentlemen, time to clean up!" Lillith called out, putting a great deal more strength behind her words than usual. "Supper is served!"

"Thank ye," Prometheus answered for all of them. "We will be ready shortly."

It did not take the heroes very long to wash their hands and faces, then take a seat at the table to enjoy the well-cooked meal. It was roast beef, done with all manner of vegetables in the pan, and the heroes ate heartily. When they finished, only a few crumbs remained on the platters, and in the bowls, and the heroes sat back for a few minutes to let their meal settle.

"Ye are the High Lord's daughters?" Prometheus asked conversationally. "He does not appear to have gained enough years to have daughters of yer ages."

"We are Daughters of the House," Lillith answered, her voice strong and filled with family pride. "Ye need have no doubt of that."

Hercules let his eyes cast over them, seeing the resemblance clearly before he offered his opinion.

"They look like Natanleod daughters to me, brothers. Perhaps we should just accept things as they are."

"Aye," went around the table, and then they fell to cleaning up their supper dishes, stacking and piling them carefully on the table. No more conversation could be heard, at least until the task was complete.

"Thank ye, Daughters of the House, for yer service to us. Please tell yer Mother the meal was delicious, as always, and that we are on schedule to turn the water off in the house overnight."

"I shall do so," Calla answered earnestly. "Yer work is proceeding quickly, gentlemen, something everyone in the kitchens will be grateful for."

With that, the two young women disappeared from the cellar, leaving the heroes to their work.

"Goddess, they remind me of Athena and Artemis," Theseus finally said aloud what they were all thinking.

"So they do, and we should simply hold them in our thoughts as if they were our sisters, aye?" Prometheus suggested.

"Aye," they all answered in unison before returning to their work of digging the trenches for the new pipes and installing them. However, several of them had difficulty sleeping that night as memories of the beautiful young women floated through their minds. Each man who experienced such a dream had it shattered however, by the entrance of the Goddess into the scenario.

"What are ye thinking?" each one of them heard in their dream. "Is this not one of the reasons ye are here in the Land, acting as my bondsmen? I would have thought this lesson well learned by now, that yer attentions should not be forced on women. Am I mistaken?"

"Ye are not mistaken, My Lady," Theseus answered in his dream. "I did not start out thinking that way about them, but I did let my thoughts stray. Thank ye for reminding me of the task at hand."

"Ye are most welcome, my son," She answered, her voice suddenly very motherly. "I want ye all to succeed, I have tasks for ye to take on in the future, tasks only beings such as yerselves are capable of doing. If ye cannot pass this test, then we must start completely over again."

"Yer warning is taken to heart, Madam," Theseus answered, his voice holding gratitude and warmth. "I shall do my best to put her out of my mind."

"Ye have learned a great deal while in My service. See ye do not throw that away now," She finished, then disappeared, leaving behind the scent of roses. The other heroes all received similar visits, since they were all having the same dreams, and when they gathered in the morning they were all ready to work hard.

Chapter 6

That day's work was some of the hardest they needed to do; installing the new inlets, laying the new pipe, and continuing to dig the ditches. However, they were able to lay the pipe leading out to the new water purifying pools, being sure to shovel in a generous layer of river gravel to provide drainage and cushion the pipes a bit from occasional earthshakes. Rounds of snacks and thirst quenching drinks were delivered about every hour, as Deborah knew one could not ask such men to work on empty stomachs. By afternoon, the pipes stretched from the new inlets to the purifying pools, still waiting to be covered because of the filters needing to be installed, as well as maintenance access points. They labored throughout that day, even though the heat was quite intense, taking their long break only after sundown that day and each one after. Deborah continued to send down snack trays and cool drinks to assist in their work, for which they were very grateful. By the time they ceased, just before supper service on the fourth day, they had installed all of the intakes, as well as the new valves, which could be adjusted to control the flow of water. They had learned that in the Spring, during the snow melt, was when the flooding happened, and that was simply due to the increased amount of water flowing through the Elan. By installing the valves and filters, they were now able to control the amount of water, as well as keep the pipes clear of gravel. More filters were installed along the outflow pipes, along with access ports that would allow the pipes to be cleaned if necessary. The next few days work would be dedicated to digging the pools for the water reclamation system, and assuring that the water flowed in just the right way to provide circulation for the system at the end of the pipes.

They were just cleaning up a bit before heading to the bath when Deborah appeared, a chilled keg beside her.

"Gentlemen!" she exclaimed, her voice warm with approval. "My goodness, ye have accomplished so much in so few days! I have something special prepared for ye tonight in light of yer successful labors. I hope ye enjoy open grilled lamb?" she teased.

Their eyes lit at the suggestion, and a round of approving exclamations went through the group.

"Madam, such a meal is considered the victor's feast," Prometheus answered for all of them as she pulled chilled silver mugs of ale from the keg and handed them around.

"Ye certainly have achieved a great victory in my eyes," Deborah smiled, handing him his mug. "I can hardly believe we are so close to having this all fixed at last. When ye have bathed, come to the kitchen, and I shall show ye where ye will be eating tonight. I have also set up sleeping pavilions for ye there, in case ye wish to sleep outside. The moon will be full tonight, and I have always found sleeping outside on such nights to be very restful."

"Thank ye, Madam. Ye are very gracious in yer hospitality," Prometheus complimented, his voice rumbling a bit with emotion. "In my life, I have not always been so welcome."

"The Goddess has sent ye here to provide a service," Deborah answered after a moment. "I would be unwise to be anything other than welcoming and thankful," she went on, a faint smile passing over her face. He bent a bit at the waist, showing respect, and another smile passed over her face, a warmer, gentler expression before she continued to lead them outside. Along the path of the new outlet pipes stood groves of myrtle, willow and hazelnut trees, and the heroes saw where a traditional firepit had been set up. A table stood beside it, where two herdsmen were just depositing four huge lamb carcasses. The heroes' mouths began to water, thinking of the feast to come, and when they got to the table, Prometheus had a few questions for the herdsmen.

"Are these yearlings?" he asked at once.

"They are, and they have been raised on apples, as well as fresh greens and grass," the oldest one answered. "My name is Russo, I am the head herdsman in the lamb pens. These were destined for the High Lord's table, but the Lady insisted ye should have them as a reward for yer work. I must say, we will all be grateful not to have the backwash this Winter," he grinned. "Some of the kitchen staff will bring out the side dishes later, ye can see the keg of cold ale over there, and the small cask beside is white wine. Tonight will be a beautiful night, Heroes."

"Thank ye Russo," Prometheus said for all of them. "The meat is perfectly marbled, and I imagine 'twill cook up to be quite delicious," he smiled.

"I think ye'll enjoy it," Russo grinned, offering the Grip before he and his assistants took their leave.

The heroes ran to the river, only a short distance away, and quickly immersed themselves, rinsing off the dirt and grime of that day's work. When they arrived back at their campsite, they found three wooden tubs, filled with hot water, an invitation to bathe. Beside them were large towels, and Priestesses stood at hand to help them wash their backs if necessary. They felt a sense of celebration wash over them, and when they were clean and dressed in comfortable clothing, they turned their attention to the waiting lamb. On the table were jars of herbs, salt and ground black peppercorns, and a few spices too. The Heroes quickly created a rub mix from what was available, and used it generously on the meat, massaging it into the meat as deeply as possible. Ale and wine were consumed liberally during the process, and laughter was heard throughout the area, as it was close to the party field maintained by the House. Once the meat was cooking, they sat back with their cups, sipping and talking quietly among themselves.

"Ye know," Bacchus said as the sun sank before them. "We have all served in worse houses," he ventured.

"Indeed," Prometheus agreed. "The food here is good, the beds are comfortable, and the people are kind. Winter is on the way, and I do not want to be wandering this year. What say ye, brothers? Should we ask to stay?"

Silence reigned for a moment or two, and then one at a time, the others raised their hands to show their agreement to the suggestion.

"Would ye speak to the High Lord for all of us, Brother?" Ares asked humbly. "Ye are the eldest, and ye speak well. Some of us are not so eloquent."

"If ye wish for me to act as representative for all, I would be honored," Prometheus agreed easily. "I shall go about making an appointment to see him concerning our Winter quarters."

"Thank ye, Brother!" he heard from the rest of them as he rose to check the lamb's cooking. As if on cue, a few women arrived from the House bearing bowls of side dishes; barley salad, roasted vegetable mélange, a green salad dressed with vinaigrette and a large basket of fresh bread, still warm from the oven.

"Good evening, Heroes," they called, laying a cloth over the table, seeing that it had been cleaned after the lamb preparation. "Is yer supper nearly ready?"

"Indeed so, ladies, and we thank ye for providing the rest of the meal," Prometheus answered for all of them. "Good night."

"Good night, and do not worry about the dishes," the leader of the cadre told him. "We will come for them in a little while."

"Again, ye have our gratitude, ladies!" the Heroes all called out, in near unison.

It was not long afterward the meat was done to perfection, and they all enjoyed the taste of rare lamb flavored with *Joy of the Mountain*, the Greek term for oregano, as well as garlic, black pepper and a sprinkle of chili flakes. The huge men ate every bite of the lamb, and emptied the bowls of side dishes too, leaving nothing, not even a crumb. Afterward, they carefully piled the plates, flatware and mugs in neat stacks, trying to make the staff's job easier. The women arrived just as they were bedding down for the night, and each of the Heroes was sure to respectfully thank them for all of their work.

"Ye are most welcome, Heroes," their leader returned with warmth in her voice. "Ye have done us all a great service by what ye are doing to the water system. We are glad to be able to show gratitude. Good night."

"Good night," they called back in a chorus. Within the pavilion they found a box of nearly black sikars, and scent proclaimed them to be anointed with the Lady's Oil.

"Look we have been gifted *Imperials*!" Prometheus announced, passing them around to those who reached for one. There was also several carafes of red wine and a large ceramic bottle of mellow whiskey, along with the proper cups for each beverage. A note stood beside the treats, and when they read it, they were a bit surprised to find it was from the High Lord.

"Thank ye Gentlemen for yer hard work. Enjoy the night, and sleep deeply," the note read, and they saw it was signed with a simple "E" instead of his full name. Such an address would be very casual, and they were all honored by the show of friendliness from the High Lord. They lit the sikars, poured beverages and watched the sky until the sikars had burned away, enjoying every puff and sip as they did so. Their sleep was deep, if short, and when they woke, they found Deborah in the camp cooking for them.

"Good morning, Heroes," she called out as she turned sausages and bacon. "First meal is nearly ready to eat, I am glad ye are awake," she smiled. The Heroes remained within the pavilion until they were dressed, emerging into the common area to the scent of cooking meat, which made their mouths water. Caffe was ready, as was tea, and they helped themselves to the beverages, as well as the huge platter of pastries on the table. Such things would not diminish their great appetites, as was prove a short time later when Deborah laid out their meal, which quickly disappeared. They all ate with very good manners, she noted as the food was consumed, and when they finished, they all thanked her in turn.

"Madam, ye are a very fine cook," Prometheus complimented for all of them. "Are ye certain ye are happy in yer marriage?" he teased a bit, testing her sense of humor.

"I most certainly am, Master Prometheus," she grinned, falling into the word game with him. "However, if I were not, ye might get a glance or two in yer direction," she laughed a bit harder. His laugher joined with hers, and then the others added theirs, a very merry sound.

"Ye'd be playin' with fire, for certain, brother Prometheus," Hercules pointed out. "Remember, she's a Phoenix Woman, and easily yer equal, as she is to all of us."

"Indeed so," Prometheus nodded, his eyes sparkling with humor. "But it might be worth the risk, just to be that close to such a beautiful woman."

"Now, now," they heard Erinn's voice enter the conversation, and the Heroes turned to face him, seeing he was smiling broadly. "Ye are talking to my wife there, Master Prometheus. We want no misunderstandings here, do we?"

"Most certainly not," he replied, his voice filled with humor, but Erinn could hear the underlying seriousness. "Good morning, My Lord. May I ask why ye are here so early?"

"I have come to join yer work party, and I have brought a few friends along to help as well," Erinn answered, smiling broadly. "Where can I be of the most help?"

"Come along, Sir. Ye can work with my group, as we are taking on the last two pools, which must be the largest and the best constructed. Where are these friends ye have brought along? I can put them to work too," the huge being beside him chuckled.

Erinn fell in step beside him as they walked the short distance from the camp to the worksite, where Prometheus and the other Heroes beheld the entire complement of the Barracks standing there waiting to work.

"I have brought along everyone not currently assigned to anything vital, and many have given up their two day to join us as well. Let us get started, 'tis already getting hot," Erinn suggested.

"Aye, My Lord," Prometheus smiled, liking his directness. They arrived presently at the first work site claimed by Prometheus' group, the final outflow pool where the clean, filtered water would house a fish pond. Erinn noted the piles of granite stones staged all about the site, as well as a huge pile of gravel and one of clean sand.

"First we must dig the pool to the proper depth, and then the sand goes in, followed by the gravel, then the stone. All of that will make it easier to clean the pool when it comes time to do so."

"And ye are setting up all of the others similarly?" Erinn asked.

"Aye, My Lord, and to aid that, I have wagons delivering fresh supplies constantly today. We can work without ceasing, for as long as we can."

"Very good," Erinn grinned, grabbing a shovel and walking to where the large circle was laid out. He began digging rapidly and efficiently, as did the others and within the hour they had the first layer of dirt removed. It was then that Prometheus suddenly noticed that Erinn's size had increased significantly, the young High Lord was now as tall as any of the Heroes and working as hard as any of them. Prometheus grinned wide, realizing now that Erinn's set of magickal skills equaled his father Drake's in every way. It made it easier to work beside him, as they could expect the same level of effort from him.

Everyone in the work crews fell to then, and soon the sound of working songs could be heard. Some of them were old tunes, some were ribald, and some very comical, but they provided a steady rhythm for everyone, which made the work go faster and easier.

While the Knights and Heroes worked, Deborah and her outdoor kitchen provided constant meals to those laboring that day. She heard many a grateful worker sigh with relief as they took their plates, then settled at one of the temporary tables set up in the shade of the trees. Lemon water with ginger was served in ample supplies, runners even taking it out to the workers in small casks so they could drink and be refreshed. After the first wave of workers hit the outdoor kitchen, Deborah turned to the young woman working beside her, ready to hand over responsibility to her.

"Now, I must go and begin the supper preparations alongside Master Klietos. I have a slightly different rub mix I would like to try on the pork, and I have to make sure we have thawed sufficient salmon to go with it. Remember, all ye need do is keep the food cooking, making certain 'tis plenty all the while. Ye have watched me do it, and I know ye have the capability of leading this crew, Brittany. Go to it, 'tis yer chance to prove yerself to everyone on the staff. I believe ye can do it," Deborah smiled confidently.

"Thank ye, My Lady," the young woman answered, her nervousness clear in her words. "I shall do my best."

"Which is all ye have been asked to do," Deborah smiled. "Ye have an experienced crew to work with here, do not be afraid to ask for advice. But ye must make the final decisions, and lead them."

"Aye, My Lady," Brittany smiled, squaring her shoulders and straightening her back. Turning to the crew, she smiled warmly and addressed them with confidence.

"Thank ye all for working with me today. We must remember to keep food available all the time today, after all, we cannot ask people to work hard on empty stomachs," she chuckled. "How is the supply of water?" she asked.

"We should make more now," one of the younger women spoke up.

"Can ye do it for us?"

"Aye!"

"Good, then please see to it today for us? We must assure plenty of refreshing drink for them, as the day is very hot."

"Aye!"

Deborah smiled as she walked away, knowing the outdoor kitchen was in good hands that day, a relief for her. She made her way directly to the Barracks Kitchen, where Klietos and his brothers were even now helping to prepare the meats for that night's meal.

"Ah, My Lady!" they all greeted her with broad, warm smiles. "Are ye hungry, or thirsty?"

"I could use a bit of cold wine," Deborah smiled. "My goodness, I dressed simply and lightly, and I am sweating as if I am wearing heavy wool. Thank ye, Master Klietos, for the wine," she said gratefully, taking the full cup and sipping a few times before setting it aside. "Now, how is the meat? Is the salmon thawed?"

"Almost, My Lady, and the herdsmen have delivered the pigs ye ordered. Ye wanted me to wait for ye?"

"I did, I wanted to try a different rub mix than usual," she answered, reaching into her pockets and pulling out several packages of a brown, crystalline product.

"What is that?"

"Master Klietos, did ye know that ye can boil the sap of sugar maple trees down so far that 'twill crystalize like this?" she asked with a grin, opening one of the packages for him. "Go, get a spoon and try it," she urged. The four men did as she requested, and as soon as the crystalized maple syrup hit their tongues, an expression of delight passed over each of their faces.

"My Lady!" Klietos thundered a bit, his surprise complete. "I...I have never tasted anything quite like this before!"

"I know," Deborah grinned. "I am going to use this in the rub mix, along with chilies, dried onion and garlic, a little bit of salt and black pepper, and a bit of red wine. I imagine the effect on the pork will be noticeably different."

"I can hardly wait, Madam!" Klietos grinned, noting her cup was nearly empty. "Would ye like more wine?"

"I would while I am working," she answered, rising and taking the apron offered to her by his next younger sibling, Cleon.

"Thank you, Master Cleon," she said gratefully, taking the cup with her as she strode to the preparation table, where the first huge porker lay waiting for her work. The four brother watched with intense scrutiny as she constructed her rub mix, making full use of the large mortar and pestle they gave her. She made bowls of the mix, using every sprinkle of the maple sugar, until finally it was all used.

"There," she said as she scraped the last crumbles of the mix into the last bowl. "Ye should have plenty to use."

"And those in the Barracks?"

"They have all been working hard today, and should be resting for their work upon the morrow," Deborah returned. "Our responsibility is to assure their comfort tonight, so they can work hard tomorrow."

"Aye, Madam. We will get this meat cooking, right now."

"Ye know my husband I and admire alacrity in all things," Deborah answered with a grin, producing a pouch of *Imperials* and handing it to the Kitchen Master. "Thank ye, gentlemen, for all ye do to assure the comfort of those in the Barracks. I have a feeling ye will be required to accommodate larger appetites in yer meals, perhaps ye should begin planning to feed at least some of the Heroes."

Klietos' face took on a look of surprise, and murmurs could be heard from his three brothers behind him at the suggestion.

"Can the Barracks accommodate such large beings, Madam?" Klietos burst out, unable to help himself. His three younger brothers began to push the carts out to the cooking area, two of them having to push the first cart due to the large carcass it held.

"Of course, Kitchen Master," Deborah smiled. "Ye know as well as I do that the Lady always finds a way."

"Indeed so, Madam," Klietos answered in an abashed tone. "I shall get to this meat so 'twill be done on time."

"Of course 'twill be perfectly timed for service," Deborah grinned, a merry twinkle in her eyes. "Ye *are* the Kitchen Master of the Barracks."

Klietos could not suppress his soft laughter at her humor, feeling as if he had been challenged as surely as if someone had thrown a gauntlet at his feet. His day took on a different aspect from that moment on, and by the time the work crew was done that day, the food was ready for them to eat.

Deborah returned to the Barracks, making a stop at the Quarter Master's room. She found the younger woman working with a wax tablet in hand, and understood it was inventory day.

"I do not mean to trouble ye, Dame Barkida, but I have need for a few flasks if we have them available," she began, keeping her voice quiet.

"Of course, Madam. If ye will give me a moment to finish counting this wall, I shall see to it."

It did not take long for the intelligent Dame to finish that part of her work, and when she had counted the last pair of unders on the shelves, she put her tablet aside and came to the High Lady's side.

"I shall return quickly," she said, turning and disappearing behind the curtain separating the lobby from the storage rooms. In what seemed just a few moments, Barkida returned, a large box on her shoulder. "Yer request is most timely, as I have found I am almost out of regular flasks, the kind we send out on patrol. I shall have to order some right away, so they will be here before Winter patrol season," she chuckled. "How many do ye need?"

"Thirteen," Deborah replied, and Barkida nodded sagely.

"I thought as much, these are for the Heroes?"

"Aye, a gift from me personally," Deborah replied.

"Well then, I have brought the correct flasks for that," Barkida grinned triumphantly, opening the box and pushing aside the cushioning straw. There were twenty four flasks in the box, all of them decorated with the Natanleod crest, and Deborah grinned to see the Lady's hand at work.

"Excellent, if ye can pack thirteen into a separate box for me, I shall be on my way," Deborah smiled. Barkida stepped back away from the counter, ducking behind a side wall, and quickly reappearing with a wooden box that looked to be the correct size. She chose the flasks quickly, examining each for any dent or scratch, choosing only those without damage. Once they were within the second box, Barkida turned to the High Lady. "Shall I help ye?"

"Thank ye Dame," Deborah said. "I can take it from here."

So saying, she picked up the box, noting the weight was lighter than she thought it would be and left the Quarter Master's office. Barkida returned to her work then, noticing just a bit later that there was a pouch loaded with largesse in her pocket. Upon opening it she found a portion of potent Herb and five smaller *Imperials*, her step was noticeably lighter as she anticipated her noon break a bit more now.

As soon as she picked up the box, Barkida seeing that the weight was no burden to the High Lady, Deborah disappeared in a *poof*, reappearing within the locked confines of her sewing room. There, she put the box on the table, then went to the Goddess' statue in the niche and lit all of the candles in their usual order. Afterwards, she lit a stick of her favorite incense, a blend of Sandalwood, Frankincense and Myrrh with a touch of Musk Oil, she let her mind empty of the day's business. Concentrating on the face of the statue before her, Deborah composed her thoughts, constructing her thoughts to speak her Will in a concise and ordered way.

"My Lady Goddess, the Heroes have given good and honest service, and I would reward them with something appropriate to their stature and appetites. Lend me Thy aid, and help me to bring forth the perfect reward for each of them?" she finished entreatingly. A wave of confidence washed over her, and she knew her entreaty had been answered. A smile appeared on her face as she nodded to the statute humbly, and thanked the Goddess for Her favor. Rising, she took a few deep breaths to steady herself before walking to the table and removing the lid from the box to reveal the softly shining flasks, decorated simply with the House crest engraved into one side. They would hold about a quart of liquor or whatever liquid was put into them, and they were designed to lay flat against the chest in an inner pocket of the Knight's tunic. Each trooper was issued one, in a plainer design of course and rendered in silver, unlike the ones before her. They were cast in Mythrill, a rare metal that combined the properties of every known metal in the Land. The ore was claimed for the family's use, and it was theirs to dispense to whom they would. Deborah grinned at the Lady's Will being worked before her, as she had intended to gift them regular silver flasks in the first place, but now seeing this was more appropriate. Taking a deep breath and letting her Phoenix abilities emerge, just a bit, she passed her right hand slowly over the flasks, seeing the perfect gift for each Hero was exactly the same. She could hardly wait to hand them out to the huge men who were working so hard to get the water system working as it should have all along, she thought as the magick continued to work, and a soft glow surrounded each flask for a few moments before appearing to be absorbed within each one. The final touch was to ensure that the cork of each could never be lost, that it would remain with the flask or at least within the reach of it. She felt the *snap* as the spell took hold, and the wave of weariness that washed over her for a short time. She dealt with it by taking a seat and letting it dissipate before picking up the lid to the box and replacing it, flipping the latch to secure it. Picking it up, she took it to the table by the door of the room, setting it on top with a bit of a thud due to the weight. Only then did she return to her usual seat by the window and call her wine carafe to her, pouring a cup of rich red wine and sipping it slowly as she recovered herself. She had the perfect gift for each of them now, she knew, one they would not be expecting in any way, which was the perfect gift to give in her opinion. When she had recovered, she summoned a carafe of very special liquor, now over twenty years old, a gift from Caius Ironhorse on the occasion of her marriage to Erinn. The cellar still held twenty casks of the mellow whiskey, and the two of them handed it out rarely. Filling each flask to the top with the liquor, she murmured over each one before replacing the stopper, sealing the liquor inside. Now she felt as if the task was finished, and with a final bow to the Lady's statue in the room, she blew out the candles, picked up the box and disappeared from within the room, reappearing within the chamber she shared with Erinn.

Her husband had just emerged from a tub of hot water and lavender bath salts when she arrived, and the remains of an antipasto tray could be seen on the table. Erinn trudged out of the bedroom, dressed in simple house clothing, his face drawn with weariness.

"Husband!" Deborah exclaimed, putting the box aside and coming to his aid. "Ye should sit down, ye look exhausted. What have ye been doing?"

"Working with the Heroes," he replied in quiet tones, and she could hear the unspoken plea for wine. "In order to keep up with them I was obliged to be as large as they. 'Tis an exhausting exercise, being as tall as a god."

"Ye are done working for the day," Deborah ordered softly, although it was unnecessary. Erinn had no intention of doing anything now except sitting and resting, as well as enjoying a wonderful meal.

"Aye Madam," he grinned. "Perhaps ye will join me for the rest of the evening? We have not seen much of each other of late. And what is in the box?"

"Something for the Heroes, a special gift for their exceptional labor," Deborah replied mysteriously.

"I see," Erinn managed a smile. "I shall have to include something from myself as well. Could I have a hint about what ye are gifting them?"

For her answer, Deborah simply summoned a flask from the box, taking it from the air and handing it to Erinn without a word.

"A flask?"

"Ye can see that one is engraved with the House sign," Deborah explained patiently.

"Aye and?"

"Open it," she instructed. With an expression of curiosity, Erinn pulled the cork from the flask and sniffed experimentally. His eyes lit as he recognized the liquor, and a smile passed over his face.

"Most appropriate, my dear. Ye are gifting them our marriage whiskey."

"Indeed, but 'tis not all," Deborah teased. "I have included a very special gift as well."

"Please my dear," Erinn smiled wanly. "I am too tired for guessing games."

"I have asked the Lady's assistance so that the flasks never run dry," Deborah explained. "And the corks cannot get lost either."

"A good inclusion," Erinn nodded.

"I shall talk to Gwendolyn right now. Ye should not be alone right now, and I would imagine yer muscles hurt badly."

"My muscles do feel tight," Erinn confessed. "If ye would just sit with me, and share supper with me, it would help me to relax."

"I shall return momentarily," Deborah grinned, kissing his cheek before disappearing. When she popped into the kitchen, she found all proceeding well and she went directly to the Kitchen Mistress.

"Madam," she said quietly.

"Aye, My Lady?"

"My husband has matched work with the heroes all day today, and has over expended himself a bit. I need to remain and tend him, if I am not needed here."

"Go and take care of the High Lord," Gwendolyn answered at once. "I have already begun to hear tales of his work, and how he assumed the size of the Heroes in order to keep up with them. Let us just say that the talk in the Barracks tonight will be all speculation about just how tall he can get," she laughed a bit. "The Barracks Kitchen is taking care of all of the cooking outside, and ye know how the denizens of the Barracks enjoy adding their help to such work. I anticipate a quiet night tonight, however."

"I do as well," Deborah nodded, noticing Prometheus approaching with Aries and Mittra behind him.

"My Lady, a moment please?" she heard him call out and paused to wait for him.

"What is it, Master Prometheus?" she asked with a smile.

"Ye granted us one more day, and the project is nearly done. We must finish up planting the trees, bushes and reeds that will provide the filtration for each pool, and we will need more plants than anticipated, as the pools are all slightly bigger than we planned. The High Lord's assistance has been instrumental in today's work, as he was able to keep us supplied with materials even though I was a bit short in my estimations," he chuckled wryly.

"If the pools are slightly bigger, then yer original calculations were likely correct," Deborah answered. "Of course, ye may have as many days as necessary," she went on. "Ye have done many months' worth of work in only six days, a seventh will not impede the project unduly. Go and bathe, I have tubs of hot water set up right by the Elan for ye, as well as the rest of yer entertainments. Thank ye for yer work, all of ye. I shall have to plan a very special meal for the morrow. Good night, Heroes."

"Good night, My Lady!" they called after her as she walked back to where Gwendolyn stood. After a short exchange of words, she disappeared in front of them, leaving them to their baths and relaxations. After a quick checking of all the preparations for supper that night, Deborah finally allowed Gwendolyn to push her out of the kitchen, promising that supper would be delivered presently.

"What are ye serving for tomorrow's feast?" she asked as Deborah prepared to leave.

"Prime beef would be most appropriate, I think. Would ye please pass the word to the Herd Master that the High Lord will be down in the morning to pick out the beasts personally? Also, I want the night crew to make up bowls of rub mix tonight, just salt, ground black pepper and garlic, with plenty of the crystallized maple syrup in it. I think 'twill add a good flavor to the beef. Good night, Gwendolyn, and thank ye for all ye do."

"I am honored to serve, Madam. Good night," she grinned, watching Deborah disappear once more, taking another two carafes of wine with her. When she returned however, Erinn was relaxed against the back of the sofa, sound asleep. She left him to it, simply sipping her wine and working on the knitted piece she was making for one of the staff's new baby. When the knock sounded on the door, he roused a bit, looked about with confusion while Deborah answered the door and took charge of the cart.

"Good night Gwendolyn," she said firmly.

"Aye, M'Lady," the older woman answered, nodding her understanding. "Good night."

Deborah closed the door behind her and locked it, causing the House Guard on duty to step to their overnight duty station at the sound. They knew that the two were in for the night now, and that their job was just beginning. While Deborah and Erinn enjoyed their meal, the Guard walked their rounds, keeping the entire Keep safe overnight, as well as the party field outside.

After the meal concluded, everyone helped to pick up the field and put away the leftovers, carrying them from the tables to the kitchen in an orderly fashion. When the night crew realized just how much meat was left, they went to work stripping the bones, chopping the meat and mixing it with all manner of roasted vegetables, as well as a bit of fresh *muzzarella* cheese to bind it all together. Others began many batches of light, flaky pastry dough that would puff up as it baked, creating a beautiful shell around the filling. The hand pies would be perfect to serve the first crew that tended the animals and did the milking in the morning. By the time they finished, there were dozens of pans ready to bake, all waiting in the cold room on steel racks with wheels to make it easy to manage them. When Gwendolyn arrived for her shift in the morning, they had cleaned up and begun the preparation for the first meal. The Kitchen Mistress could smell caffe, hot tea and fresh fruit as she entered the busy area, calling out her usual morning greeting.

"Good morning everyone. How did the night pass?"

"Easily Madam!" the chorus of voices answered tiredly. "The ovens are almost ready to begin baking the hand pies we have made!"

"Excellent, let us get the first five trays baking then, so that the people doing the first morning chores can eat heartily!"

When the first shift began to arrive, their eyes still sleepy, they went at once to the beverage counter to pour out their chosen cup, many of them also taking a bowl of fruit and yogurt to begin their day.

Into this strode Erinn, his stride determined, his face wearing an expression of purpose. He was up early to make good on Deborah's warning to be ready as beef was on the menu for that night's meal. Prime beef would be a satisfactory meat to serve in celebration of finishing the water project, and Erinn always attended to such a task personally.

The animals in question had been raised to be tame and docile, they would follow their keepers about, knowing that an apple or carrot was available if they did so. The beasts were bathed daily, their stalls large and luxurious, and only the most skilled of people were chosen to care for them. Now he stood in the kitchen, thanking the staff member for the cup of caffe in his hand.

"Ye are most welcome, My Lord. I have heard that the water system will be finished today? Can it truly be so"

"Indeed 'tis so," Erinn smiled faintly. "By the end of the day, the system will be functioning as it should, which will be a relief for all of us."

"Aye, My Lord!" the young woman responded with a smile. "We have hand pies for first meal this morning, and the first few trays are baking right now."

"Is that what I am smelling?" Erinn sniffed appreciatively. "I can hardly wait to have one! The odor of them is most appealing."

"I think so too!" the young woman smiled. She watched as the young Smith, Polemusa, walked into the kitchen, and moved to be ready to be of service to her, as was her duty. Other eyes watched the beautiful young smith, as she was quite aloof from most of those in the Barracks, preferring to work alone and in private. She had even strung a heavy curtain across the front of her area, so she could work barely clothed and not attract undue attention. The smithy was hot on sunny days, and she found that being barely clothed kept her from getting too hot and having to stop her work before she wanted to.

After Erinn consumed one hand pie, he took another and wrapped it in napkin, taking it with him as he went out to the worksite. The Heroes were already out there, and Erinn noted they all had a partial pie in hand, which was quickly disappearing.

"Good morning!" he called out in warm tones. "Good meal, aye?"

"Aye!" the collected response returned, and Erinn noted their mood was a bit lighter today.

"Shall we be about it, after we finish our first meal?"

"We have only one concern, My Lord," Prometheus answered. "We may not have enough plants to fully landscape the area. Especially necessary are the reeds, the cattails, and the water greens, which provide the filtering and cleaning necessary."

"I shall speak to the High Lady at once then, and arrange for more to be onsite," Erinn answered seriously, sending his thoughts out to Deborah. "Madam, a moment of yer time please?"

"What is amiss?"

"Master Prometheus tells me we need more plants for the water system. Could ye be of assistance?"

"Of course, please tell him not to worry, all will be provided," she answered, a touch of humor in her tone.

"I shall tell him exactly that," Erinn sent back, ending the conversation, knowing she was busy too.

"The High Lady has spoken," he said, turning to Prometheus, his face wearing a broad smile. "She said to tell ye not to worry, yer needs will be supplied."

Prometheus' face creased into a grin at his words, and he found himself anticipating the day's work. The day was already hot, and the heat intensified with each passing hour. By the High Lady's order, the water bearers worked continuously bringing water, cold herbal tea and lemon/ginger drink. When the supply of plants began to run low, they found the supply replenished as necessary, much to Prometheus' wonder. In the end, they had exactly enough to finish, so that as the water traveled from pool to pool, the solids would settle out, and the plants would filter the water completely clean before it entered the Elan downstream of the House. This was kitchen water, not from the necessities, which was handled more discreetly due to the odor it produced. The system was very similar, but the water moved much more slowly to allow the solids to settle. Those pools were cleaned weekly on a regular schedule, and the solids were composted for use in the decorative gardens, completely away and out of sight from everyone except those who tended the system.

When the work was finally finished, late that afternoon, the valves were opened and the water began to flow through, exactly was it was supposed to. Prometheus wore a satisfied expression as he watched it, turning to the others with a great burst of enthusiasm, catching each of them in an embrace in turn.

"We have done it, and in only seven days, my brothers!" he exulted a bit. "Look at it, 'tis exactly as it should be, and 'twill last as long as the Land as long as 'tis properly maintained. I find myself with a great thirst, and the longing for a swim in the Elan. 'Tis bloody hot out here, has anyone noticed?" he chuckled. The others joined in with his mirth, especially when he bolted for the river, clearly meaning to have his swim right then and there. The others followed after, arriving just in time to see him leap from the shore and enter the water cleanly with barely a splash. Erinn's brow crinkled, for he knew that section was usually not so deep, until Hercules explained.

"We dug that section out carefully, removing all of the crystals and metal before doing so. Did you know that Master Bacchus has an extremely organized mind? One might even go as far as to describe him as obsessive at the exercise," Hercules chuckled. "We let him go first to collect what was necessary, and he did so in just a few hours, packing everything carefully into trays in order. When we finished digging that section out five feet deeper, we reconstructed the bottom layer by layer, finishing with Bacchus putting everything back exactly as it had been taken out. As ye can see, the river is as it should be, and the deeper channel will allow the outflow to work better."

"And we have a diving pool now," Erinn grinned. "I am ready for a cold drink and a pipe of Herb before I go swimming. I am off to find my lady, gentlemen. I shall see ye all later."

The Heroes watched him walk away, their opinion of him now much higher than when the project was begun.

"He works like his father," Prometheus observed later as they all sat in the wooden tubs of hot water, soaking their muscles after the long day's work. "I have rarely seen the like of him, and his ability to assume our height and size is also quite impressive. I wonder where Drake is, 'tis not like him to be absent from such an event as a major renovation of the House."

It was just at that moment when Drake himself appeared in the busy kitchen, right in the midst of the bustle.

"What is going on?" he thought to himself, letting his mind run over the possibilities for feast days. "The Summer Solstice is still days away, have I missed something?"

Deborah noticed him from her testing kitchen, where she had stored the box filled with flasks for the Heroes. She came to greet him, taking him aside out of the way of those coming and going, bearing pitchers and casks, headed out to the party field.

"Hello Father," she said with warmth and affection, kissing his cheek chastely. "To what do we owe the pleasure of yer arrival after so many months?"

"Months?" Drake echoed.

"Aye, ye have been gone since around Yule or so, if my memory serves me correctly. Much has transpired in yer absence, but I cannot explain at the moment. As ye can see, meat is cooking outside, and people are in a very good mood."

"What has happened?"

"The water system has been fixed, at long last, and 'twas done in seven days," Deborah responded, a bit of a teasing tone in her voice.

"Seven days?" Drake's voice rose in volume at the news. "Did ye both work magick to get that done?"

"I did very little, except feed an extraordinary group of men," Deborah smiled, still teasing Drake and enjoying it.

"What?" Drake asked as realization hit him. "The Heroes, they are here?"

"Indeed so Father, the Goddess sent them to our aid, and they have performed magnificently," Deborah declared. "Ye should go out and look at the new drainage field for the kitchen water."

Drake's face took on a look of surprise and wonder, and after Deborah put a cold mug of brown ale in his hand, he stepped out of the back door and walked the short distance to the worksite. His eyes lit as he observed all of the new workings, and how they were laid out.

"My goodness!" he exclaimed with a grin. "Does it work?"

"Perfectly," Deborah assured him. "The Heroes are still here, and I would imagine one would find them cavorting in the Elan after their labors."

"Seven days?"

"Aye, and I have a gift ready for them, to thank them for their efforts."

"Of course ye do," Drake smiled warmly. "Ye are the most generous woman I have ever met. I think I might wander down to the cooking area though, that meat smells good, but ye have done something different, haven't ye?"

"Ye are the ascended one, it should be easy enough for ye to ascertain what has been done," Deborah laughed, embracing him. "I am glad ye are here. Much has transpired in the Land, and yer son has not had the benefit of yer counsel."

"I shall find him at once then," Drake assured her. "Would ye like for me to carry the box for ye?"

"I have work to do first," Deborah chuckled, waving her hand around the kitchen. "I shall join the party shortly, when I can take a break from the jam making."

"Very well then, I shall go in search of my son," Drake grinned, accepting a third mug of ale from her before leaving the kitchen through the back door. First, he went right to the worksite and walked the entire length of the new water system, sipping the ale and nodding appreciatively at the practicality of it all. Next, he went to the cooking area to taste the rub Deborah had made with the crystallized maple syrup. There were chickens cooking for the hungriest of appetites, and Drake took a piece when offered. The meat was spicy and sweet, with a deep rich flavor that contributed in the best way, and Drake found himself finished with the piece before he wanted to be.

"Delicious!" he pronounced with a grin. "Have ye seen my son?" he asked of the man tending the grill where the chickens cooked.

"Not since the project was finished," the man answered. "I heard him say something about going to look for his wife. She's a busy woman, I would imagine 'twill take time for him to find her," the man chuckled a bit as he answered.

"Perhaps so," Drake chuckled with him.

Erinn was in the office, sorting through his large, cedar box filled with black *Imperials*, sikars treated with the Lady's Oil. He picked out five for each Hero, packing them into the proper-sized silk bags and including a smaller packet of extremely fine, heady Herb. Afterward, he went to his room and bathed, donning light, comfortable clothing in anticipation of the afternoon's fun. Sending his thoughts out to his wife, Deborah told him she would soon join him, adding a request.

"Would ye please tell the Heroes I want to talk to them for a bit?" she asked.

"Of course," Erinn agreed. "I shall see ye shortly then?"

"Aye, the second shift is finally here, and I can turn over the jam making," she replied with a sigh of relief.

"Good, I look forward to ye joining me," Erinn sent back. He left the room then, returning to the office to gather up his gifts, tucking them into his pocket. Walking into the hall and shutting the door behind him, he made his way back to the kitchen, then out the back door, grabbing a cup of ale on his way. It was perfectly cold, and the brown ale was the perfect thing to celebrate a job well done, Erinn thought to himself. He passed the Heroes as they soaked in the wooden tubs filled with hot water and repeated the High Lady's request.

"The High Lady would like to speak with all of ye for a bit, when ye have a moment," he told them.

"The High Lady wants to speak with us? Why? What have we done wrong?" a smallish voice answered from their midst, and the great harper Orpheus stepped forward. "She scares me," he added quietly, and a murmur of agreement ran around the group.

"If truth were to be told," Erinn answered in a quiet tone, stepping into their midst. "She frightens me as well. I have seen what she can do as a Phoenix, and 'tis quite intimidating, even for the son of a dragon," he chuckled.

"I would have liked to have seen that," they heard Odysseus' voice.

"I would be happy to tell ye the tale of how she burned Nateri the Great, from tail to head from the inside out, while she grew to twelve feet, summoning a cup of wine in a golden cup, and a large sikar to enjoy while it happened," Erinn proposed.

"Nateri?"

"Aye, and though we lost the skin, 'twas a great victory nonetheless," Erinn smiled at the memory. The Heroes suddenly found they could see his memories, and they gasped in unison as the events unfolded, until the end of Nateri.

"By the Goddess, yer lady is something to be feared!" Prometheus breathed softly.

"Indeed so, but only when the Goddess empowers her to act," Erinn agreed. Reaching into his inner pockets, Erinn withdrew the packets he had prepared for the Heroes, passing them out and receiving their earnest thanks. "Now gentlemen, she is waiting to speak with ye."

"We will finish up bathing and dress appropriately, My Lord," Prometheus responded.

"Very good," Erinn smiled, taking his leave of them. They hurried to finish then, and after wrapping their waist in a towel, they gathered their things and returned to the room in the Barracks they shared. All of them changed into their formal wear, despite the heat, wanting to greet the High

Lady appropriately, especially with the memory of Nateri's death fresh in their minds. When they appeared on the party grounds, everyone turned to stare, for all of them wore the distinctive armor of their Greek heritage, their weapons sheathed, and their shields on their backs. Deborah stood waiting, still wearing her kitchen wear, her hair unruly and her apron stained with drops of jam from the day's work. Her expression upon seeing them turned from one of repose to one of surprise, and their expressions were similar to see her so casually dressed.

"Gentlemen, ye do me honor," she said, snapping her fingers. A circle of fire appeared at her head, and travelled the length of her body, her clothing being replaced and her hair taking on a dressed appearance. When the fire dissipated, she stood arrayed in a scarlet bolt of silk cloth, twined artfully about her, the informal tiara of her rank firmly in place among her loose tresses. They knelt as one, showing their respect, and she waved at them to rise at once, summoning the box containing the flasks at the same time. When it appeared, it simply floated beside her, a few inches off the ground, so she did not have to bend to retrieve the contents.

"Now that we are all appropriately dressed, allow me to present a gift to each of ye in thanks for yer work. Ye have accomplished a task in seven days that would have taken many, many men months to finish, and I and all of the residents of the House are extremely grateful," she said, throwing back the cover of the box, exposing the clean straw underneath. "Master Bacchus, if ye would please come forward to receive yer gift?" she asked, reaching under the straw. He approached and bowed, receiving a warm smile in return as she put the flask into his hands.

"My Lady," he breathed as he felt the soft metal, and observed the satin-finish of it. Turning it, he saw his name and sign engraved on the back in Greek, and a fond smile appeared on his face. "I thank the High Lady for such a gift!" he said. Unable to help himself, he raised the flask to his ear and shook it, hearing the sound of liquid within. "And tell me, what have ye filled it with?"

"I shall leave that for all of ye to find out later," she grinned, a mischievous twinkle appearing in her eye. "Master Aries, if ye would please come forward?"

One by one, the Heroes received their flasks and admired them, seeing them a both practical and beautiful gifts. Whatever was within them would also be appreciated later, with one of the *Imperials* they had each been gifted, and they all anticipated that.

Prometheus was the last to receive his, and he bowed deeply to Deborah, having gained a great deal of respect for her in the last seven days. "I shall enjoy this later, My Lady. I thank ye for the opportunity to serve."

"I hope to see the Heroes remain here in the Capitol City," she answered. "I have grown accustomed to yer presences, and find them a comfort. Enjoy the party," she finished, nodding to them to show her respect for them. Erinn appeared at her side just then, and whispered in her ear softly. She smiled and took his arm as they walked away, and the Heroes watched their progress all the way back to the House until they disappeared through the back kitchen door.

"What say ye, Brothers," Aries finally said. "Shall we go and don more comfortable attire?"

"Aye, I see a fresh cask of the brown ale being breached right now!" Hercules answered, bolting for the Barracks entrance that led directly to the kitchen and dining room. The others pursued him, and soon they were all within the large comfortable room they had been given upon their arrival. It did not take them long to put off their formal attire and don lighter clothing and sandals before heading back out to the party field and the fun awaiting there.

By then everyone in the Barracks was outside and some of them had brought out their gitars and harps, as well as fiddles. Merry dancing music soon sprang up, and the Heroes were treated to the sight of Knights and Dames enjoying the music.

"It reminds me of the old days, before we warred with the Titans," Prometheus spoke up at length. "Ye know brothers, we have served in worse places than the High Lord's Barracks. I for one am tired of wandering and traveling, what say ye all? I vote we remain here and continue our service, if the High Lord will have us. 'Tis no need to speak up now, let us continue to consider the question as the day passes," he proposed. Nods of assent could be seen around the group as they sipped their ale and enjoyed the sikars, as well as occasional pipes of the sweet and heady Herb. When supper was ready it was served communally, the meat sliced right from the roast and laid on their plates, and then spoonfuls of this and that put alongside it. They ate slowly, enjoying tastes and textures, especially the beef.

"I have never had anything like this before," Bacchus commented in wonder as he laid the last slice atop a thick slab of bread and cheese to nibble on. "After all, Hera was a terrible cook, as I recall."

"No patience," Prometheus commented dryly. "But Artemis was a good cook, especially with wild game!"

"Aye, and so was Demeter," Hercules sighed. "I miss those days, the days of peace."

"Perhaps they will come again," Prometheus proposed. "In the meantime, we all still have service to offer, and I cannot imagine a better place than right where we are."

"The High Lady scares me," they heard Orpheus confess again in soft tones.

"She scares us all, boyo," Aries growled a bit. "Even me."

"YE?" they all said together.

"Aye, if ye want to know the truth. I have never met anyone like her, not even Penthasilia and her sister Hippolyta! And even they were not as gifted as this woman. The High Lord is a most fortunate man to have such a woman as his mate, is it not so?" Aries continued, for he did indeed feel a few pangs of jealousy. What man would not be just a little envious, he thought to himself, laughing internally at his own reaction. "I, like ye brother Prometheus, am tired of the endless wandering. I would like a home for the Winter, and have work to do. I think the Goddess has brought us here for more than just a water system problem. Perhaps we should make our application to remain very soon, in fact, I think we should talk to someone about it today!"

As it happened, Calla and her sister Lilith were attending the feast, marveling at what had been accomplished in the seven days past.

"Just think, no more flooding in the basement," Calla giggled a bit, having indulged in a cup or two of wine.

"Aye, and have ye ever seen better representations of male body perfection?" Lilith asked in return. "If only every man looked like that," she sighed.

"Sister?"

"One cannot help but admire their musculature, look at them!" Lilith went on. "Did ye ever think to have the opportunity to meet such men?"

"Nay," Calla grinned. "However, I think I shall keep my distance, as their reputations are not unsullied."

"But surely, 'tis why they are here in the Land!" Lilith countered. "To help them redeem themselves!"

"Ye are wiser than me sometimes, Sister," Calla sighed. "Still, I do not think any of them suit me."

"Nor me, but to listen to their stories and hear them relate history would be a great learning experience!"

Calla simply laughed harder and embraced her sister, enjoying being part of such an extraordinary family. They continued their walk until they finally met up with Drake on his return from inspecting the recent project.

"Grandfather!!!" Calla greeted him joyfully. "Where have ye been?"

"Grandfather!!!" Lilith echoed. "I am glad to see ye!"

"Granddaughters!" Drake greeted them in return, coming to embrace them in turn. "I have been on the Goddess' business, to answer yer question, Calla. Ye know I cannot talk about that. And I am very glad to see the both of ye, Lilith. Perhaps ye can tell me what is going on?"

"O Grandfather, all is going very well!" Calla said. "Now that the water will not flood the basement anymore, the House will run much better!"

"And Father is going to open up the Scout Camp next Spring!" Lilith chimed in.

"What?" Drake questioned. "Scout Camp?"

"Aye," Calla confirmed. "He has put Sir Mittra in charge of it."

"A good choice," Drake nodded, sipping his ale. "Tell me both of ye, what do ye have planned for the day?"

"After this morning's exercise, we have planned naught," Calla answered.

"Then ye could spend the day with yer Grandfather, and tell him all about what is going on?"

"Could we?" Lilith asked in an excited tone, always happy to have time alone with her fascinating grandfather.

"If yer Mother agrees, I see no reason not to," Drake grinned.

"I shall ask her!" Calla volunteered.

"Me too!" Lilith chimed in.

"Well then it looks as if we have our day planned. I want to see yer workout too, if I may?"

"We would welcome ye!" both young women said together, holding out their hands for his. Grinning wide, Drake clasped them and the three walked quickly back to the kitchen, finding Deborah in the midst of the work of the day. Making their requests succinctly, they quickly found a huge basket of food in their hands, along with Deborah's jovial order to leave and get out of her way.

Chapter 7

Making their way downstairs, the three passed the Heroes as they sat there trying to recuperate from the day before. They watched as Drake and his granddaughters passed by them, and a curious expression appeared on most of their faces. Those who wanted to know what was happening rose from their seats and followed after, leaving the others to commiserate together. All of them had tried their best to drink their new flasks dry, only to find that no matter how much they drank, the flask was always full, at least until it was not. They had all reached their capacity, but due to the amount they had consumed, they were slow to realize that fact. They drank them down one last time, thinking they would simply fill again, only to find that they remained empty.

"What is this?" Bacchus thought to himself as his brain worked on the problem. "Ah! I see! The flask only fills while one is capable of enjoying the contents! After a certain amount of drink, I know I hardly even taste it anymore! The High Lady is a clever woman!" The realization amused him greatly, and when the others discovered the secret of the flask, he was quick to offer his explanation. The others listened intently, nodding their understanding carefully, so as not to jar their brains too much. "I believe that upon the morrow, these will be full again," he speculated reassuringly. "And, I think 'tis time for bed," Bacchus had suggested. All of them had rose together, helping to support one another as they wove their way from the fireside outside to their room inside. It was a comical sight to watch as they moved together, walking closely together so that those who could not stand exactly straight would be supported. It seemed to take a long time to all of them, and they thought they might be lost until they came upon a squire and asked him for directions. The young man looked them over, a grin appearing to see the Heroes of Legend so very inebriated, and he volunteered to guide them the rest of the way.

"Thank ye, young man," Prometheus managed to say clearly, if slowly, and the young man grinned wide. His name was Darius, he was one of those rescued recently from a Naga fortress, and the young man was fitting in well. He had been chosen to join the Squire's Corps already due to his diligence, and he thrived in the environment of sponsorship and support. Now he guided the thirteen huge men through the twisting hallways, until he found their room and opened the door. Standing aside, he watched the Heroes prepare themselves as a group, then launch themselves at the open doorway, barely making it inside before their loose association broke up and most of them fell to the floor.

"Are ye all well?" Darius asked with concern.

"We are fine," Prometheus managed to speak clearly, at least this one last time. "Just close the door boyo, and have someone summon us when first meal is served."

"Aye, Master Prometheus," the young man nodded, closing the door as he left the room. Hours passed, first meal began to be served in the Barracks Kitchen, and finally Klietos sent a squire in search of the Heroes. That squire was again Darius, and he knocked on the door tentatively. It took several rounds of knocking to rouse them, and when the door opened, Darius was not surprised to see them all sitting about, looking somewhat miserable.

"Master Klietos summons ye to first meal, all of ye," he told them in quiet tones. "Ye'd best come now, before he puts the food away and starts cooking second meal!"

"Ugh," he heard then, "Ow," several times as the large men tried to compose themselves long enough to eat a meal. Darius could tell they were all suffering the effects of too much drink, and his mind tried to calculate just how much it would take to put such men into this miserable state.

"I shall make sure to put out the big bottle of willowbark powder," Darius chuckled, unable to help himself. He knew their pain well enough, he had occasionally taken one or two too many cups of ale and suffered for it the next day, even at his young age. "Come Masters, let me guide ye?"

"Aye, we will need yer help," Aries put in, his voice in a near whisper. "And keep yer voice down, would ye please? I cannot recall the last time my head hurt this bad."

"Aye," the others mumbled in agreement as they readied themselves to follow Darius. When they appeared outside their quarters, they still wore the clothing from the night before, their hair basically uncombed, most of them wearing no boots, shoes or hose, and one of them completely barefoot. Darius led them through the hallways, arriving at the common room, where the sounds of sword practice could clearly be heard. Such sounds drew the Heroes without exception, and all thirteen of them gathered in the entry of the arena to see the exercise. They all stood dumbfounded to see the two Daughters of the House, clad in the briefest of Amazon uniforms, wielding sharp blades against each other in a deadly dance. All of them could not move due to their astonishment, and all of them watched the two young women work with deadly accuracy, laughing all the while.

"By the Goddess," Aries finally said. "They are both magnificent!"

"Aye, they both remind me of Artemis or Athena, they are graceful and deadly in their work," Hercules agreed. The others simply nodded and mumbled their agreements, as they could barely tear their eyes away from the scene.

Calla and Lilith were completely unaware of their audience, but Drake saw them enter and stop to stare. A smile crossed over his face, and he mentally encouraged the young woman by explaining they had an audience.

"The Heroes are watching, granddaughters. Ye might as well show them what ye can really do," he suggested.

The two young women laughed aloud, increasing their pace as they did so, and soon they were surrounded by a cloud of arena dust, kicked up from their bare feet as they worked. The Heroes were covered with sand by the time they called a halt to their work, and a round of applause broke out among the thirteen men.

"Well done, young ones!" Aries spoke out enthusiastically. "Ye are most skilled, both of ye. 'Tis clear ye have benefitted from yer Grandfather's training."

"Aye, and the training of a few others as well, including our Mother and Father!" Lilith answered, a bit of challenge in her tone. "Ye are welcome to come find out what we know, anytime!"

"They do indeed benefit from my training, and the training of a few very skilled others," Drake said quietly to the huge men, knowing the pain they were in by the expression on their faces. "Ye would be wise to remember they can defend themselves, physically and magickally. They are Natanleods, both of them, and they are not to be touched without permission."

"Aye," he heard their collected response, and knew by the tone they were sincere. "If ye will please excuse us, My Lord Drake, we are on our way to first meal."

"Ye'd best hurry," Drake grinned. "Master Klietos is not known for his patience with overdue diners. Come my dears, let us seek our packed lunch from the kitchen, and perhaps we should take fishing gear as well? What say ye two?"

"Aye!" Calla echoed fiercely. "I am ready for a swim!"

"I am too!" Lillith echoed, and the two of them disappeared from the arena, leaving only their footprints behind to show they had been there.

The rest of their day was spent by the three at the riverside, discussing everything that had transpired in Drake's absence while they snacked and took occasional dips in the river.

As for the Heroes, they continued on their way to the dining hall, where Klietos took care of them, giving them their first dose of willowbark powder before he would serve them any food.

"And no caffe, only herb tea!" he ordered, knowing that would help them recuperate that much faster.

"Aye, Master Klietos," Bacchus mumbled. "Please keep yer voice down for a bit longer? I just got my dose of willowbark powder," he moaned a bit.

"What has put ye all in such a state?"

"The High Lady's gift to us, and we cannot say more than that. Our sensibilities were sorely tested last night, and we failed the test miserably. As such, we are in a correspondingly wretched state this morning, which will pass soon enough," Orpheus put in softly and sensibly. "Thank ye for the meal, Master Klietos. Everything tastes good, as usual, in yer kitchen," he managed to finished before falling forward into his crossed arms, asleep before his head came to rest.

"I think we had best finish up, and then seek our quarters," Prometheus suggested, chuckling a bit. "We must see the Knight Commander first, however."

"I shall pass on word of yer illness," Klietos offered at once, as he would have for anyone in the Barracks. "He will understand, of that I am certain. Ye have just finished a huge project, and celebrated robustly. Ye are due a day or two off, I should think."

"Thank ye, Master Klietos, we owe ye," Prometheus put in, rising from the table slowly. "Come brothers, 'tis time we sought our beds."

"Aye," Orpheus agreed. They fell into step beside one another in two lines, shoulder to shoulder, as they left the dining hall. Finding their way back to their quarters without assistance, they entered the room again, cleaned up as best as they could, then fell into their beds to sleep away the morning. After their second meal, they felt much better, and used the rest of the day to clean their room, change out their bed linens, and sit quietly to rest, drinking many, many cups of lemon water throughout the day.

Later that day, as evening approached, a group of six very large people approached the front gates, asking for permission to enter. They were clearly Giants, with their red hair and their great size, and the guards hesitated to admit them, at least until the Knight Commander was called to the gate.

"Ho there!" Tristan called up to the man in the lead of the group. "What is yer business here?"

"We have come a long way to join the High Lord's Tournament of Skills!" the man rumbled back in deep, resonant tones. "Our women have come too, as they are some of the finest warriors among us. May we enter?"

"Aye, come in and be welcome!" Tristan called back to them indicating the gate should be opened. The huge men ducked under the top of the gate, despite its height, and once they were inside, the gates creaked shut once more, locking behind them.

"If ye will all come with me, we will see about getting ye into the Tournament. If no open slots remain, ye will have to prove yerselves to the High Lord in combat to gain his approval."

"We thought to simply compete amongst ourselves," their leader answered, a puzzled tone in his words. "Who else would have the size and mass to equal us?"

"We have thirteen Heroes in residence, most of whom are ancient gods of legend," Tristan answered, his face completely composed and serious. "I do believe that at least one of them might be able to offer good challenge for yer skills."

"The Heroes... they are here?" one of the others asked, his voice filled with hope and astonishment. "We had not heard anything of them for many, many years now. In fact, 'twas only recently that the Postal Riders began traveling to the far reaches of our District. The news of the Land has been quite sketchy of late."

"Once ye are in the Barracks, 'twill be easy to catch up quickly," Tristan grinned wider, knowing how warriors loved to talk and tell stories. "Come with me, the High Lord will want to meet ye at once."

"Hadrian will be getting grey by now," one of the women speculated, chuckling a bit. "How is he?"

Tristan's face showed pain, and he hesitated a moment before answering. "My Lord Hadrian is dead. He gave his life to save citizens from being consumed and overtaken by Nagas. I am sorry ye had not heard that."

"I would like to pay my respects if possible," the lead Giant responded respectfully. "My name is Balor and I would like to present my woman, Cethlenn. That man over there is my First Sword Cuchulain, and his wife Ériu. She is First Sword among our women warriors, and \he is very skilled. The man and woman standing behind them are my Second Swords, Cormoran and Banba."

"Welcome to all of ye," Tristan nodded his acknowledgements to them. If ye will come with me now, we will see the High Lord at once. He is in the arena right now as a matter of fact, allowing other late entries to prove themselves. Ye are not late at all," he chuckled, leading the way. The group followed after him, occasionally ducking to miss overhangs and such due to their height, until they arrived at the entrance to the arena. They again had to stoop a bit to enter, but once inside, they saw the High

Lord at work, stripped to the waist and bare-footed, using a real weapon against someone dressed and armed similarly. As they watched, the Moorish man facing the High Lord launched a flurry of cuts, making the classic "X" pattern taught in so many martial schools. The Moorish man was clearly at his maximum effort, and so it did not take long for him to exhaust himself, and as soon as it was obvious he was nearly finished, the High Lord called a halt to the exercise.

"Azeem ben Cain, ye have acquitted yerself well," he said in warm tones. "My Lord Tristan, would ye please find him a spot in the opening round?"

"Aye, My Lord!" Tristan called back laughingly. "My friends, we start at the seventh hour in the morning," he announced with a grin, turning to those gathered there.

"Aye My Lord," they all answered, and a collective chuckle ran around the arena. "My Lord, may I present Master Balor and the Giants from the Iron Mountains. They have come to enter our Tournament."

"Good then, let us proceed at once!" Erinn answered, and in front of everyone's eyes he grew to match their height. His weapon grew with him, so that the challenge would be equal, and their leader Balor grinned with anticipation. "Now, come at me, all of ye!" he commanded. "Hold nothing back, give me everything ye have!"

"All of us?" Cethlenn asked in astonishment.

"Aye!" Erinn confirmed. The six all shared a progression of expressions then, starting with astonishment and progressing to humor.

"Very well then, My Lord!" Balor chuckled. "Come my friends, let us have at it!"

The next half an hour of time was one of the most thrilling the Barracks had ever seen. Erinn stood in the center of the arena, surrounded by the Giants, and they all attacked at once with a fierce battle cry. Erinn's blade worked quickly and efficiently around the circle, finding their skills to be better than just competent. He pushed them just a bit, to see if their temper would flair, but they remained calm and focused. Erinn began to think they would be excellent additions to the Army, especially the women, who were artful in their swordwork, and teamed up constantly to press their attacks. Erinn was elated, they were truly testing his skills and he answered each sortie, until Karpon called out that half the hour had passed.

"My Lord, the allotted time has passed," the War Duke called out, and Erinn whirled out of the exercise, a sheen of sweat on his forehead.

"Marvelous!" he commented at once, and Balor noted the High Lord's breathing did not seem labored at all. "Ye are all accepted! Karpon, find these folk slots in the opening round!"

"We will begin at the eighth hour!" Karpon called out, laughing a bit.

"Come, Master Balor, let us get ye quarters. I am certain we have the right rooms," Erinn invited cordially.

"We will only need one large room," Balor spoke out. "We are used to living communally."

"Very well then," Erinn nodded. "See to it, Knight Commander. Now, who is next?" he asked.

"Ye have met with everyone who missed their chance to sign up," Karpon called out. "Is there anyone else who wishes to try for a slot?"

No one else came forward, and that suited Erinn, who now wanted to bathe and spend time with Deborah, discussing his bout with the Giants.

"We will begin the competition on the morrow so that the finals might be held on the Summer Solstice," Karpon said at length. "I would suggest ye all get some rest, I think this year's Tournament will have many, many fine bouts."

"Indeed so," Erinn nodded. "Now gentlemen, if ye will excuse me, I think I shall go and find my wife," he grinned, throwing them a wink as he walked off.

Erinn knew exactly where Deborah was at the moment, in the kitchen supervising the harvest processing and storage. When he walked in, he found her exactly where he thought he would, in her testing kitchen. Master Orpheus was in there with her, assisting with the production of crystalized maple syrup, to that the Army could have the concentrated sweetener for their ration packs.

"Good morning," Erinn called out in a jovial tone. "And good morning to ye, Master Orpheus."

"Good morning, My Lord," the young Hero called back, keeping his eyes on the boiling pot of syrup in front of him. A cup of iced water stood at hand, and every so often, the musician would drip a few drops of the boiled syrup into the water.

"Look My Lady!" he said excitedly. "I think 'tis ready!"

"Indeed so, Master Orpheus," Deborah smiled. "We can pour it out now and let it just set up. Afterward, we will use this, to break it up into a rough powder," she went on, brandishing the beautiful silver hammer made for her by Hephaestus recently. It had a broad peen, and a short, sharp spike at opposite ends, a tool Deborah employed to good purpose.

"How long will it take to be ready?" Orpheus asked anxiously.

"I like to wait 'till the next morning," Deborah replied, and Erinn heard the stress of weariness in her voice. "Ye will join me after first meal, aye?"

"I would love to continue to help and learn!" Orpheus replied with a wide smile. "I shall see ye in the morning then, My Lady."

"Thank ye for yer assistance today, ye have the knack for candy work. Perhaps ye would consider joining the team this year to help make all of the candies for Yule?"

"O, could I?"

"Yer help would be welcome, since ye seem to grasp the technique so well, and so quickly. Good night."

"Good night, Madam," he answered, bowing a bit at the waist to show respect. "I shall do the clean-up for ye, if I may?"

"Ye are doing me such a kindness, Master Orpheus. I thank ye," Deborah smiled warmly, truly grateful for the offer. He beamed a bit as the smile on his face was wide, and he bent to the task as Erinn ushered Deborah out of the kitchen. She made him stop so as to speak with Gwendolyn, who was waiting for the next shift to come on duty.

"Sister, is there aught I might do to assist?"

"Ye are done," Gwendolyn answered sternly, her eyes twinkling merrily. "Go and rest, so ye can work on the morrow. 'Twill be hot all day, I think, and we will need lighter foods than we had planned."

"I suggest turkeys," Deborah answered at once. "We have dozens downstairs from last year's slaughter. We need to use them quickly, and I cannot think of a better way than to let the Barracks cook outside, aye?"

"Ye are a brilliant woman, ye know," Gwendolyn laughed a bit as she responded. "I shall have them pulled up at once, and send word to Master Klietos, before he makes his own plans."

"Very well, I can retire without worry then," Deborah said. "Good night, Sister."

"Good night, My Lady," Gwendolyn answered, curtsying a bit as was her habit. Erinn swept her out of the kitchen then and down the hall to their room, locking the door after they entered.

"I shall draw a bath at once," he offered. "Ye look very tired."

"The day has been a long and hot one," Deborah sighed. "A bath would be most refreshing, and then perhaps we might cook on the patio?"

"I would like that," Erinn smiled. "I shall arrange for it at once."

"Thank ye Husband," Deborah said, kissing his cheek as she passed by him. Off she went to her closet to pull out light, comfortable house clothing for the night, while Erinn turned the spigot in the bath and started the water for her. He made certain to adjust the temperature to a lesser one than usual, knowing she would need to cool off a bit. Next, he sent his thoughts out to Gwendolyn, finding her mind ready to receive them.

"I can bring ye what ye want right now," she offered. "I shall ice down the meat, so that ye will have time to enjoy wine and Herb."

"Ye are a wonder Madam," Erinn chuckled. "Thank ye for taking such good care of us."

"Ye need someone to take care of the both of ye, otherwise ye might work yerselves to exhaustion!" she said, a note of indignation in her voice, and Erinn could not help but laugh a bit as he closed his mind to her. Turning back to the bath, he saw the level was nearly to the proper height, and he began to remove his clothing, meaning to share the bath with her. The place had been remodeled recently, and the tub enlarged, much to their common liking. They spent their night talking, sipping wine, puffing the Herb and smoking a sikar or two, while broiling a side of salmon on their patio. Gwendolyn had sent along a simple salad with fresh herb vinaigrette, and some fresh haricot verts, a basket of fresh rolls on the cart as well.

"Wife, why do ye think the Giants are here?" Erinn asked as they sat after supper, enjoying an after supper sikar and the appropriate beverages for each.

"Husband, why do *ye* think they are here?" Deborah asked in return. "It seems to me that the Goddess has assembled quite the work force, and ye have an epic project in mind."

"Indeed so," Erinn chuckled. "All I need now is the Dwarves to come down from the mountains to help mine the local stone we will need. As well, their expertise in setting the footings for the bridge will be essential. We will see, perhaps the Lady will simply send them. If not, I shall send a troop out looking for them. Either way, I shall invite the Dwarves' help for the Crevasse project before next Spring. I had planned to open the Scout Camp before Winter, but it appears that project will not be finished in time. I am building Mittra and Zenobia a house out there, as they will be permanently in charge of the thing. Also, the camp itself is in rough condition, and the remodeling crew will need more time to assure the place is ready for habitation," he explained. Deborah nodded as she sipped her cordial, her mind turning on what other reason there might be for the presence of such folk in the Land. If she only knew what her daughters were doing out at the family house, she might have started preparing for more residents at the High Lord's house.

In the morning on the next day, the sun rose warm and continued on until by the sixth hour, it felt like it was already mid-day. Those slated for the first round of bouts arrived early enough to stretch and warm themselves, as well as to have a few cups of lemon water after indulging in the comforts offered by the Barracks. The Giants seemed most especially affected, the men walking slowly, their heads hanging a bit. The women were also under the weather, so to speak, and there was little discussion around their table as they sipped lemon water. Only after a few cups did they seem to rally a bit, and hot cups of mint tea soon appeared on their table, courtesy of Master Klietos, who could appreciate their depleted conditions.

Finally, their appetites roused and they were able to take some scrambled eggs with cheese mixed in as well as a basket of fresh biscuits, still hot from the oven.

"By the Goddess, that smells fine!" Balor exclaimed as he twitched the cover off the basket and inhaled deeply. "My appetite is returning!"

"Aye," his second mumbled in agreement, and his third said nothing, simply taking small bites of the plateful and chewing slowly, enjoying the flavors. They ate until their plates were empty, and did not ask for more, their appetites sated for the moment. Klietos then brought the big bottle of willowbark powder, and all of them had a generous portion at his invitation.

"Thank ye, Kitchen Master," Balor said after his portion was down. "I look forward to this taking effect, so I might focus on the task at hand."

"Ye just sit there and let that work," Klietos advised. "Yer people are not slated to fight in the first round today. I suggest ye check the board to see when ye are to prove yerselves. Ye will have plenty of time to take a bit of a warm-up before yer first bouts," he went on.

"Would ye have someone come and fetch us at the appropriate time?" Balor asked, feeling the medicine start to take effect.

"Of course," Klietos smiled warmly. "Ye are our guests, and here to participate in the Tournament."

The group of them sat in the kitchen then, letting the powder do its work and soon their headache and neck tension faded, leaving them ready for their morning exercise. Rising to leave, they neatly stacked their used linens, flatware, cups and plates, despite not knowing the routine. When the squire came to clear their table, he smiled in recognition of their lack of knowledge, as he had experienced the same upon his arrival in the Barracks.

"Thank ye for helping me," he said with a smile. "Welcome to the High Lord's House," Darius went on, using the platter to assemble the dishes and such.

"Did we do it correctly?" Balor asked, glad that his headache was finally gone.

"Ye are our guests, ye needn't concern yerself over it," Darius replied genially. "If ye win yer way into residence, there are other procedures ye will need to follow."

"I hope someone will educate us?"

"Everyone will help with that," Darius chuckled, knowing it was true from his own experience so far. "I shall take care of this. Ye all need to get to the arena and start warming up for yer bouts. The crowd is gathering out there, and they are expecting a show, I think," he chuckled a bit harder.

"Very well then, we would not wish to disappoint," Balor grinned. "Come my friends, let us attend to the business we came to do."

"Aye," he heard them agree as one, and the group of them walked from the dining hall to the arena in short order. Room was made for them to practice their usual stretches and other warming movements, so that they could work without hesitation or fear of over-straining cold muscles. Retrieving their weapons from the armory, they found that they had been completely cleaned and fresh edges put on them. Even Cormoran's huge mace had been freshly cleaned and sharpened, the *lorg* (handle) freshly sanded and oiled, and a grin passed over the huge man's face to see the work done overnight.

"They surely take care of things quickly down here," he chuckled. "Look at it, 'tis practically brand new!"

"Look at all of our gear, even the armor," Balor pointed out. "All of it has been cleaned, repaired and refitted! Mine feels better than it has for a long time and I think they have even replaced the lining and padding!" he exclaimed.

"I think ye are right, my husband," Cethlenn agreed, turning her breastplate around to show the new cloth and leather. "Husband, they have used a blending of fibers in this cloth, I have never seen the like of it!"

"We have much to catch up on, it appears," Balor chuckled deep in his throat. "Come my friends, let us prove our worth!"

Just as they finished dressing in their armor, the call came for them to enter the lists. As a group with Balor in the lead, they walked from the armory to the arena, taking their place in the center of the circle of sand.

Across from them stood those Heroes who were participating in the arena events that day. Balor's eyes widened, and a wide smile crossed his face as he realized they would have the proper opponents to help them practice their skills. Prometheus, Aries, Hercules, Perseus, Theseus, Mittra,

Chiron, Odysseus and Achilles were all famous warriors of legend, and the Giants began to anticipate the competition much more now.

"Balor, 'tis been many years since we have spoken," Prometheus spoke first, stepping forward. "How have ye all been?"

"Ye would ask that of us?" Balor answered defensively. "Yer folk and mine have always been on different sides of things, at least 'till now. We want our people in the Barracks, whether 'tis us or others. 'Tis time we came down from the mountains," he finished his simple address.

"And 'tis time for us to stop wandering," Prometheus answered earnestly. "Surely, we can find common grounds to forge a friendship between us after all these years?"

Balor stood there, watching their faces, knowing his kin were doing the same. There had been trouble between their people in the past, due to the fact they were all of rather large size and liked living in the same areas. There was only room for one huge race of people in an area, and so they had sought separate parts of the world to colonize. Eventually, however they had found their way into the Land, all of them, and they all knew that they were enjoying the Lady's grace because of it.

"A friendship between us?" Balor asked after a bit. "Can we have such a thing after the difficulties between yer folk and mine?"

"We could just put all of that aside, forgive each other for those offenses and drink a cup or two together over it," Prometheus proposed in a friendly tone. "The Lady has called us all here for a purpose, let us work now to achieve harmony. We will need it in the near future, I think," he grinned, offering the Grip.

Balor took his forearm and gripped it, not too tightly he hoped, and put a warm smile on his face. He could not have expected to have gone so well, he thought as he exchanged the familiar greeting with someone he had regarded as an enemy in years long past. When they released each other's arms, both turned to their fellows to encourage them to do the same, finding some resistance from both groups.

"But... the ancient war between us," Cuchulain whispered. "What if 'tis a trick?"

"Would we seek to deceive here, in the High Lord's Barracks?" Prometheus answered sensibly. "Think about it brothers, and put yerselves in their shoes for a moment. We have both committed sins against the other, and 'tis time for us to put all of it aside. We cannot be enemies out there, on the honor sands. We are here to compete and demonstrate our skills."

"Prometheus is right," Mittra put in as soon as he could. "The war between us was pointless anyway, we do not rule, the Lady does. Let us become brothers and sisters again, if we might?" he offered, stepping forward and extending his arm. There was only a moment of hesitation and then the group of them fell into a mix of embraces and greetings. They had all been friends at one time, before the war between them, a foolish mistake acknowledged by both sides. Now it was as if the years of distrust and dislike had never been, and they quickly caught up on each other's lives, at least until they were summoned for their bout.

"Come my friends, let us put on a bit of a show for the High Lord and his Lady, what say ye?" Prometheus urged with a grin.

"I like it!" Balor nodded. "But we will not show them everything, not at our first meeting, aye?"

"Aye!" Prometheus laughed out loud and the two groups lined up beside one another to enter the outdoor arena. A hush fell over the crowd to see the two groups of huge people walk into the center of the sands where Karpon waited to Marshall the bout. Erinn and Deborah arrived just then, appearing in their seats, which had a good view of the entire arena.

"Ye have all been briefed on the rules, which are the old and ancient rules. The fight, once it starts, continues 'till blood is drawn. It ends at that, do ye all understand?"

"Aye, we are not fighting a blood match," Cormoran's voice could be heard.

"Good, I am glad ye understand the rules then," Karpon's voice rapped out sharply and Balor's first in command found himself silenced, especially when his commander swung around with a look of disappointment on his face. "Come then, let us get this started. The sun is risen, and the heat will continue to intensify."

He dropped his hand then and they leapt at each other with no anger or hate, just the desire to show their skills. The women teamed up at once, while the men fought singly, Erinn noted the difference at once as the three women took on the mighty Aries, driving him back more than a step or two. The god of war's face wore an expression of delight, and he answered their advances with his mighty blade of red steel, a huge ruby set in the pommel. The women's response was epic as they surrounded him on three sides, completely cutting him off from the rest of the group, and then concentrating on him alone. Aries' skills were sorely tested as he fought all three of them at once, the grin on his face slowly fading as he defended himself. Balor soon made his way over to them after disabling Theseus and Perseus, leaving them with bare scratches on their right shoulders so that they withdrew from the fray, walking to the wall and then following it around to the entrance to the lists, seeking the few stitches necessary to stop the wounds from seeping blood.

Balor soon saw his assistance was not needed as the women of his clan had Aries caught between the three of them, looking like a beleaguered bear. He was clearly limping as well, and Balor looked him over quickly, concerned he was bleeding from an unseen place. He could see naught, and so assumed one of the women had dealt him a blow from the flat of her blade. He moved on then to engage Prometheus point blank, and the elder of the Heroes laughed heartily in anticipation. He and Balor had battled before, sometimes in play but more times in earnest, and Prometheus knew that Balor's skills were considerable. He also knew how to use his weight to his best advantage, and so Prometheus gave him respect. One by one around them, the groups and pairs of combatants struggled against one another, each engagement continuing until Karpon called out for them all to hold.

"Hold there!" he called out, checking the sand clock in the arena. "The time has expired for yer match, and I think we have a draw! What say ye, My Lord and Lady?" he called up to the Natanleods sitting there.

"I concur!" Deborah called back.

"As do I!" Erinn added. "Allow them to advance to the next round!"

The crowd roared out their approval as the Heroes and Giants helped each other out of the arena, their muscles weary from the engagement. Aries limped to a seat, settling himself carefully on the wide stone bench.

"What is amiss, brother?"

"I pulled that muscle in my ass again," Aries confessed in a whisper. "I can barely walk thanks to those three women," he went on, wincing painfully.

"Come on, I shall help ye," Prometheus responded with a straight face, although on the inside, he could not help but laugh a bit. "We need to get ye back in shape for the next round!"

"Ow!" Aries grunted as Prometheus offered him a hand up. Taking his limping brother to the infirmary, he helped him up onto a table then called for help. A very large, broad woman stepped out, and Prometheus' first thought was that she might have the muscles for the job.

"What is amiss?" she asked in a deep toned voice.

"He has pulled a muscle in a sensitive place," Aries answered for himself, chuckling ruefully. "My ass hurts, and I must advance in the Tournament. Can ye help me?"

"Lay on ye stomach and try to relax as much as possible. I shall do what can be done," the woman answered warmly. Aries did as she requested, dropping his trous first to expose the aching area. "My name is Bridgetta, my specialty is muscles," she introduced herself quickly.

She could see once he laid on his stomach that one of his butt cheeks was clenched like a fist, twitching in spasm visibly. She said nothing, simply bunching up her fist and punching the twitching mass of muscles right in the center.

"Ahgh!" Aries cried out in pain, and then the aching was gone.

"Now lay still," she ordered, using some of her own massage balm, which was heavily laden with oil made from the Lady's Herb. As she worked Aries could feel the twitching stop, and a sigh of relief could be heard many times, until she stopped and stepped away. "I would just lay there for as long as ye can," she advised. "Let that work, and as soon as ye are done for the day, soak for a long time in the bath. That mineral water will be good for ye."

"Aye Madam," Aries nodded respectfully. Off she walked to her next task with no further words to them, for none were necessary. The two Heroes remained there until a squire came to summon them back to the arena.

"Yer bout is coming up soon," he said to them urgently.

"We are on our way," Prometheus answered, watching Aries rouse himself. Upon sitting up, he smiled a bit, noting that the pain was completely gone and there was no sign of the muscles twitching.

"I am cured!" he laughed a bit as Prometheus helped him down. Walking carefully for a few steps, Aries was relieved to find out that the cramping was indeed gone, and he felt confident enough to return to the competition. "She is very good!" he grinned. "I have never felt better!"

"Well, ye'd best come on then," Prometheus grinned. "I shall let ye take the lead, since ye are so much improved!"

Aries did take the lead in the next round with the Giants, and before it was over, one of the women and one of the men of their group had been eliminated. Two of the Heroes would also be sitting down for the next round, as Perseus and Theseus both had fresh stitches on their shoulders. When asked about them, both men had the same answer.

"Ye watch out getting in close with those Giant women," Perseus warned. "They are wickedly fast and their teamwork is well practiced and precise," he continued as the healer covered the shallow wound with a clean bandage.

"I am going to clean up, then find a seat in the viewing area," Theseus grinned as another healer finished his shoulder. "I should like to see how *ye* deal with them!"

Prometheus and the others sat in consultation with their sidelined brothers, until they felt confident to meet the challenge of the next round. Taking the opportunity to rest in the cool shade of the lists, they watched with interest as the bouts proceeded, including watching both Lillith and Calla perform well in their contests.

"The High Lord's daughters are very skilled," Hercules pointed out.

"And beautiful," Aries chimed in.

"Brothers…" Prometheus said, a hint of warning in his tone. "They are not for us."

"Nay, they are not," Aries nodded. "However, they do not have older brothers, or uncles about, do they?"

"Aye, 'tis true," Hercules agreed. "And if we are having such thoughts, just imagine what those boys out there are thinking."

"Those girls do indeed need an uncle or two," Chiron said in a flat tone. "How else can they walk about without being accosted constantly due to their beauty and position?"

"Uncles?" Prometheus repeated, as if trying on the title. A smile appeared on his face at the very thought of such a duty. "We have rarely been called upon for such a task," he went on in a thinking tone.

"Perhaps 'tis time for us to do so," Chiron pointed out with a grin. "We are uncles already, however we have missed the opportunity to offer guidance or counsel. What say ye, should we talk to the others?"

"Aye, tonight! And if they agree, ye'll talk to the High Lord for all of us aye?"

"Of course, brothers," he smiled. After all, he was the eldest, he thought to himself as they readied themselves for the next round.

When the time came for them to compete again, the Heroes focused their attention on just staying in the arena with the remaining Giants. They came out fighting hard, knowing they were down two of their number, leaving only the four of them. They teamed up to take control of the center of the sand, leaving the Heroes to circle them, looking for any opening. It was Ériu who led most of that round, her sword flashing, slicing and cutting as she defended her ground against any who faced her. She showed no fear, even when confronted by Aries himself, simply laughing at him as she held him off, assisted by those closest to her. Chiron was watching however, and the older of the Heroes noted that the tall Giantess favored her left side a bit. He began to press her then, making her turn on the left leg until finally she began to limp, a little a first, but more and more as she tired. The men tried to help her, but found themselves completely engaged with the rest of the Heroes, until finally the round was over and Ériu sat heavily in the sands, unable to move.

"Ye will all have to help me up," she chuckled breathlessly. "I cannot stand on my own."

The Heroes immediately offered their hands and Ériu accepted, letting them pull her to her feet while she panted for breath. They escorted her over to a seat in the lists, and brought her some water while the rest of the Giants watched in shock.

"Are ye well, Sister?" Prometheus asked. He had been the first to offer his hand to her, and when she accepted, he felt her weight as he helped her stand. She was thin, he thought to himself, too thin for someone her size. He wondered if the rest of them were equally underweight, and concern for them grew within him as he watched them struggle with stamina issues. On the last round of the day, Cormoran took a slice to the thigh which was deeper than any other that day. The healer came out into the arena as soon as Karpon halted the bout, and ordered him taken to the infirmary at once. All of the Heroes volunteered to carry him, and they did so carefully so as not make the wound any worse, Cormoran dribbling blood the entire way. It was the healer on duty, Alma, who treated him, then dosed him to sleep so that the stitches could set. When she saw his bones clearly visible under his skin, her surprise was complete. One could not tell just how thin he really was under all that armor and padding, she thought, and it occurred to her that it was a deliberate attempt at concealment. Once he was asleep, she went up to the kitchen to find Deborah, concerned with the physical condition of the rest of the Giants.

"Madam, I have just treated one of our Giant guests for an injury from his combat today. I could not help but notice that he is vastly underweight. My goodness, he is naught but skin and bones under his clothing! I believe that they have tried to hide that by layering extra clothing under their armor to avoid questions."

"I see," Deborah nodded, filing the information away for later thought. "Thank ye for telling me, and make sure he gets fed well. I am concerned that such people might be suffering under the High Lord's rule."

"Of course, My Lady," Alma smiled. "The Giants are usually strong, healthy and the most vital of people here in the Land. 'Tis hard to see them in such a state."

It was not long after that the competition was called for the day due to the heat, and the rest of the Giants wandered into the Barracks, finding a repast of cold fruit, yogurt and iced mint tea waiting for them.

"Eat up and be refreshed," Klietos told them, having already heard the rumor concerning the health of the Giants. "We are cooking outside tonight, and I have assured a generous meal. Everyone should eat hearty tonight, and rest well, so they can perform well upon the morrow."

Balor and his people ate their fill, glad to be able to do so and feeling a little bit guilty about it. The people at home were waiting for them to return with good news, after all the reason they were there was not simply to participate in the Tournament. They had come with a different purpose, and soon they would have their opportunity to see it through.

Chapter 8

The second day of the Tournament dawned just as hot and bright as the first. The Heroes and the Giants shared one bout in the arena, and then they were done until the next morning.

"Ye will finish yer bracket by early tomorrow, and then the High Lord will ask for those who remain to give a demonstration during the noon rest period," Karpon told them efficiently, Erinn having passed on his instruction before the Tournament's beginning.

"We would be honored to give such a demonstration," Balor nodded.

"Aye, and so would we," Prometheus answered for the Heroes. "Master Balor, would ye share our table tonight?" he asked.

"I and my people would be honored," Balor smiled warmly, glad the difficulties between them were settled at last.

"Good, we will find one in the shade," Prometheus grinned, whispering conspiratorially.

"Perhaps one by the river?" Banba asked wistfully.

"We will see Madam," Prometheus nodded. "One of us may have to go and stake our claim early," he chuckled.

After finishing with their first meal, the two groups retired to the indoor arena to stretch and warm themselves in preparation for that day's bouts. Those of their number who were now sitting on the sidelines dropped in to wish them well, and Balor mentioned the table by the river requested by Banba.

"One or two of us will go and secure the one we like best! Perhaps our brother Heroes will also join us?"

"I would imagine ye will find volunteers for such a cause," Prometheus grinned. Indeed, several members of both groups combined to search for the perfect place, then working together to ready it for that night's usage. That night was spent by the two groups in companionable conversation. It was as if the old hurts had never happened, and their friendship was rekindled. They helped each other to their rooms that night, and slept well due to their exertions of the day.

The last morning of the Tournament passed uneventfully, the rounds of bouts proceeding without incident until the event concluded. The Heroes and the Giants gave a demonstration of sword play and other weaponry skills unlike anything that had been seen in the Land for many decades, and the cheers of the crowds rang pleasantly in their ears. As the bout continued, shouts of encouragement began to be heard from those in the Barracks. It seemed equally divided to Erinn as he listened, and so he said naught, wanting to know the opinions of those who served him and the Goddess. Then one by one, starting with the Heroes, they began to withdraw from competition. Afterward, the night of the Tournament's conclusion was a bit riotous and everyone slept late the next morning, except for Erinn and Deborah. They were up at their usual time, and about their usual duties, waiting for their opportunity to sneak away for a few days at the family house in Dragon Valley. Every time they wanted to go, something came up to stop them, for instance, the arrival of Lillith astride a huge black Roc. Such birds had not been seen in the Land for a century at least, and so Erinn was more than a bit astonished to see the three huge birds land in the party field, then Lillith sliding off the back of the largest one.

"Hello Father!"

"Greetings Daughter," Erinn returned, eyeing the huge bird behind her. "Ye have brought guests to the house."

"I have indeed Father! May I present Barnabas Lightningclaw, the leader of his clan?"

Erinn turned to the huge Roc standing behind Lillith, smiling to watch the bird change slowly into a man's form. "Master Lightningclaw, welcome to my home."

"My Lord, I would be honored if ye would use Barnabas?" the man replied, shaking himself a bit as if unused to wearing his man-shape.

"Very well, Master Barnabas," Erinn smiled easily.

"These are my Wingmen," Barnabas continued, turning to the other two Rocs, who were now changing form. "My General of Armies, Roderick Brasseye," he said, waving his hand at the man on his right. Brasseye was a broad man with a glowering face, as if he never smiled. Erinn briefly wondered what it would take to break his seriousness as he walked forward and offered the Grip. "Master Brasseye, I am pleased to meet ye."

"Call me Roderick," the man grumbled a bit, accepting the gesture.

"Very well, Commander Rodrick," Erinn responded genially.

"And this young woman is my sister, Marion Broadbreast. We have the same father, but different mothers," Barnabas explained automatically, as if used to doing so.

"Barnabas, the High Lord could care less if we have the same parentage," Marion laughed lightly, offering the Grip to the High Lord, who accepted readily. "I am very glad to meet ye, My Lord…" she trailed off, eyeing him a bit. "I thought ye would be older by now, My Lord Drake."

Erinn grinned widely as he turned to find Deborah's eyes meeting his, amusement twinkling within the hazel depths.

"I am not Drake, I am Erinn, his son," he introduced himself.

The eyes of the Roc-man widened expressively, and Erinn found himself enveloped in a penetrating gaze. Finally, a grin appeared on Barnabas' face and a laugh emerged.

"So, he actually managed to get himself a son," Barnabas laughed merrily. "Yer father still owes me some gold, is he about?"

"One never knows with my Father," Erinn answered evasively. "His skills have improved a great deal since ye last spoke, he has become an ascended being."

"WHAT?" Marion exploded. "Drake Natanleod, the *philanderer*?"

A ripple of laughter ran around the collected folk, all of them warriors from the Barracks who had served with Drake, or been ruled by him as High Lord. Drake's reputation with women was a famous one, and most men stood in admiration of his skills, which had been put to use during the war to collect information and to gain access to the Naga's keeps. Such things had kept the Black Dragons alive many times, and more than a few Naga Lords had met their demise due to his secret, night-time work.

"It sounds like ye have first-hand experience with My Lord Drake's reputed skills. Perhaps ye could confirm a few things for me?" Deborah's voice countered the laughter. Marion's face flushed bright red, and the corner of Deborah's mouth curled with amusement, knowing her instincts had again come to her aid.

It was at that precise moment that Drake made his appearance within the kitchen, startling Gwendolyn more than a bit.

"My Lord!" she said in a shocked tone. "When did ye get here?"

"Just now, I heard my name being impugned!" he answered, a trace of comic outrage in his tone. "Where is my son?"

"Outside at the moment," Gwendolyn answered as she opened the back door and he saw the assembled crowd in the field below. "I think ye might want to go there now, we have guests for supper, I think."

Drake glanced at the crowd and recognized three faces he had not seen for many, many years. "Marion!" he whispered with a bit of shock and without another word he strode out of the kitchen, headed for where Erinn and Deborah stood surrounded by those from the Barracks. There was a bit of tension in the air, he noted as he walked into the circle to greet his son.

"My Lord Erinn," Drake announced himself in mellow tones.

"My Lord Drake," Erinn answered coolly. "I am glad to see ye, we have guests to welcome, and apparently ye know them well."

"I do indeed!" Drake acknowledged, walking to where Barnabas stood. "My friend, I am glad to see ye again. Yer people, they are thriving?"

"Indeed so, My Lord. The place ye suggested for our retreat was completely defensible and private, as ye promised 'twould be. We only saw a few Nagas, and they did not return to spread the word of our Aerie."

"Good!" Drake nodded, turning to Marion. "My dear, I have something to say to ye in private, if yer brother would allow it."

"My brother does not speak for me. I am a free woman among my people," Marion answered in a cold tone. "I will hear what ye have to say, in private then, but ye had best attend to it tonight. Otherwise, ye know the cost."

"I do," Drake nodded. "I came specifically to deal with this, now and forever," he went on. "We will not speak of it ever again after tonight."

"Very well," she nodded in return. "I look forward to that."

Jovita also appeared, right beside Deborah, but she said nothing as Deborah handed her a pipe silently, followed by a cup of wine that simply appeared in her hand.

"Ye have naught to be concerned about, ye know," she said quietly after a few moments had passed.

"I know, and I am ashamed to show any trace of jealousy at all," Jovita sighed, sipping the wine appreciatively. "I hope someday to be over all of that."

It was not long before Marion reappeared and stalked off towards the Elan, Barnabas behind her. Drake appeared a moment or two later, his handsome face wreathed in regret. Deborah simply handed him the pipe, newly refilled, and a cup of the same wine as Jovita was drinking, which materialized in the same fashion.

"I shall not ask, as 'tis none of my concern," she whispered to him, and he was grateful for her attitude, as he was feeling regretful at that moment. He and Marion had shared a very brief, but passionate time together, causing Marion to believe they were promised. When Drake had simply left them at the site of the new Aerie, her anger had been kindled and resentment had grown in the years following. Drake's explanation and apology were late, but they were sincere enough, and after a few hours, Marion's anger cooled.

"I was certainly stupid at times in my youth," he finally muttered. "Jovita, would you mind if we talked just a bit?"

"Of course," Jovita answered archly, stalking off the opposite direction from where Marion had gone. Drake sighed heavily and took the pipe with him, wine in hand, walking after her as if he carried a great load on his shoulders. Deborah realized at once that this was the Goddess at work, helping Drake to resolve anything left that might keep him bound to the Land.

It was a long time later when Drake and Jovita reappeared, holding hands and sharing the last of the wine in Jovita's cup. Deborah could hardly repress a grin as they walked to her, the aura about both of them calm and serene.

"Do ye have the room I usually use available?" Drake asked simply.

"Ye know I do," Deborah answered. "And we would be honored by both of yer presences. We have honored guests, 'twould be good to have ye at the table with such old allies."

Meanwhile, Erinn had already gone to Lillith, a determined look up on his face.

"Daughter, come with me. Ye have some explaining to do," he said in a quietly commanding tone.

"Very well, Father. Are ye angry with me?"

"I am not, however ye have been missing for over two weeks. Not even Oracia has been able to find ye. Where have ye been?"

"With Adalinda, of course," Lillith answered simply, and Erinn nodded his understanding. "But I never left the family valley the entire time."

"Come, let us talk privately. I want to hear the entire tale without being interrupted."

Nodding, Lillith came to stand beside him and they disappeared, reappearing within Erinn's office. Erinn waved her into a seat by the hearth, then poured wine for both of them, loaded a pipe and took a deep inhalation. Waiting for Lillith to do the same, he sat there with an expectant look up on his face as she finished the pipe while composing her thoughts.

"As ye know, Calla and I like the Valley. 'Tis quiet and we can think more clearly," she began and Erin nodded, agreeing with her. "We went out hunting for our supper the morning after our arrival there two weeks ago, and a fierce storm blew up out of nothing. We got separated, but I am not exactly certain how it happened. I ended up at Adalinda's cave after falling and hurting my arm a bit," she went on, showing him where the limb was still bound. "I was only there a few days though, I think, because when she said I needed to go and that I was healed up enough to do so, I did not question her. I simply took the pack I had brought and walked out, finding myself walking higher up into the mountains. I have never been up there, I wanted to see what 'twas like, and the view was magnificent!" she declared with a grin.

"I know, I have been up to the top of Dragon Mountain. Ye can see almost the entire Land from there," Erinn agreed. "Go on."

"Well, I rounded a corner and saw a rock wall I had never seen before," Lillith went on, smiling hesitantly. Erinn nodded, knowing of her love of climbing, and nodded again to urge her to continue the tale. "I climbed and climbed, for what seemed like hours. The sun traveled across the sky into near twilight before I reached a ledge and pulled myself up onto a large plateau that led into a beautiful valley. As soon as my feet touched the top of the mountain, I found myself surrounded by huge black birds. I thought they were eagles at first, until I realized their size was far too large for that. I knew then that the old stories were true, that Rocs existed in the Land before the Nagas, and here they were!"

"And then?"

"I was taken to their leader's nest and introduced to him. I explained who I was, and how I had arrived at their Aerie. They were very kind and considerate of my health, and I was treated very well while with them. It took me many discussions to convince Master Barnabas to send a representative, and I was shocked when that person was himself. Apparently, he felt a personal responsibility to bring me home," she finished.

"I would have felt the same if the situation were reversed," Erinn answered thoughtfully. "Thank ye Daughter, for bringing them. I see the Goddess' Hand at work here. I shall simply stand back and allow Her Will to be worked. Now, have ye heard from yer sister? She has been missing for as long as ye have, and I am beginning to worry."

"Father," Lillith smiled ferociously. "Calla is more than capable of taking care of herself. Have ye and Grandfather been wasting yer time training her then, if ye think she requires any help? I think she wants this time alone in the woods, as I did. My experience has certainly expanded my horizons," she finished.

Erinn cast an assessing eye over his daughter, finding that she stood a little straighter, or was it that she had grown a few inches while out on her adventure, he wondered.

"How are yer clothes fitting?" he asked her mentally.

"What?"

"They seem a little short in the arm and leg to me," Erinn went on warmly. "I think ye need to go to the market with me tomorrow."

"I would love to go to the market with ye!"

While daughter and father made plans for a social outing, Calla was still out in the woods. She found she enjoyed the challenge of foraging for her meals, and building temporary shelters to spend her nights. Even the sound of wolves howling did not dismay her, instead she found herself wanting to wander deeper and deeper into the woods. One night, she heard noises outside her shelter, and a deep resonant growling from several throats.

"There are wolves outside," she thought calmly, reaching for her bow and the spring-loaded lance beside it. The lance was compactable, and when fully expanded it reached almost six feet in length. Made from steel, it was lightweight and strong, she had used it once already to defend herself from a wild pig, which ended up being supper for several nights before being smoked into travel rations. She reckoned it would keep the wolves at bay, at least as she set it close at hand and waited, bow at the ready. She could hear them sniffing and investigating, all around her shelter, but none of them tried to enter, much to her relief. She liked wolves, seeing them as necessary to the health of the forest as they scavenged as well as hunted. Killing them would have been regretful, she thought.

Hearing them leave gave her a sense of relief, but she kept her weapons at hand, and only rested within the shelter for the remainder of that night. Emerging at dawn, munching on a meal of smoked pig, she found their tracks everywhere, as well as where they had marked around her shelter. Calla did not linger there, she packed her things and burned the place, remaining to assure the fire did not spread into the surrounding wildwood until it had reduced its fervor to just a few smoldering places. By then it was past mid-day, and she ran for a few miles towards the mountains across the valley from where Adalinda's cave lay. The climb was an easy one at first, but as the day went on, she found the terrain more and more challenging and began to look for a place to shelter overnight. Just as the trees began to thin significantly, she spied an opening in the piles of rocks and investigated quickly. She found no evidence of a permanent resident of any kind and so claimed the place for the night. Despite the fact that it was still late summer and warm below, the temperature where she was seemed chilly. Calla spent a great deal of time gathering firewood for that night, piling it close to the mouth of the cave before returning to the rivulet of fresh water for a few rocks to make a firepit within her shelter. Once that was done, she quickly split up some of the driest wood she had gathered, making certain to provide plenty of tinder by way of the birch bark she had stashed in her provisions. The fire took hold of the bark, consuming it rapidly and beginning to lay down a bed of good coals while she slowly added sticks of firewood in ever-increasing size. At length, she had a good fire going, it put out enough heat to warm her without feeling overheated, and she could put together a hot meal as well. She felt relaxed and confident that night, right up until the wolves could be heard outside the entrance to her cave shelter. She was awake when they arrived and she was armed as well, sitting in the mouth of the cave waiting for them. She could see at once these were young wolves due to their actions, but they were of an incredible size.

"Direwolves!" she thought at once in astonishment, for such creatures had not been seen in the Land for decades. Her mind pondered the advantages of having such creatures as allies, for they could run fast and far, they were fierce fighters and had tight family bonds from all she had read about them. She sat there until finally, one of them made eye contact with her, and she sent out her thoughts hoping they could be heard.

"I am Calla Natanleod, I mean ye no harm. I am traveling to learn more about the family valley here under Dragon Mountain," she thought to them as simply as possible. She heard a whine or two, then a growl, and then they were gone, melting into the surrounding woods not to be heard from the rest of that night. She was finally able to sleep a bit, resting easily without disturbance until morning. When she did wake, she took her time rising, meaning to remain where she was for another night before moving on. Finally, after a meal and a quick detailed cleaning of her shelter, she stepped outside, fully armed and ready to hunt fresh meat for supper that night. Her surprise was complete when she found herself surrounded by two dozen huge, fierce wolves with long sharp fangs. She showed no fear, even though her heart was beating harder than usual, and her mind worked clearly if rapidly.

"Ye are Calla...Natanleod?" she heard in her mind, a gruff male voice with deep rich tones. "How is that possible?"

"I am the daughter of Erinn Natanleod, the High Lord of the Land," Calla answered without hesitation.

"Who?"

"Erinn Natanleod, the son of Drake Natanleod, Hero of the Land," Calla answered proudly.

A chuckle ran around the circle of males, and from that, Calla understood they were familiar with her Grandfather's reputation.

"I see," the voice in her mind said, the tone tinged with humor. "Well then, Daughter of the House, night is fast approaching. Ye had best come with us, so ye will be safe. 'Tis not wise to linger out in the night."

"The war with the Nagas is over, my father even now searches for their last strongholds with the determination to wipe them out," Calla responded evenly. "My Grandfather and the Black Dragons defended the Land, while your clan retreated and hid here in the mountains. The same with the Roc Clan, they retreated as well to hide while my family stood and defended. My father will want to talk to ye all about that."

"My father is the leader here, human!" one of the younger of the wolves assumed his human form to say. A murmur went around the group, it was not usual for one of their kind to do such a thing in front of a human. "He determined that we would be better off in hiding, and our clan has prospered because of it."

"And how many in the Land died because ye would not stand and serve?" Calla challenged, and the young man felt a thrill of desire run through him. She was beautiful in a way he had never seen before, her green eyes fierce and her dark red hair was different than most of the girls he knew in the clan.

"What do ye know about it?" he answered. "Can ye imagine the danger if we had been taken over by those, those *things*?"

Calla heard his voice break a bit, and realized he was much younger than her. She was unconcerned about his ability to shift into a wolf, she had long since mastered her dragonform and could easily assume it now.

"I do, and I watched it happen to the people of the Land, over and over again," Calla responded. "Not a pleasant prospect, for anyone, which is why we should have all stood as one against them."

A long, uncomfortable moment passed until finally the outspoken young man broke the silence. "Ye had best come with us now, 'twill be full dark soon. Ye will be a guest in our cave, and no one will harm ye, my father will see to it. Ye have naught to fear."

Calla stood there in the gathering darkness, finally nodding in assent. "Very well, I shall accept yer offer of hospitality for the night. My father will want to know everything I can tell him about ye when we speak next. Lead the way."

They all fell back into their wolf forms, Calla watching with interest as they did so. The small pack of five surrounded her, and walked her to their family cave, where all of the clan was now assembled and preparing for their nightly meal. When they approached the cave mouth, they were challenged by the sentries, who asked about Calla at once.

"Who is she? Where did ye find her?"

"She is Calla Natanleod, a Daughter of the ruling House," the young man spoke up. "Bring my father and mother, if ye would please?"

It did not take long for a huge, burly man to appear with his equally large wife.

"Sable, my son, who have ye brought into our enclave?" Sirius, his father and leader of the enclave, asked.

"She is Calla Natanleod, my father," Sable answered.

"Calla... *Natanleod*?" Sirius stumbled a bit. "Drake has such a young daughter?"

"Drake is my grandfather," Calla spoke up for herself. "My father, the current High Lord, is Erinn Natanleod."

"Drake... has...a...son?" Sirius enunciated each word loudly, and Calla heard the murmur pass through the others around them.

"Aye Master Sirius," Calla acknowledged, giving him his title easily. "And through his son, a grandson and granddaughters as well. The Goddess has been good to him, since he has been good for the Land. He saved us all."

The huge, hairy man stood there, and Calla realized he was an intelligent person as he stood there considering her words.

"And tell me, is he still about?"

"Of course, despite the fact he has gained a certain state of grace due to his heroism and sacrifice," Calla responded. "He has been granted the state of ascension."

Sirius stood there, his face wreathed in shock and admiration at what he had just learned.

"He did it!" the huge man finally whispered. "He actually did it!"

"The first one to do so in many centuries," Calla affirmed.

"And tell me, Daughter of the House," Sirius went on. "Does he still reside in the Land? He owes me a bit of gold, plus interest," he chuckled merrily, the sound a low growling rumble in his chest.

"I hear that quite often," Calla grinned back, unable to repress her humor over the situation. "He does return from time to time, but no one can predict exactly where and when."

"That sounds *just* like him," Sirius laughed aloud, his humor spreading throughout the group. "Calla Natanleod, I am glad ye are here to share our meal tonight. Come, supper is nearly ready. I hope ye enjoy yer meat a bit on the rare side."

"I do!" she grinned, falling in between him and his wife.

"Forgive me, my dear," Sirius addressed his spouse. "I should have introduced ye right away. Calla Natanleod, meet my wife Aurora."

The large woman smiled broadly, and from that Calla gathered that he often overlooked such presentations in the heat of the moment.

"I am happy to meet a Daughter of the House," the older woman spoke clearly, in a husky tone. "Our clan is honored by yer presence, come and join us and be refreshed," she invited formally.

"I am the honored one," Calla answered, understanding the forms of manners and protocols. "I am a bit thirsty, may I have something to drink?"

"Of course!" Aurora nodded, turning to make a gesture. Her cupbearer came forward, and poured a clear liquid into the simple stone cup. Garnishing it with a slice of lemon, she handed it to Calla with grace, who received it gratefully, nodding her thanks before partaking. The liquid tasted like spring water, but she noticed the effects at once. This was *not* spring water she thought, sipping carefully, appreciating the slightly astringent taste.

"We call it *Tears of the Wolf*," Sirius explained with a grin, watching her reaction to the potent spirit. "Yer Grandfather favored it, however it might not favor him so much. Ye seem to be handling it well, but I would advise caution and temperance."

"Of course, I would not wish to embarrass myself, or my House," Calla replied carefully. As she sipped the drink, she found herself wishing Drake was there with her, and she fell back upon her training with him now to deal with the situation.

"Come, the meat is finally done," Sirius growled, and Calla interpreted his tone as hunger, not anger. She went with him and Aurora to find a large circular stone table, crowded with people around the inside and out. Servers circulated around the table with trays and bowls, serving to each person's choices, much like they did at home, Calla thought. When she sat, she saw that the meat was steaming hot, but bloody rare within, which did not dismay her. She was used to eating rare meat, and enjoyed the flavor, so when her portion was served, she smiled in anticipation.

"Ah, ye look a bit like yer Grandfather," Aurora said quietly. "I never met a person of the Land who enjoyed his meat as rare as he."

"He is my Grandfather, I have eaten the game he hunts and cooks over an open fire. I like my meat tender and rare," Calla smiled. Aurora grinned with her, already liking the beautiful young woman, and then she glanced across the table, where Sable sat with his group of best friends. She could not miss the expression on his face, which was openly lustful, and it was fortunate that Calla did not appear to notice.

"My son, do not even consider her as a mate," she sent to him through their pack link. "She is not for ye, nor any of us. She is a Daughter of the House Natanleod, and ye will treat her with honor. Do I make myself clear, or shall I have yer Father reinforce it?"

"I hear ye," he said shortly, embarrassed at being observed.

"Ye are yer Father's eldest son, and my first born. I shall not look kindly upon any embarrassing incidents as have occurred in yer past. Hear me, my son, and obey," she ordered.

"I said I heard ye," he repeated sharply, and cringed a bit when he saw her expression turn cold. "I mean no disrespect, Mother."

"I am glad to hear that," she answered coolly, knowing her son's temperament well. After he had started maturing, there had been incidents with the young girls of the enclave, none of which were their doing. Sable had been forced to apologize and do labor for the offended families, such was their way in their clan. He, of course, would never put his full effort into such things, and therefore the lesson went unlearned. He was, however, about to receive his full lesson from the Goddess in the matter of how women should be treated.

Calla drank sparingly, eating just enough to satisfy her hunger, knowing she would be sleepy soon after she finished. She sat and talked with Sirius and Aurora until her eyes began to droop a bit, and Aurora stood to walk her to their quarters.

"Ye will sleep among us," she said in a semi-commanding tone. "I know ye will be perfectly safe that way."

"I appreciate everything ye have done to make me welcome, Madam," Calla answered warmly. "My Father will be glad to hear how hospitable ye have been to me."

Sirius smiled, exposing his large, white teeth, genuinely glad to see all was going so well. He did not see the lustful expression on his son's face, and he passed it off when Aurora tried to discuss it with him later.

"Husband, ye need to speak with our son about our guest. I do not like the way he looks at her, and I do not like the tone of his thoughts."

"She is a beautiful young woman, any young man would have lustful thoughts," Sirius defended his son. "I do not think we need have any concern over it, especially after the last incident, and how long it took him to make it right."

"Sable is more like ye than me in temperament," Aurora persisted, rousing Sirius' ire a bit. "Ye've said it yerself, that he needs a stronger hand to guide him. Perhaps we should send him to the High Lord's Barracks, and have a trainer see to him?"

"Send him away?" Sirius gasped a bit. "Aurora, he's done naught to earn exile!"

"I do not wish him to be exiled," Aurora answered disdainfully, thinking Sirius was acting a bit childish himself. "But he needs discipline, more than ye seem to be able to exercise. He keeps making the same mistake, over and over again."

Sirius' face took on that stubborn mien she had come to recognize well. The conversation was over and he had made up his mind not to do anything about their son.

"Very well, but if ye do not tend to it, the Goddess will. Ye know that, and 'tis naught ye can do to stop it now, since ye refuse to deal with him," Aurora answered, rising from the bed and donning a thick robe. "I am going to sit up for a bit," she said, struggling to control her anger. "Good night," she finished, her tone dripping with icicles.

"Aurora," he started, only to stop when she whirled and he saw the look on fury on her face. After she walked out the door, she slammed it hard, punctuating the situation sharply. He did not sleep the rest of the night, and when he rose, he found his first meal waiting for him in the oven and a short note from his wife.

"I and some of the women are going hunting. We have taking young Calla with us, for her protection. We may be out all night, do not worry, we will be well. Think hard, husband, about what ye intend to do about yer son."

It was signed simply with a print from her wolf paw, and he sighed heavily, knowing her anger was his fault. Perhaps he was being too lenient with the boy, he thought to himself as he ate the simple meal of barley porridge. When he finished, he washed the bowl and spoon, putting it on the drying rack before taking his leave for the day. He spoke to some of the older men about Sable and what could be done to mend his attitude. The oldest man in the enclave had an answer for him, one that Sirius did not like.

"Ye want to help yer son?" the old man asked.

"Aye!"

"I'll be right back, with just the thing to help ye," the old man responded seriously. Rising and walking slowly into his quarters, he was gone for only a short time before returning, bearing a good sized paddle with holes drilled throughout its surface. "Ye know how to use one of these, aye?" he asked of Sirius, handing it to him.

"What's this for?"

"Would ye like a demonstration?" the old man asked, chuckling a bit. "Or can ye figure it out on yer own? Honestly Sirius, are ye certain ye are still capable of leadership? If ye cannot discipline yer son, how can ye expect anyone to follow ye?"

Sirius found he could not meet the old man's eyes, the question was a hard one to consider after all. He took the paddle, rose from his seat, and gravely thanked the elder for his time.

"Remember, it don't work 'less ye use it," the old man cautioned, being very serious while doing so. Sirius nodded, and trudged out of the man's quarters headed for his own and the duty that awaited him.

Arriving back at his family's home, he walked inside and found the place cold and dark. Aurora was still gone, and now Silver was late to get home. Sirius wondered what was amiss, and stowing the paddle in the room he shared with his wife, he went in search of his son. It took a few stops, but at last he pieced together the story of how Sable had organized his best friends into a "hunting party" and gone after the females led by Aurora. Sirius frowned a bit, an uneasy feeling suddenly settling into his innards, instead of returning home he visited the families of each of Sable's closest friends and learned they were also missing their sons. Now Sirius' anxiety rose another notch, and he walked out into the woods, his thoughts searching for his wife and finding nothing. She was not using the pack link, he thought in frustration, which would make it harder for her to be found.

"Which is exactly what she wants," Sirius growled a bit, angry until he remembered why she had left in the first place. Turning to the other fathers, he quickly issued a few orders, including where they would be meeting in the morning to go in search of them all if they did not return at dawn.

While the uproar continued at the enclave, Calla and the other women of the clan were enjoying themselves out in the wildwood. Calla had no idea of the tension between Aurora and her mate, she was simply enjoying being with other strong, intelligent women. As they hunted, they talked in hushed tones, at least until Calla realized she could hear their thoughts and told them so.

"Ye can hear the pack link?" Aurora questioned with surprise. "Ye would be one of the only humans able to do so."

"I am a Natanleod," Calla answered simply. "I have always been able to talk to the animals."

"Yer Grandfather could do the same," Aurora smiled a bit. "Which is how we met. He was injured, hiding in the wildwood close to the Blessed Realms, when I and Sirius found him. He stayed with our clan for over a month recuperating from some very serious wounds. I believe that only his extraordinary nature kept him alive long enough for him to be found," she finished.

"Grandfather is extraordinary," Calla smiled fondly. "But my Father is truly his son, and therefore heir to all that Drake was and still is. I think he will be very happy to meet all of ye, and discuss how yer Clan might be reintegrated into the Land. I know we could use assistance patrolling the borders, especially up in the more remote areas of the border."

"Our Clan would be very useful in such a purpose."

"Exactly," Calla grinned, liking her very much.

"And tell me about yer Mother. Is she still in the Land?"

"Of course, she is High Lady," Calla answered, her face adopting a more serious expression. "Her name is Deborah, and her abilities are still manifesting."

"O?"

"Indeed, but ye will learn all about that as time goes forward. Shhhh," she said suddenly, and the others reacted at once, silencing all talk. "Do ye hear that? I think I hear an elk in distress!"

"I hear it too!" Aurora nodded. "We should go at once! An elk is a great deal of meat!"

Off they ran, those of the Clan adopting their wolf forms in order to close the distance more quickly. Calla found she was easily able to pace them, to their astonishment, and it did not take too long for them to find the injured beast.

"The leg is broken," Calla noted at once with a sigh. "The Goddess has provided for the Clan, and we should give it the quick death."

"Would ye do the honor?" Aurora asked, for it was an honor among their people to attend to the kill. Calla simply nodded and carefully approached the thrashing elk, murmuring to it in soft tones until it calmed enough for her to kneel beside it.

"Let me release ye from this pain, my brother," she said in a near whisper. "I promise, ye will have a beautiful death."

She could feel the elk's response at once, and the tickle of its thoughts within her mind, expressing relief and thanks. Drawing her blade, she attended to the deed with no further conversation, pulling the wickedly sharp edge across the throat of the elk, severing the artery without staining herself with blood.

"Go now," she whispered to it. "Be at peace. Thank ye for the nourishment yer body will provide."

With a final shudder, she felt its breathing cease, and then the slow thumping of its heart stopped at last. She patted it gently a final time as the Direwolves watched in wonder, they had rarely seen a human demonstrate such care for a game animal. Aurora was moved a bit, as were several of the other ranking females of the Clan, and Calla's acceptance among them was settled. She helped them skin the carcass and field dress it, leaving the entrails as an offering for the others of the wildwood, then they rigged a travois and two of the Direwolves volunteered to pull it. They had just loaded up the meat when Silver and his friends arrived on the scene.

"Mother! Congratulations!" he called out jubilantly, for elk was a favorite meal.

"The congratulations should go to the Daughter of the House," Aurora countered. "She gave an injured elk a perfect death, I doubt it felt her stroke whatsoever. She is very skilled, and a good hunting companion."

"And very beautiful," Sable added in an ingratiating tone. Calla did not care for it, he sounded servile and whiney to her. She wanted naught to do with him, and told him so right there in front of the others.

"Yer compliment makes me feel uncomfortable. Do not speak to me," Calla said plainly, and Sable's face took on an expression of anger.

"Ye cannot order me about," he answered flippantly.

"She is the Daughter of the High Lord of the Land," Aurora pointed out, stepping in. "She outranks me, and yer father as well. She can order ye about if she wishes, and ye owe her yer service."

Sable glanced at his mother, and Calla almost gasped to see the look of hatred and despite on his face. So, she thought, he is one of those kind of men, the kind that think women are beneath them, her thoughts went on, and her face took on a determined expression.

"Ye will do as I ask, or ye will pay the price," she said simply, in a quiet and cool tone, keeping herself balanced on the balls of her feet, her hands near her weapons.

"Very well," Sable said after a few tense moments, his tone seemingly amused. "Ye certainly have a temper, Daughter of the House."

"Ye have seen naught concerning my temper," she growled at him, not liking him at all now. "Ye keep yer distance, or ye will find out all about it."

"Ye are a girl, what can ye do to me?" he laughed derisively, and his mother stepped in between them.

"Sable, go home," Aurora ordered. "Now! Ye and I will be talking to yer father when I get home, and ye had best be there when I do. Go and take yer friends with ye!" she ordered again, pointing the way. Sable stood there for a long moment, wondering if he could beat her in a battle and finally deciding that discretion would be the best course. He called to his friends, they all assumed their wolf forms again and they ran off, headed in the direction of the enclave. Aurora stood there for a long time, struggling for composure until finally she took a long, deep breath and turned to the group.

"Come, we must get this meat home," she said, forcing herself to smile. "Calla, ye will come with me. I do not want ye staying out here by yerself."

"I would be happy to come with ye!" Calla grinned. "I like a good piece of elk grilled over a fire too."

Laughingly, they all helped to pull the huge carcass along, lifting it up over small rocks and clearing the larger ones out of the way of the travois. It was nearly dark when they returned to the enclave, and everyone was glad to see them, and the load of meat they brought with them.

"Ah my wife," Sirius greeted solicitously. "Ye are one of our finest hunters, and this just proves 'tis so. Welcome home, and congratulations."

"Actually, we were disappointed with our hunt until we found this elk, laying and suffering with a broken leg. It was Lady Calla who gave him the perfect deal, I must say that I admire her skill with a blade after seeing her at work."

"Thank ye, Lady Calla, for yer help to feed our people," Sirius turned to the young woman to say, showing good manners. Aurora's eyes narrowed a bit, she was more than a bit suspicious of his manner and tone, especially after their harsh exchange earlier that day. Turning to Aurora, he continued. "I have the bath ready for ye, and I am certain that the other mates have the same waiting for ye all. If ye will come with me, my dear, I have something I would like to say in private."

"Is Sable home?"

"What? No, I thought he was with ye!"

"That little…" Aurora said, pursing her lips. "I told him to go home."

"He and his friends will be fine out there," Sirius chuckled a bit. "He is just trying to make ye worry enough to come looking for him."

"He would not want me to find him right now," Aurora growled. "But, ye are right, 'tis something he has done before. I refuse to worry about him, as I am ready to celebrate a bit. Our hunt was successful, and from the signs we saw, we will have meat in the locker this year."

A cheer rose from the others around them, for such a year was good news. Less rationing of meat meant fuller bellies and better health for the Clan, a blessing in their minds. The rebellious sons were put aside in light of such joyous news, at least in everyone's minds but Calla's. She determined to remain vigilant, for she did not trust Sable and his friends whatsoever.

Chapter 9

Calla retired early that night, meaning to leave for home in the morning. She had much to report to her Father, and wanted to do so right away, while the details were fresh. She slept well within the confines of the headman's quarters, and rose easily with the dawn to dress and ready herself for departure. Sirius and Aurora were still abed after a very late night, she wrote a simple note thanking them for everything and saying farewell. Leaving it on the common room table, she left quietly, closing the door with barely a click as she left.

It did not take her long to make her way out of the enclave and head towards the family house in the valley. She was sure to stop at the sentry post on the way out, to express her thanks for the welcome she had received.

"We were honored to host ye, Calla Natanleod," they all said in one way or another. "Good journey to ye."

"Thank ye, I hope to see ye all again soon," she called back, turning to go. They watched her walk down the mountain, until she passed out of their sight, and wished her well before returning to their duty.

Calla felt free again as she lost sight of the enclave, however she put her mind to remembering how to return to the place as she walked down the mountain. Keeping her wits about her, she plunged into the thick wildwood that stood between her and the family house, at least a good day's hike away. She set a good pace, passing her former campsites as she made her way back along her approach route, until suddenly she became aware that she was being followed. No, I am not being followed, she realized, I am being hunted. A strange expression crossed her face as she stood there, thinking of how best to deal with what she reckoned was Sable and his friends tracking her. Deciding to stand and confront them, she found a good place, assembled stones for a fire circle and lit a blaze to warm herself, spreading out her rolled up reed mat on the ground before it to wait. It did not take long for her to catch sight of them, lurking around the firepit area.

"What do ye want?" she called out in a challenging tone, remaining seated to conceal the fact she had her expandable lance and bow at hand.

"Just to talk and share yer fire," Sable called back, trying to keep his tone friendly. He was not fooling Calla at all however, she could clearly hear the lust and malice in his tone.

"Go home, I want naught to do with ye!" she said in a stern tone, standing with the lance in hand, and her bow across her back. "Ye should not be following me!"

"I just want to talk to a beautiful woman, is that something so wrong?" Sable returned, keeping his voice as friendly as possible. "Surely the great Natanleods have a moment or two for those who live under their rule?"

"I do not rule, my Father does," Calla answered, seeing no way out of the hospitality trap before her. "Come then, I am only taking a short break to rest my legs before I return home."

"Home?" Sable questioned. "Ye are going to walk all the way back to the Capitol?"

"Nay, of course not," Calla snorted. "I am at the family house here in the valley, overseeing the re-staffing of the guardhouse there. I need to return to my work, I have dallied enough in the wildwood."

"Perhaps ye have not," Sable questioned in low and seductive tones as he approached the fire, his friends lurking behind him. "Ye spent no time with me or any of my friends, after all and we are closer in age than the rest of the enclave."

"I do not want to spend any time with ye," Calla replied, putting a harder edge on her voice.

"Why not? I am a handsome man, am I not?"

"Not to me," Calla replied at once, not liking how close he and his friends were getting at all. "Back away, all of ye, lest ye wish to feel pain."

"Pain is not want I want at all!" Sable shouted back and leapt for her. Even with her quick reactions, she was startled a bit and so hesitated, which was all that Sable needed to wrap his arms around her and try to press a kiss to her neck. Once Calla realized what he was about, she pulled her belt knife and used it to good purpose, cutting a deep slice under his eye, right across the right cheekbone so one could see the bone. Sable screamed in pain, released her and clapped his hand to his face, trying to stop the copious bleeding. His fellows did not know what to do, they were ashamed by Sable's actions and did not know how to respond.

Calla had no difficulty acting however, she stood there and calmed herself before calling out in her mind, instinctively wanting Deborah's presence;

"Mother, I need ye, now!"

Far away, at the High Lord's house in the Capitol, Deborah was sitting in her sewing room, putting the last touches on the latest batch of clothing for Arthfael's two children when she felt Calla's mind touch hers, and then the urgent summons. She stood, put the clothing aside carefully, then went to stand before the statue of the Goddess in its niche.

"What is amiss?" she whispered, her eyes beginning to turn color as her hair took on streaks of flaming red. No answer came, but a feeling of urgency persisted, in response Deborah called her war regalia to her, including the small diadem that announced her rank, then sent Erinn a quick thought or two.

"Husband, I must go. Our Daughter…"

"I heard that, I shall be right behind ye," Erinn responded coldly, for his anger was roused. Calla would not call them in such a way unless the need was urgent, and he also called his war armor to him, watching it appear around him in place of the clothing he had been wearing. After he was dressed and armed, he called to Tristan, Knight Commander and leader of the Black Dragons.

"Commander, I shall need a troop of the Dragons to accompany me. My daughter is in peril."

"Aye, My Lord," he heard Tristan's terse response, and moments later the man appeared with twenty of his best, war-hardened Black Dragons, all dressed for battle.

Meanwhile, Deborah had already disappeared from the sewing room, appearing next to Calla in a flash of fire and a peal of thunder.

"What is amiss here?" she called out in a cold, commanding tone. Looking at Calla, she saw the mark on her neck, and her anger was fully roused. "Who…has… *touched*…ye?" she enunciated clearly. Calla could not speak due to her own anger, simply pointing at the offending young man from the clan of the Direwolves.

"He did!" Calla finally managed to say. Deborah noticed the cut under his eye, and saw the exposed bone without emotion. "Well done, Daughter," she said, turning to Calla and seeing the rage on her daughter's face.

"Yer training paid off well, Mother," Calla answered, her words dripping with ice. "He did exactly what you said an attacker would do!"

"Ye have learned well then," Deborah complimented.

Erinn now appeared in a thunderclap, the ground vibrating under their feet at the concussion.

"What is amiss here?" he thundered, and Sable felt his words as a vibration throughout his body. "Ye! Who are ye?" Erinn continued, pointing at Sable.

"I…"

"*He* is the son of the leader of the Direwolves Clan, Father," Calla interjected, her tone full of scorn.

"Direwolves?" Erinn questioned.

"Aye, 'tis a long story, but I found them and have been staying with them for a day or two. I was on my way back to the family house when he and his *friends* attacked me!"

"I see ye have defended yerself well, Daughter," Erinn chuckled despite the situation. "I daresay that cut will leave a scar no matter how skilled the healer might be who treats it. What say ye, Wife?" he asked, turning to Deborah, who was fully aflame, surrounded by the figure of the Phoenix bird. Sable's friends were awestruck, and trembled on the ground in fear as she walked towards Sable. Putting her finger under his chin, she raised his face so as to observe the cut, and a faint smile passed over her face.

"I agree, 'tis a deep cut. 'Twill take a long time to heal properly, and I think 'twill leave a visible scar. I could assure that with a simple touch," she menaced and for the first time, Sable realized he had bitten off more than he could chew. He had never met anyone like Deborah before, and as she stood there, the heat of her presence began to make him sweat furiously. The salty liquid trickled down his forehead, over his nose and right into the cut, which was extremely painful and he moaned a bit.

"Where are yer parents?" Erinn demanded, and Sable blanched visibly. "Never mind, I shall call them to attend. They have some explaining to do, and so do ye, young wolf," Erinn growled a bit, and Sable could suddenly smell sulfur.

The High Lord straightened himself, took a deep breath to compose himself. Using his extra abilities, he used his senses to find Sable's parents, far away in the enclave. They were still abed, he noted as the summons was sent, and when it was received, the effects were startling. Sirius came awake suddenly, as did Aurora, hearing the commanding tone in their minds.

"Sirius and Aurora of the Direwolf Clan, ye are summoned to the High Lord's presence. Yer son has committed an act of violence, and ye must be there to attend his judgment!"

At the same time, all the other fathers and mothers of Sable's friends heard similar summons, and soon found themselves in the High Lord's presence, ready or not. Some of them came unclothed, as they were bathing when called, others came in rumpled bed clothing, with messy hair, as they were summoned from their sleep. All of them were a bit grouchy as they stood there, wondering what was amiss. As soon as they saw their sons all gathered around Sable, their faces changed from confusion to a mix of resolution and rage.

"Yer sons have been involved in an attempted claiming of a woman from outside of your clan," Erinn began, over-enunciating each word. "They helped *him* to hunt my daughter!" he went on, pointing at Sable, bleeding on the ground. "They attempted to keep her from escaping their custody, at his orders! As well, they stood by while *this* one tried to mark and claim my daughter as his own, according to the ways of yer people. My daughter is no Direwolf, and she is not to be claimed in such a fashion. He has done her harm, look ye can still see the mark he put on her!" Erinn went on, pointing at Calla, who obligingly tilted her head so that the purplish, slightly circular mark could be seen clearly.

"But My Lord!" one of them tried to object, only to have Erinn cross the short distance between them rapidly, so that within moments of his speaking, Erinn stood before him, looking down at him with his face cool and composed.

"What?" Erinn barked. "Ye are that one's father, why have ye not taken his discipline seriously? And ye!" he turned on Sable's father, pointing a wrathful finger. "Ye know all about his behavior, but do naught. Instead, ye have raised a spoiled and willful son, and now he must pay the price for it!"

"My Lord, please do not kill my son," Sirius answered simply. "If ye give him to me, I shall see to it he is punished within the laws of our people."

"Hold there!" Deborah rapped out. "My daughter has been harmed, I claim the right to discipline her attacker. 'Tis my right, according to the laws of the Land."

"She is right," Erinn nodded, and now Sirius was truly concerned, for Deborah was now outlined in flames, and the shape of the outline was that of a Phoenix bird, the wings fully unfurled. Her hair looked like it was aflame as well, and her eyes burned a hot, amber color. He could feel the heat from the flames all the way across the rough circle, where she stood opposite him beside Calla, and a shudder of fear passed over him.

"But…"

"What?" Deborah cut him off. "If she were yer daughter, what would ye do?"

"He would be exiled from the pack," Aurora spoke out at last, having seen and heard enough. "I beg ye, My Lady, to take him and teach him the lessons we do not seem to be able to teach him. He does have a good heart, underneath all of that ego, could he not be saved?" she implored with passion.

"Everyone deserves a second chance," Deborah answered after a moment. "But, he will have to work for his. Very well, yer son is now bonded to my house, and I shall oversee his service myself personally. He will remain a Bondsman until his lessons are learned, one way or another!" she proclaimed.

"Indeed," Erinn nodded, seeing the wisdom of her choice. "So be it then," he went on, making a gesture and a thick, leather collar with a sturdy steel buckle appeared around his neck. It was not uncomfortable, but Sable still chafed a bit at having his freedom so restricted. Deciding he would just avoid all of the unpleasantness by changing into his wolf form, he soon found himself unable to do so, and an expression of panic passed over his face.

"Ye will not be able to change into yer wolf form 'till yer debt is paid, and yer name will be simply "Bondsman" 'till the High Lady chooses otherwise. My Lord War Duke, take this Bondsman back to the High Lord's house and install him in proper quarters," Erinn revealed, his voice cold to the point of iciness.

"Aye, My Lord," Karpon nodded, motioning for two troopers to come and collect the young man. Erinn simply opened a portal, and most of the troopers returned to the Capitol City, leaving only Erinn, Deborah and a small group of Black Dragons to act as their guard and escort.

"When may I see my son again?" Aurora asked plaintively.

"When he has paid his debt, and not before," Deborah insisted. "I think 'tis best for him to be completely isolated from both of ye, and the rest of the pack, so that he might be able to concentrate on working. I shall send ye periodic reports of his progress, have no concerns."

Sirius and Aurora stood there, knowing there was nothing further to discuss. Nodding, they simply accepted the situation, knowing it could not be changed.

"Thank ye, My Lady and My Lord," Aurora spoke up at length. "At last, my son is going to receive the lessons he should, and the discipline he needs to improve himself. Ye are taking a boy, and I expect to see a man when he returns to us. Come my mate, we have work to do at the enclave," she said, turning to Sirius.

"Aye, we would not want the other parents stirring up the rest of the pack. Farewell, My Lord and My Lady. I hope that we might still be able to discuss an alliance between our people and the people of the Land?"

"Of course, that has naught to do with the actions of an immature boy," Erinn nodded. "We shall talk soon then, perhaps Samhain would be a good time for that? Yer son will have had time to adapt to his new situation, and ye will have had time to think about yer proposal of alliance. What say ye?"

"And we would be welcome at the Capitol House?"

"Of course," Erinn smiled suddenly, offering *the Grip* as a token of friendship. Sirius took his arm and used the opportunity to test Erinn's strength, finding his muscles more firm than most other men he had tested. Erinn made certain to grip the man's arm hard enough to leave a single finger bruise, just to demonstrate his strength, which impressed the leader of the Direwolves. Later on, when he readied himself for bed, he found a small purplish mark on his arm right where the High Lord's fingers had gripped his arm, just one mark and it struck him that it was about the size of the mark on Calla's neck. When he showed it to Aurora, his wife said something similar, and they just stared at each other in wonder at the workings of the Goddess.

Once Sable had been dealt with, Deborah was ready to leave. Turning to Erinn, she made mental contact with him to make a suggestion.

"My Lord, do ye not have yer two day on the horizon tonight?"

"I do indeed, and so do ye," Erinn replied with amusement.

"Should we just stay at the family house?" she asked, and Erinn heard the need for peace and quiet in her tone.

"I would like that very much," he answered mentally before addressing Calla aloud. "And what will ye do, my daughter?" he asked.

"I am going home to the Capitol," she replied, her voice still filled with emotion. "I need to work off my anger, and the Barracks is the best place for that. Enjoy yer two day, both of ye, and thank ye for coming to my aid so quickly," she said in a much calmer tone.

"We will see ye soon, Daughter," Deborah replied with a soft smile, embracing Calla warmly. "That mark on yer neck will heal quickly, and most people will be empathetic concerning it. If they are not, ye should let me know," she smiled fiercely.

"No one in the High Lord's house will make a fuss over it," Erinn replied. "Except to express their love for ye. Perhaps ye should seek yer sister out? She has also just returned from her adventures with the Roc Clan. Ye should talk to her."

"O that sounds wonderful!" Calla smiled. "I think I shall go and find her now to see if she wants to have supper together! We have so much to talk about!"

With that, Calla simply disappeared in a flash of light, reappearing moments later at the High Lord's House. As soon as she arrived, she made her way to Lillith's room, and after they greeted each other warmly they agreed that a shared supper would be grand. It did not take long for them to make their requests at the kitchen, and they spent the rest of the day and most of that night talking, drinking, laughing and sharing their meal, along with tales of their adventures.

As for Deborah and Erinn, they settled into the family house in Dragon Valley, ready for two days of rest. They had no idea that the Goddess had other plans, however.

The two of them chose a roast for supper out of the frozen area of the cold room, as well as a small basket of vegetables to go with it. It did not take long to prepare the meat for the oven, and soon it was roasting away, while the vegetables were peeled and set into cold salted water to wait. Deborah put on a batch of simple biscuits, leaving them to rise on the counter, while Erinn brought up wine and ale from the cellar, arranging it on the center table in the common room, along with the pipe and Herb, as well as a few sikars. By the time Deborah had the meal cooking, Erinn had the common room ready to relax in, and after both changed their clothing from their usual day wear to the comfortable, cozy house clothing they preferred. The rest of that day was spent talking, sipping their drink and planning, and they were not surprised that when after dark fell, Drake appeared in the room.

"Good evening ye two, what is going on in the Land?" he asked at once, his voice heavy with concern. "I feel as if something has happened."

"Sit down, Father," Erinn grinned, handing him a pipe and turning to pour him some wine. "We will tell ye all about it while ye enjoy a few comforts. Did ye know that the Direwolf Clan is back in the Land, and ready to be of service?" he asked casually. Drake stopped sipping his wine, put his cup aside and sat up.

"Is that so?" he asked, a trace of sarcasm in his voice. "And tell me, what miracle has been wrought to make that happen?"

"Yer Granddaughter brought them in, actually," Erinn grinned, reloading the pipe for his father.

"WHAT?" Drake asked in a shocked tone. "Ye *are* going to explain, aye?"

"Of course," Erinn chuckled a bit at Drake's reaction. "But my wife is going to have to tell some of the tale, after all."

"Well?" Drake asked impatiently. "I am waiting to hear all about it!"

And so Deborah told him of Calla's meeting with the long-absent clan of shapeshifters, right up to the point where Sable had marked Calla. Drake's rumble of disapproval shook the table, at least until Erinn told him how the incident had turned out.

"So, the young wolf is at the Capitol House as a Bondsman?" he chuckled at the very idea. "And who is going to direct his service?"

"The Mother of the offended girl, of course, which is the Law of the Land," Erinn supplied, winking at Deborah a bit.

Drake glanced at Deborah, noting she looked very satisfied with the prospect of monitoring the Bondsman's labor. He shuddered a bit, knowing how hard Deborah worked all the time, and that she would expect the Bondsman to work just as hard or harder. The young man had no idea what to expect, Drake thought with a grin as he sipped his wine and enjoyed the sikar Erinn handed him.

"Well then, most of our old allies have returned to the Land," Drake mused as Deborah served supper a bit later. "The only ones missing are the Ents and their Druid Keeper, but I do not expect to see them again. I believe they have passed into the Blessed Realm, where they were safe from the Nagas' machinations. I gave them my permission to go, seeing that I could not guarantee their safety. Just imagine having a Naga take hold of something as powerful as an Ent?" he finished, his tone heavy with concern.

"I can imagine," Erinn nodded. "It would be as bad as if they possessed a Direwolf, or a Roc. The sooner they are all eliminated from the Land, the better off the world will be."

"Indeed so, my son," Drake sighed. "Is my room ready, my dear?" he asked Deborah.

"Of course, it always is," she replied in an overly patient tone.

"I thank ye for that," Drake replied sincerely. "I am not as welcome in other places."

"I can imagine not," Deborah answered seriously. "If ye are doing the kind of work I think ye are, then most people would fear meeting ye."

"How do ye know that?" Drake demanded, having always been careful not to discuss what work he was doing as an Ascended being.

"Ye will not talk about it, which leads me to believe ye are doing something the Goddess does not want many people to know about. I am not stupid, Father. I can reason things out," she went on in a somewhat scornful tone.

"I never thought otherwise, daughter," he answered. "The last thing I would ever accuse ye of being would be stupid. But I must be cautious about what I say."

"Indeed, since what ye are doing is so very secret," Deborah smiled faintly. "I think I shall go put myself to bed, gentlemen," she said, standing gracefully and sipping the last of her wine. "Good night husband, good night Father. Sleep well, both of ye, when ye do."

"Good night," they both called after her, watching her walk up the stairs and hearing a door close behind her. After sitting in silence for a bit,

Erinn rose to pour whiskey for both of them, then lit a final sikar to enjoy. Drake took the moment to ask a very serious question.

"Erinn, if the Goddess asked something of ye, ye would do yer best to accomplish that thing, aye?"

"Of course," Erinn nodded.

"And what if She should propose that the entire Earth should become the Land?" Drake asked.

"Father, that She would task me with such a huge project would be an honor, of course. 'Twould be a difficult, arduous task, but very worthwhile. We would need many, many more troopers to accomplish such a thing. The Army is far too small at the moment, unless She wishes to invest all of them as gods and goddesses," Erinn answered in a sensible tone. Even as he answered, however, his mind was already working on the idea, which appealed to him greatly. Drake saw it, and inwardly, a sense of pride filled him at how his son had turned out.

"And if She would grant ye more troops, as well as armies of healers, builders and every manner of Guildsmen to assist in the rebuilding?"

"Such would be necessary for such a project," Erinn replied at once. "Such a thing would require everyone in the Land, and more."

"Ye are right about that," Drake nodded. "I was being theoretical with my questioning, as 'tis something I let myself consider from time to time. That world out there is barbarous, and growing more so all the time. Be wary of anyone who comes to the Land from out there, very wary."

"I always am Father," Erinn replied seriously. "And not all of them are allowed to stay either."

"Ye are wise to be so discriminatory," Drake nodded, sipping the mellow liquor. "Tell me all about the Direwolves reappearing in to tathe Land?"

"I shall tell ye what I know," Erinn replied, pouring a bit more whiskey into both cups. It took a bit longer for Erinn to explain the circumstances, and when the incident with Sable came up, Drake sat up, and expression of wrath on his face.

"He touched her, marked her?" the elder Natanleod asked, a frown on his face.

"He did, but she gave him a mark in return, a cut under the eye. 'Tis one that will last his entire life," Erinn explained. "He is now a bondsman, awaiting his Mistress at the Capitol House. I am certain that he is receiving the treatment he deserves in the Barracks for his crime, and when Deborah returns, his labors will truly begin. I almost feel sorry for him."

"She is a hard taskmaster, for certain," Drake acknowledged, a grin on his face. "I think I am ready for some rest, dawn is nigh."

"I need to go lie down for certain," Erinn yawned. "I am glad ye are back in the Land, Father. I miss yer counsel."

Drake smiled a bit as they shared *the Grip*, then retired to their respective quarters for the night. When Erinn slid into bed, he was careful not to wake his wife, who he knew slept lightly. She said nothing, and so he simply closed his eyes and let himself slip off to sleep.

As they slept that night, Erinn dreamt a strange dream. He was standing far away, just outside of one of the smaller worlds within the Land, a vague shape appeared just outside of the magickal barrier that separated it. With a flash of light, and a word of power, the barrier opened wide, and the vague shape entered. A short time afterwards, the ground around the area shook, and a rumbled could be heard, growing louder and louder as the dawn rose. Just as the sun peeked up over the mountains, a small herd of massive bovines stampeded out of their world into the Land, the vague shape following after them. They were Aurochs, an ancient, massive breed of cattle well-known for their hearty nature and uncertain temperament.

Not bothering to seal up the barrier, the individual stood there watching the Aurochs run wildly, trampling everything in their way. A cruel laugh emerged from the person, and in the gathering light of the morning sun, he was revealed as a tall, dark-skinned man wearing a very unusual outfit. He looked as if he had stepped into the Land right out of ancient Egypt, his black eyes cold, and his face drawn into a haughty expression. He seemed very pleased with what he had done, and a great shout of laughter could be heard as he disappeared from the place, leaving the Aurochs to run.

The huge cattle thundered on, looking for pasture but finding only farmer's fields, and the much smaller domestic cattle found themselves overwhelmed by the much larger animals. Even if the herd bulls of each farmer tried to withstand the Aurochs, they were simply pushed aside and trampled if they refused to move. Several farmers lost animals this way, and some of the others had their cattle join the stampede, running wildly among the Aurochs.

Despite the hour Erinn woke, felt the *wrong* in the Land, and sent out his senses to discover the reason.

"Aurochs are loose in the Land?" he questioned inwardly, rising to call his war gear to him. "How is this possible?"

"They have been released, 'tis the only explanation," Deborah's voice answered him as she roused. "Erinn, they must be rounded up at once, before they hurt someone! And we must discover who was able to release them as well!"

"Is it not fortunate then, that we have Heroes and Giants to help us herd them?" Erinn asked tersely. Taking a moment to compose himself, he sent his thoughts out to his War Duke.

"My Lord War Duke!" he commanded. "Summon the Giants and the Heroes, as well as many of the Black Dragons as ye can. We have a serious threat to deal with. There are Aurochs loose in the Land."

"Aurochs?" Karpon asked, his voice sounding very surprised. "But My Lord..."

"I know, they should be confined in their peaceful little part of the Land. Someone has deliberately released them, and I must discover who and why. But we must deal with the Aurochs first, they are a danger to everyone now. I shall be in the Barracks shortly."

"I shall begin summoning everyone now," Karpon replied, feeling their connection cut off. He did what was necessary, using his own magickal abilities to summon the personnel necessary, telling them to assemble in the common room.

When Erinn arrived a few moments later, Karpon was dressing in his own war gear, and quickly explained that all was in preparation when Erinn asked.

"Good, I am glad to have someone so organized as my War Duke," Erinn smiled thinly. "Come, let us join them in the common room."

Karpon stamped his foot into the second boot, tightened his sword belt around him and nodded his readiness as they left his office, heading for the common room.

As they went, the mental summons passed throughout the Barracks, and the Lady chose who She wished to accompany the High Lord. In the end, all of the Giants, all of the Heroes, and all of the Black Dragons available stood in the common room, waiting for their orders. Erinn could hardly suppress the smile of gratitude and satisfaction to see them all there, and he took a deep breath before addressing them aloud.

"Ladies and Gentlemen," he began in his best parade ground tone. "We have a new threat to deal with. There are Aurochs running loose in the Land. 'Tis our task to stop them before they can do more damage, or before they hurt, maim or kill someone. Auroch meat is delicious, or so I have read. Perhaps our friends the Giants might have more information?" Erinn asked, turning to Balor.

"Indeed so, My Lord," the huge man answered with a grin. "We were the keepers of the Aurochs before the war with the Nagas, and I can remember times when we cooked an entire beast to feed our camp. The taste is that of prime, wild beef, but better," he went on, feeling his mouth fill with saliva at the very thought of such a meal. Murmurs went around the room, and Erinn felt the rise of excitement and anticipation concerning the hunt.

"Remember that these animals are completely wild, they have never been handled by men. As such, they will view ye as predators, most likely, and will be very aggressive. I suggest boar spears be added to yer weapons, my friend. We have a hard task ahead of us, and I want ye all to return to the Barracks when we are done," Erinn advised. He was gratified to see over two thirds of the group hold up the expandable lances. "Good then, some of ye have the ken of how dangerous this could be. Go now, ready yer steeds so that we might depart. I want to be gone soon."

"Aye, My Lord!" he heard their reply all at once, and the room quickly emptied.

"I have had yer steed saddled along with mine," Karpon said quietly. "If ye will come with me, My Lord, we will be ready to meet them when they are ready. Is yer wife coming along?"

"Nay," Erinn replied. "I need the exercise, and if she is here, the thing will be done too soon," he grinned widely.

"Very well then," Karpon nodded, unable to shake the uneasy feeling that gripped him.

"What is amiss?" Erinn asked, feeling the man's anxiety.

"Well, my mind keeps wondering just how the beasts were able to escape their confinement, My Lord," Karpon answered quietly as they walked along, headed to the stables and the rear entrance to the House. When they arrived, Erinn's horse was waiting and ready, as was Karpon's, while the rest of the troop was in the final stages of saddling their horses. The Quarter Mistress, Barkida, came to see them off and to ask Erinn if this would be an extended campaign.

"If ye are going to be out, perhaps I should send a wagon after ye?" she worried.

"They have their usual travel supplies for patrols?" Erinn asked.

"Aye, My Lord!"

"Then we will be well-supplied," Erinn reassured her. "The weather is warm, and even if we must seek shelter overnight, we have our tents and rations. All will be well," he finished with a winning smile, knowing how the young woman worried over her responsibilities.

"As ye say, My Lord," Barkida nodded.

Finally the troop was ready to depart, and they did so with no ceremony, simply riding through the town as quietly as possible, headed for the back gate of the Capitol City. As soon as the first crossroad came into view, Erinn opened a portal and took the entire group through to the place Oracia said the Aurochs were now grazing quietly.

Arriving at what looked to be a usually pastorally serene place, the damage was obvious. Fences had been broken through, fields trampled, gardens eaten and wrecked. Erinn noted at once that there were no animals in any of the fields, and suspected that the Aurochs passing through had simply swept the animals along with them. Turning to the troops behind him, Erinn hardly had to issue any orders, as all of them were eager to assist.

"My Lord War Duke, take the troopers and offer what assistance ye might. See if there are other places where the beasts have done damage, and assist there as well. Help them sort out their animals as well, as I am certain there are domestic beasts in their number. I am taking the Heroes and the Giants with me in search of the Aurochs. Aye, I am taking a few Black Dragons along with me, including the brothers, ben Cain. I shall be well protected."

"Very well My Lord," Karpon nodded, knowing Erinn was making the right choice. "I shall begin at once!"

With no further conversation, the War Duke turned to his men and barked out a few orders.

"I want half of ye to form up and go in search of more victims of the Aurochs' passing. Be of what assistance ye can be to them, if ye find them. If ye find no one, return before dark."

"Aye My Lord!"

"Commander Tristan?"

"Aye?"

"Ye will lead the search and rescue party," Karpon ordered.

"Aye My Lord," Tristan grinned a bit as he acknowledged the order. Turning to his group, he told them to mount up and assemble, leaving as soon as they did so. Karpon led the rest of the troop into the village, and Erinn heard the cheers at their appearance. Turning to the Giants and Heroes with him, Erinn motioned for them to follow and they went in search of the huge, wild cattle.

It did not take long to find them, as they had left a wide swatch of damage behind them. The beasts were not cruel, they were simply huge and a bit clumsy too, and they did not care for fences or barriers in their way. As they followed the Aurochs, Erinn took note of the damage they had caused, meaning to send more troops to be of assistance to the people whose farms and homes were damaged.

Finally, just before noon, they came upon the huge herd of beasts, quietly grazing in a field of wheat. The farmer just stood there watching his crop be ravaged, and as Erinn approached, he could see the older man's eyes were wet.

"I am here to take them away Grandfather," he said quietly as he approached the man.

"But...my crop," the old man sighed heavily. "The wheat was good this year, for the first time in many. I thought the Goddess had blessed my house, but She is still wroth with me for some reason. Why else would She send such a calamity?" he sighed again.

"Ye need not worry, yer family will be provided for," Erinn promised him, meaning ever word. "I am the High Lord, Erinn Natanleod, and yer people will have everything they need to get through the coming Winter."

The old man turned and looked Erinn over from head to toe before a small grin appeared on his face. "Ye *are* Drake's son! I can see it all over ye! Thank ye, My Lord, for coming to our aid, and for the promise of help. I wonder what Auroch tastes like?" he said aloud, a mischievous expression coming over his face.

"I would imagine we will find out soon Grandfather," Erinn chuckled a bit at the expression on the old man's face. It was both hunger and satisfaction, and Erinn realized that they needed the meat in the village. Nodding to himself, he turned back to those with him, and when he stood among them again, out of the old man's earshot, he quickly gave his orders.

"We will round them up and take them somewhere they can be easily confined. To take them back to the pocket world they escaped from would simply cause more damage," he began. "However, it appears this village could use some meat. What say ye, my friends, shall we assure they have it?"

The Giants nodded, as did the Heroes, both groups eager to prove their worth in a fight. Since Deborah had undertaken restoring the Giants to full health, they had all gained a considerable amount of weight that was not fat, the spring in their steps had returned, as had their sense of humor. They laughed more often than before, and were easier to get along with too, now that they were getting enough to eat. Erinn had already sent wagonloads of provisions to where the Giants were ensconced, along with Temple healers, to see to returning their entire tribe to full health. Part of that was discovering why there were no children, and when Deborah heard of the conditions they lived under, it only confirmed her own suspicions about the cause. They were all simply malnourished to the point where the women's cycles had ceased and the men's potency had faded. She had ordered all of those at the House to eat three full meals a day, and insisted on mid-day snacks for the women too. She had ordered the same regimen to be established at the Giant's village too, and when reports of weight gain came back to her, both she and Erinn were delighted at the news.

Now Erinn cast an assessing eye over the Giants, seeing the new muscle developing and guessing they felt much stronger. He decided it was time to see just how much they had recovered, and so he had asked them to join the rescue team.

"My friends, let us go to it then," he said quietly. "I shall take half the group and circle to the right. Master Balor and Master Prometheus, take yer group and circle around to the left. We will surround them, and cut out one of them as a gift to the village. Once we have done that, we will need to take the rest of them away. Where shall we herd them to?"

"My Lord," Balor spoke up. "In the days before the Naga Wars, we were the keepers of the Aurochs. If we could take them to our old fortress, 'tis plenty of grazing and wild fruit to keep them content."

"And do ye know how to guide us there?" Erinn asked calmly, thinking this would be the perfect solution.

"I do, 'tis not all that far from here after all," Balor answered. "I think the Aurochs were headed there, as their path is a straight one, headed exactly in the right direction. I think they would be easy to herd, if they reckoned we were taking them there."

"Good then, let us round up these beasts and get them on their way," Erinn grinned.

Cutting out a young bull to slay and skin for the village did not take long, the Giants proved their abilities with the Aurochs in short order, working together to separate one from the others, then quickly putting it down and dressing it out for the villagers. Once the carcass was up on the spit, the villagers laughingly told Erinn they could handle it from there, and after Erinn magically summoned additional supplies from the House in the Capitol city, they said their farewells and began the task of herding the large group of huge beasts in the right direction.

Erinn let the Giants take the lead, as he began to feel a bit of discomfort and soon realized the reason.

"I smell the machinations of a Naga here," he said in his mind to Deborah. "My wife, summon Drake and our daughters and come to me. I think we have a problem to deal with, and I want to meet it with everything we have."

"I shall be there shortly," he heard her respond, and felt the wave of heat through the mind link before it severed. A smile crossed his face, knowing she would be with him, and that whichever Naga it was in front of them, they would face it together.

As soon as Erinn's mind left hers, Deborah called to Drake first.

"Father, are ye ready for a bit of exercise? Erinn thinks we may be dealing with a Naga in the case of a herd of Aurochs running loose in the Land. He has asked for us to join him, feel like a bit of sword work?" she said in a laughing tone.

"Nagas again?" she heard him answer in a growling tone. "Aurochs? They should be confined to their pocket world!"

"Aye, someone has freed them from their confinement world, thus the implication of a Naga at work. Only someone of their sorcerer class could take the barrier down, and 'tis most likely still down, since they are sloppy workers. Erinn is even now leading a rescue team, and going in search of the herd."

"I should be there," Drake nodded, calling for his war gear.

"Aye, so ye should," Deborah acknowledged.

Next, Calla and Lillith appeared, already dressed for war and eager to be of assistance.

"Good, both of ye understood the urgency of the summons," Deborah smiled warmly. Down to the stables they went to dress their steeds, then they were on the road out of the city. Stopping at the same crossroads used by Erinn earlier, Deborah summoned up her abilities. Quickly, she let the energy of the Phoenix emerge, just enough to open a portal, and they all stepped through, appearing right beside Erinn as he rode with the Giants and the Heroes. Both groups of men were startled to see her simply appear with her daughters and Drake, as they did not understand the full extent of her abilities.

"Wife, I am glad ye could come," Erinn said, riding to her side and reaching for her hand. "Do ye feel it?"

"I do, and I can almost smell snake," Deborah answered with a shudder. "Whichever one we are facing, 'tis an old one. There are not many of those left, and so those who remain are notable. I suggest we might be meeting one of their elders and someone who is quite accomplished. Who else could have countered the spell that held the barrier between the Aurochs' place and the Land?"

"There are not many of the elders remaining," Drake growled. "But one of them has evaded me for many, many years, and I hope we are facing him right now."

"Ye refer to Apophos, of course," Deborah stated.

"I do," Drake nodded. "He will be looking for ye."

"Well, perhaps I should allow him to find me," Deborah smiled ferociously. "Let him meet me, if he dares. I wonder if he will burn from within as well as all of the others have?" she asked, as both Erinn and Drake's faces took on an expression of amusement.

Ishmael ben Cain happened to be close enough to hear her as he rode beside Azeem. He wondered if she could truly accomplish such a feat of control to destroy the Naga, leaving the skin intact. If so, it would be a masterful display of her powers. I should like to see that, very much, he thought to himself as they covered the short distance to the besieged district. It was clear to Erinn as they approached which way the Aurochs had run, as they had left a wide, trampled swath in their wake. Counting the hoof prints, and multiplying them by four, Erinn reckoned the herd had more than two hundred members.

"I wonder if we have enough personnel?" he thought to Drake. "I count over two hundred in the herd."

"I do believe that between yer wife and ye, the Aurochs will come under control soon enough. Remember, ye can speak to them," Drake reminded. "And so can yer wife."

"Which is a comfort to me," Erinn nodded. "Very well then, let us round them up, and get them somewhere more remote, so they can graze peacefully."

As soon as they had the Aurochs surrounded in a loose ring, open only on one side, Erinn urged them through the opening, the rest of the Knights and Dames assisting. The Aurochs moved slowly now, being tired from their run, and they were easy to point in the direction their keepers wanted them to go; North to the old cave fortress of the Giants, long abandoned at the outbreak of the Naga war. It took them all day, and as night fell, Erinn simply opened a portal to take them the rest of the way. The Aurochs simply walked through the whirling aperture as if they were domesticated cattle, and as soon as they were on the other side, they streamed out into the lush, green meadow, contentedly grazing.

"Come, My Lord," Balor invited with a smile. "Allow me to welcome ye into my home."

Stepping up to the huge door, which Erinn noted was bound in forged steel, Balor put his hand on the latch and murmured a few words.

"Hello, 'tis me. We are back. Please open the door?"

A moment or two passed, then a creaking groan could be heard as the huge, thick oaken door opened for the first time in many, many years. A rush of stale air blew past them as they made their way inside, the rest of the Giants following after, opening doors to help circulate out all of the stale air. Erinn assisted by summoning the elementals to his aid, and soon the dank smell was replaced by clean, fresh air.

"Balor, we are home," Cethlenn finally said, her voice filled with wonder and gratitude. "I am going to the Chapel, to light candles and offer our thanks. 'Tis good to be home again."

"Thank ye for seeing to that for me," Balor smiled warmly. "Please add my thanks to yers?"

"Of course," she smiled. "And then, we need make a meal. The cooking fires in the kitchen have been cold for far too long."

"I agree," Balor smiled. "My Lord and Lady, Heroes, Black Dragons, Knights and Dames, I invite ye to remain tonight and feast with us! Auroch makes a fine meal!"

A cheer went up from everyone gathered there as a small party was put together to take care of selecting, dispatching and preparing one of the huge beasts for the spit. Erinn himself drew the blade across the throat of the beast, after Balor picked him out of the herd of huge beasts.

"Why that one?" Erinn asked, curious as to the choice.

"He has a deformed back foot. Look!" Balor pointed out as the men worked to remove the hide carefully, so it was all in one piece. Erinn followed his pointed finger, and saw the deformity at once.

"I approve of yer choice," he said as Cethlenn brought huge mugs of cold ale. "I would have chosen him as well, had I seen that. What spices and herbs will ye use for the seasoning?"

"My Lord, I was hoping ye would assist with that," Balor asked quietly. "I have enjoyed all of the meat cooked at the House, and I understand that all of the meat served is treated with a rub mix that suits it. I know I like garlic and black pepper, but perhaps ye might suggest other additions?"

"Come along, Master Balor," Erinn grinned widely as a cup of the stout ale was pressed into his hand by Cethlenn. "Let us work together, and learn from each other."

"I would like that!" Balor grinned as they walked into the busy kitchen. Men and women worked side by side there, busily cleaning counters, pulling dishes, plates and cups out of the cupboards and cabinets, while water heated in the boiler. Everyone was laughing or singing as they worked, their joy at being at home evident in their manner. Deborah was working with them, of course, and soon the great stoves and ovens were lit and heating, readying for their work that day.

"My goodness, the ventilation is remarkably good in here!" Deborah remarked to Cethlenn.

"When we renovated the cave to be our home many decades ago, Balor's grandfather engineered the circulation system so it would work well even if the doors and windows were all closed," she revealed. "Come, I shall show ye how it works."

Deborah followed her to the main chimney of the kitchen, which looked like a tall, oval structure until she got close enough to see it better.

"O my, ye have a natural vent here!" she realized. "It goes all the way up and out of the cave, aye?"

"Aye, and it vents naturally in places that are concealed by trees and bushes," Cethlenn explained. "Despite all of that, the Nagas were able to infiltrate our compound, and take over some of our people. It was hard to end their lives, but it convinced us to leave this place and find somewhere even more remote to safeguard our people. I am sorry it caused so much discord, but what else could we do? Drake was fighting for all of us, and Hadrian's abilities were not equal to his brother's. Drake could only do so much, we all thought it best to remove ourselves from the Land, thinking to protect people. I know it makes little difference now, but I thought that perhaps an explanation might help."

"Ye are under the impression that I disagree with yer choice," Deborah smiled a bit. "I do not, I think ye did the right thing, and who knows how many lives were spared because ye chose what ye did. Yer people have certainly paid the price for it, ye nearly starved yerselves to death living in such a harsh place where agriculture was so hard. I am glad ye are all back in the Land, and that ye are beginning to recuperate a bit from that."

"Thanks to yer diligence and care, My Lady," Cethlenn smiled, gesturing for drink to be served now that cups were clean. "Do ye like wine?"

"Ye know I do," Deborah smiled back.

"Good, then ye should enjoy this vintage very much," Balor's lady replied. "The grapes that provided the juice have grown wild here in this valley since our people first settled here, their flavor is rich and not too sweet. What we are serving now was made just before we left, 'tis almost fifty years old. I am looking forward to a cup or two as we cook," she chuckled deep in her chest, a pleasant rumbling sound.

That night was merry as they divided the Auroch into two halves, so that it might cook a little faster. After the rub was put together, Erinn and Balor applied it to both halves, then they were hung over perfect fires and the turning began. No one turned the spit more than half the hour at a time, and after they were relieved, a cold cup was thrust into their hands. It was loud and boisterous, a happy celebration of returning home. Calla and Lillith stood by, out of the way, wishing they could return to the quiet of the family house. Finally, they went to Deborah as she stood with Cethlenn, for each of them felt tired and wanted to retire.

"Excuse me Madam Cethlenn," Calla began politely. "Could we be shown to our room? We are tired and would like to sleep."

"Of course," the Giant woman answered. "Ye both come with me, I have a nice quiet room for ye with a good view of the valley meadows."

"Thank ye Madam," Lillith said gratefully, for she was truly tired. Deborah joined them as they left the party, and after a short walk down a hallway, Cethlenn opened a door and stepped inside.

"We finished cleaning this one so that ye would all have a nice place to sleep," she explained, turning to light the lamp on the table. Deborah simply snapped her fingers and the rest of the lamps on the walls lit, throwing a great deal of light out all at once. The room was spacious, with two suites, both with private doors. Cethlenn opened both rooms to show how they were set up, including private necessities for each suite.

"We will be very comfortable here," Calla said, stifling a yawn. "Thank ye so much."

"What about yer supper?"

"I am not hungry," Lillith answered truthfully. "I just want to sleep."

Deborah was momentarily concerned, knowing how the Natanleod appetite was voracious at times, until Cethlenn reassured her all would be well.

"My Lady, now that our people are eating better, it seems our appetites have also resurfaced. Our kitchen always has food to serve, much like in yer own Barracks. Yer daughters will have plenty to eat when they are ready."

Deborah smiled warmly, offering a friendly embrace to the large woman. "I thank ye for that, I shall rest easily knowing they will be well cared for."

"Now Madam," Cethlenn smiled warmly. "May I fill yer cup again, since ye are able to relax?"

"Aye, and I thank ye. 'Tis delicious! I would love to see the vines, and I think someone I know would also like to see them," she finished in a thoughtful manner.

"O? Whom?"

"Master Bacchus, who has an intense interest in improving the quality of wine in the Land," Deborah answered. "He has increased the vigor of the vines at the High Lord's House, which means our cellar is fuller than it has been in past years."

"Would he take the time to have a look?"

"Most certainly," Deborah chuckled a bit, thinking of the Hero's reaction to the inquiry. "He most likely run out there if asked, 'tis most likely he is just yearning to get out there. Come, let us ask him," she said, holding out a supportive hand. The two women walked to where Bacchus sat, slowly sipping out of a great cup, the size usually reserved for Giants. He seemed to be handling it remarkably well, despite the size however, Deborah noted.

"Excuse me, Master Bacchus?"

"Aye, My Lady?" he answered at once, his tone sober as if he had not imbibed a drop. "How may I serve?"

"Our friend here has a question about the wild vines here in the area, and I suggested to her than ye would be the one to ask about such things."

"If I may be of assistance, I would be happy to offer an opinion," he smiled broadly.

"Perhaps on the morrow?" Cethlenn suggested.

"I am at yer service Madam," the man smiled warmly. "If what I am drinking comes from those vines, they need to be tended. Ye say this place has been abandoned for fifty years?"

"Aye, and the vines were only trimmed enough to provide wreath material for our craft work in past times."

"I see," Bacchus nodded sagely. "Then they are truly wild vines. Excellent! I can hardly wait to talk to them!"

Cethlenn started a bit at his statement, but Bacchus only smiled reassuringly, and Deborah added her support as well.

"Did he say what I think he said?"

"He did, and I can tell ye, the vines listen to him," Deborah told her seriously. "Ye should see the vines at the High Lord's House. I thought they were well tended before he spoke to them, but this year's harvest is nearly double the year before due to his contribution. The juice is rich and sweet too, I think 'twill make fine, fine wine when it has aged sufficiently."

"How long will it have to age then?"

"Master Bacchus suggested that it might need to sit and age no more than six years before we could consume it. Such a thing would be a blessing to most of the Land, I should think," Deborah added with a grin. "I must say, ye are looking very well these days."

"If so, 'tis because of yer regimen," Cethlenn replied seriously. "My courses have even returned, after being absent for over twenty years. Some of the other women have also reported the same, and so we have hope again because of yer work."

"I was happy to help where I could," Deborah replied warmly, taking more wine when it was offered. "I noted that yer men seem to have regained a bit of their vigor too, it should not be long now until yer people are restored to their full capacity."

"We all look forward to that, My Lady," Cethlenn smiled, her gratitude apparent as they gazed upon their men interacting with both the Heroes, and those from the Barracks.

Even as she stood there with Cethlenn, Deborah was uneasy of spirit. Something was definitely wrong, she kept thinking, despite the smiles and warm camaraderie being exhibited at the moment. It was as if something was slowly rotting in the Land, and finally Deborah had had enough of it.

"Oracia!" she summoned the beautiful golden-skinned Fae that inhabited the Great Map of the Land.

"Aye, My Lady?" she heard the response, both timid and respectful at the same time.

"Where is the wrong?" Deborah asked simply. "Show me."

"Aye, My Lady," Oracia's voice quavered a bit. "I do not have to go there, do I?"

"Nay, all ye need do is show me where he is," Deborah responded coolly. Oracia shuddered a bit, for she feared what the High Lady could do, having seen some of it. It did not take long, and soon Deborah could see a small compound over ten leagues from where she stood now.

"He is close," the thought came into her mind, and she realized it was not her own thought, but the Goddess'. "Now we have him, Daughter, and he has no idea ye are here. Take yer rest, go to it in the morning," Deborah heard the Goddess in her mind.

"Aye Mother, as ye say," Deborah nodded. "As long as we are in no danger at the moment."

"He does not know ye are here, he believes he is safe in his remote compound," the Goddess chuckled a bit. "He is one of their nobles, one of those who is directly responsible for the Nagas being here in the Land."

"Apophos?" Deborah asked quietly.

"Indeed, he of the bright, golden skin," she heard the Goddess answer. "We have waited a long time for this, and 'tis time for his reckoning. Morning will be soon enough."

"As ye say, Great Queen," Deborah nodded.

She was not the only one to receive a short visit from the Goddess that night, Drake was also alerted, as was Ishmael ben Cain. The message was the same to both of them, that the time to die had finally come for the rest of those associated with the Nagas and their war.

"I want them all gone, one way or the other," Drake heard the command.

"Of course," Drake grinned coldly. "Have I not wanted that all this time as well?"

"Then go hunting, which is yer forte, and find them all," he heard Her response.

"Thank ye, My Lady," he whispered, having finally received an order he had been awaiting.

Ishmael heard something similar, but the Goddess added something to his instructions. "Make certain yer brother is truly of the Land now," she said. "Ye will need his assistance very soon. Ye will have a skin to tan, I think, a very, very special one."

"I await the opportunity," Ishmael replied respectfully. "And I shall attend to my brother. I do believe that his loyalty is with ye, Great Mother, but I shall not rest 'till I find out the truth."

"Thank ye," he heard a grateful response, and felt a rush of warmth within him. "Ye will both soon have the opportunity to work together for Me."

"I look forward to that, My Lady," Ishmael responded reverently as he felt Her presence fade from his mind.

When the meat was cooked to perfection, they sat down for a hearty supper, enjoying the meal while talking among themselves, occasionally peals of laughter could be heard too. Afterwards, they all worked together to clean and straighten the dining and living area of the cave fortress, sharing the work without rancor. Finally, everything was clean and tidy, a stew made from the Auroch meat simmered on the stove for morning service, and pans of fresh bread were put to rise. Only then did Deborah finally say her goodnights, Erinn by her side, retiring to the room they had been assigned.

"I am glad to be alone at last," she sighed, changing into comfortable clothing and readying herself for bed. "Erinn have ye *felt* that something was off?"

"Aye, since we arrived here," he confirmed, climbing into the huge bed and pulling the quilts over him wearily. "I reckoned that the Goddess would let me know what was amiss soon enough."

"I told ye before that I felt the presence of a Naga," Deborah replied, climbing in beside him. "He is here, less than ten leagues north of our current position. And if 'tis who I think it might be, we must deal with him now, while we are here in such numbers. Apophos is out there, and we must deal with him. His knowledge of their breeding program is a danger to every world in the Universe, he could just escape here after all and start again somewhere else. And ye know he would be taking what belongs to the Goddess with him. He must be stopped."

"Agreed, but not tonight, surely?" Erinn asked gently. "We could use the rest, as could the rest of the troops. Karpon will rejoin us in the morning, along with the rest of those we sent to be of assistance to the citizens affected by the Aurochs' passing. We will be at full strength then, and ready to face such an enemy."

"Aye," Deborah nodded, knowing that sleep would be hard to find that night. Nonetheless, she managed to do so, waking early and feeling rested. Erinn was already up and dressed in his war gear to bring her caffe and pastries from the kitchen.

"Ye are up early, husband."

"I wanted my pastries to be hot out of the oven," he replied with a grin, handing her one on a plate with a napkin before pouring her caffe and sweetening it according to her likes. "I know ye enjoy them that way too."

"I do indeed," she agreed. "Thank ye, Husband."

"Ye are most welcome, Wife."

They ate their pastries and enjoyed their caffe before Erinn disappeared to summon the troops. Deborah gathered up their morning dishes and took them to the kitchen, finding an ever growing crowd there helping themselves to hot drinks and warm pastries.

"Feed them well, we may have a fight on our hands shortly," Deborah whispered to Cethlenn.

"How so?"

"We have a Naga close by here, which I believe is what led ye to leave this place originally. Is it so?"

"Aye, My Lady, 'tis so. As I said yesterday, they took possession of a few of us at first, to use our strength and stamina to build their fortresses before sacrificing our people to the snakes," Cethlenn's voice shook with outrage, and Deborah felt a wave of empathy wash over her. No wonder the Giants had simply packed up and left, she thought to herself as she reached for Cethlenn's hand, squeezing it a bit.

When her plate was handed to her, she took it and sat by Erinn, eating mechanically, knowing she would need the sustenance for later, no matter what she had to do. All the while, she could feel her power growing within her, a great, burning sensation that seemed to consume her more and more as time passed. Erinn could feel the heat of it, but he said naught, knowing that his wife would not be experiencing such a thing unless it would be necessary. Finally finishing his own plate, he got Balor's attention and asked if he could speak to those gathered.

"Of course, My Lord," Balor answered, wondering what Erinn was about.

"Thank ye, Master Balor," Erinn responded, rising and clearing his throat. The room fell silent almost at once, giving Erinn the opportunity to be heard. "My friends, we have a problem to deal with," he began in a serious tone. "A Naga installation is less than 10 leagues from here. We have no idea who or what might be there, but it must be investigated, and if a Naga is hiding there, they must be slain. Who is with me?" he called out in a ringing tone, and everyone in the room stood as one.

"We are all ready to help rid the Land of the Naga threat!" Balor answered for all of them.

Chapter 10

It did not take very long for them to garb themselves appropriately, reassembling in the huge dining hall afterward.

"My Lord, he will see us coming," Balor whispered to Erinn, his concern tinging his words.

"I think not," Erinn grinned, pointing to Deborah, who was now nearly completely aflame. Balor was shocked at the transformation, as her hair was flame red, and her eyes a shockingly bright amber color. She was surrounded by flames, or so it appeared to Balor, and she also seemed taller than usual to his eyes.

"Yer Lady is aflame," he said in a rumbling tone.

"Indeed, as she is a Phoenix woman, 'twould be usual for her to go into battle like that," Erinn explained. "I assure ye, she has complete control, and no one in our group will be harmed by her. I have seen it before," he grinned. "This Naga has no idea what she can do, and so 'twill be a most entertaining experience, I think, to watch her."

"Entertaining?" Balor questioned within his mind, thinking that would not have been the word he would have chosen. Still, he had heard the tales of the Phoenix woman, and was curious to see if they were true.

Finally, the order was given to move out, and a brilliant portal of light appeared just outside the door to the cave fortress. "We will return soon," he assure those who remained behind. "And we will return victorious, I am certain of it. Cold ale would be most appreciated up on our return," he suggested with a slight smile.

"All will be ready for our troops, My Lord," Cethlenn assured him. "The hunters have been out this morning already, and I am told that two huge wild boars have been snagged. I daresay with the Auroch meat we have left over for hand pies, we will have plenty for a hearty meal upon yer return, My Lord. Bring our people home to us?"

"I shall, Madam, and I shall bring them home alive," he promised, his tone filled with confidence, as he could feel the Goddess was with them.

"Thank ye, My Lord," he heard several of the women say as he bowed and took his leave of them. He was the last one to pass through the portal, closing it behind him, and once they were all on the other side, they quickly formed ranks and began the short journey.

When they found the compound, it was clear why Erinn had not been able to detect it until now. The place was in an underground cave, the entrance secreted by magickal means, which is how Deborah found it.

"Here My Lord," she said, pointing to it. "I know it looks solid enough, but once the magick is dispelled, ye will see a huge opening."

Erinn simply waved his hand a few times and suddenly, the screening spell shattered, falling like broken pieces of mirrored glass to the ground. However, it was a nearly noiseless shattering, and it allowed Erinn's troops to further penetrate the place without raising an alarm. No guards stood at hand anywhere, a testimony to the Naga's arrogance, but Erinn knew they were being watched nonetheless. Deborah kept to the middle of the group, not wanting the Naga to detect her presence just yet as she used her will to rein in her powers.

Finally, they arrived in a huge chamber with vaulted ceilings, and Erinn suddenly realized why he had not seen the place for so long. There were silver tracings all through the walls, which Erinn recognized as *Mythrill*. No wonder then, he marveled, as he reckoned the vast store of the rare metal that was locked into the stone of the cave.

"Ye see that?" he asked Drake mentally, pointing to the walls and ceiling.

"I feel that," Drake answered with a grin. "I do believe this entire cave is one large deposit, one that rightfully belongs to our family. I think 'tis time to call for our host, aye?"

"Be my guest," Erinn laughed a bit at his father's feral anticipation. "I know ye have been looking forward to this battle for a long time."

"Hold there!" they both heard, and turned to see Deborah now completely surrounded by flames. Her voice was different as well, and both men understood it was not just Deborah speaking now, that the Goddess herself had come to speak through her. "Whatever ye might think, the Naga is *mine*! Without his leadership, they would have never lasted so long, nor been able to advance their perverse breeding program so far. It all must end here, and so I claim the Naga as my prey!"

"As ye will, Great Lady," both Erinn and Drake said at the same time.

It was just then that a huge roar could be heard, alarms began to sound and people came streaming out of every door in the room. They were all armed in some way; kitchen knives, pitchforks, shovels, axes, whatever they had been able to pick up when the Naga's magickal compulsion had come upon them. They rushed the armed Knights and Dames wildly, by the compulsion they were under, they were uncaring as to their own deaths. Even the Giants were confronted by members of their own kind, those who had been taken years earlier and been kept to do the Naga's will. They came to fall upon their fellows in a blind, mad rush and was no choice but to defend themselves. Cries of pain could be heard, and trickles of blood began to run on the floor of the cave compound.

Erinn and Drake took opposite sides of the conflict, managing each side equally due to their mental link, while Deborah stood on the dais in the room, waiting for her prey to appear. Calla stood on one side, Lillith on the other, the two daughters set to guard their mother against any assault. It did not take long for them to be engaged, especially when another roar could be heard and a gigantic beast with seven heads made its way into the room. Deborah acted at once, using her abilities to assure he remained a Naga, knowing he would be vulnerable that way despite the virulent poison in its teeth.

"Let me go!" the thing commanded, used to getting its way. "I am Apophos the Mighty. I cannot be contained!"

"Is that so?" Deborah asked, a hint of humor in her tone. "We will see about that. I am Deborah Natanleod, the High Lady of the Land, and ye will remain as ye are, *worm*!"

"Ye are no one to command *ME*!" Apophos roared out in frustration, finding that he was indeed confined to his snake body.

"Ye are mistaken," he heard the response, and everyone in the place felt the change of presence occur. "I can command anyone, anywhere on this world. I am the Goddess here, not ye!"

It was only then that Apophos took a closer look at the woman wielding all that power, and a gasp could be heard as he regarded the Phoenix aura around her.

"Impossible!" he finally said. "Veronica's daughter is dead!"

"She is *not* dead," he heard the response, tinged with cold laughter. "She is very much alive, and now High Lady of the Land, which means she can channel MY abilities in full. Yer plans and machinations have come back to haunt ye, and ye will be utterly destroyed by yer own creation. I find that intensely satisfying, and I shall watch with pleasure as she takes yer life, at last. Once ye are gone, the others will be easy to find and eradicate, and then, victory will be mine. I hope ye enjoy the reward that awaits ye," She finished with a cold laugh.

By this time, Deborah's height had grown to that of one of the Giants, and she was floating a good distance off the ground. Everyone noticed, even those fighting for the Nagas, and the battle ceased as they stared at Deborah. A cup of wine appeared in her hand, a loaded pipe followed after, and she took a deep dosage of the fragrant Herb that appeared, floating in front of her. Once the dosage had been consumed, the pipe disappeared, a sikar replaced it, and a smile of satisfaction appeared on the High Lady's face.

"Ye are making a mockery of me, and I shall not have it! I am the rightful ruler here, and ye are MINE!" Apophos screamed out, struggling to throw off the spell that kept him as a snake,

"She is not yers," Erinn's voice came into it as he came to stand beside her. "She is mine, ye are too late, and now ye will pay the price for bringing yer invasion force to the Land. Go to it, my dear," he looked up at Deborah to say.

She said naught, simply calling up more of her abilities, until the Flameblades appeared around her, looking like fiery feathers. Apophos screamed and struggled, trying to loosen the magickal bonds around him, to no avail as Deborah simply tightened them further. The pain that caused him set off a long and angry diatribe, all of which ended dramatically for the vile creature.

"Ye are mine, I made ye! Ye will not defeat me!" he screamed out, and Deborah chose that moment to launch a single Flameblade, which went through his wide open mouth and down his throat, settling into his innards. Apophos screamed in agony, but such would not be the worst of it for the evil Naga. The flaming feather set him afire inside, and as he was a fat, bloated thing, he burned hot and quick. Deborah simply watched with a curious expression on her face as he died a little bit at a time, screaming and writhing throughout the entire experience. In the end, all that was left was a flaccid snake skin, which fell to the ground with a loud, wet thump, and Deborah's Phoenix aura faded at once. She fell into Erinn's arms then, exhausted from her exertions and from channeling the Goddess' presence, and he caught her easily, as if she weighed nothing.

"Master Ishmael," she called out, her voice still strong despite her physical weariness. "I have a task for ye."

"Ye have only to command me, My Lady," he said, kneeling at her feet.

"I would like ye to tan this hide for me, and keep it very supple. I think I shall make a dress from it," she laughed a bit in Erinn's arms, and a ripple of chuckles ran around the room at the very idea of her wearing the skin of such a creature as a dress.

"I shall keep it all one piece then, My Lady, and assure that 'tis soft and very flexible."

"Thank ye Master ben Cain," she said softly, the weariness beginning to show. "Husband, I am tired. May we go to the family house for some peace and quiet?"

"Aye, at once, Wife," he agreed, turning to Karpon. "Take command, My Lord War Duke, and see that our troops get home. I shall return in a few days to hand out largesse to all of those who have been with us, and ye have my thanks for yer service."

"Thank ye My Lord, but to see Apophos destroyed in such a manner is reward enough for us," Balor spoke for all of the Giants, who stood there silently astonished at what they had just seen. The force that had come with Erinn was equally astonished, except for those who had already seen what Deborah could do when her abilities were roused.

Azeem ben Cain stood rooted to where he stood, his mind going over and over what he had seen. Finally, he was able to move a bit, and walked to where Ishmael now stood beside the steaming snake skin.

"Brother, what *was* that?" he asked quietly.

"Azeem, do ye remember the stories our Mother used to tell about the Phoenix bird's magickal abilities? How they could summon and wield fire as if it were a weapon?"

"Aye, I remember now," Azeem answered, his mind suddenly accepting what he had seen. "I only thought of that as a story, I never accepted that such skills could be real," he said softly. "She is a Goddess."

"She can certainly channel one," Ishmael chuckled. "Come brother, help me lift this skin so we can carry it back to my tannery. I shall need yer help to get it on the stretching rack, and to finish scraping the inner side. My Lord, may we go?"

"Of course," Erinn grinned, simply thinking that a portal should be there. It appeared right where he wanted it to, big enough to transport any amount of people who wished to go. "Ye are all excused to go home now that the battle is over. I shall see to cleaning up the place," he said and Karpon nodded.

"Very well, My Lord. Come my friends, let us depart, so that our Giantish friends might celebrate their homecoming in private. Farewell, Master Balor. I hope ye and I might speak soon about putting a small detachment of troops here."

"We would be honored to house them," Balor responded sincerely.

"Excellent!" Erinn smiled, wanting to extend the Grip, but since he was holding Deborah in his arms, he could not. Balor understood the situation, and a smile appeared on his face too. "Calla? Lillith? Are ye coming to the family house?"

"We should return to the Capitol House, Father, since ye and Mother are going to take a few days' rest. We will be there to organize yer correspondence, at least."

"Such an act would be muchly appreciated," Erinn answered, his gratitude obvious. "I would imagine 'twill be a feast, since Master Balor is sending an entire Auroch to the House for the occasion."

"O! How fun!" Lillith said, for she loved parties, especially those held outside.

"I can hardly wait!" Calla added, her excitement just as clear. "How are ye getting the meat to the House?"

"Just like this," Erinn grinned, snapping his fingers dramatically. A small portal opened, and the girls could see the party grounds on the other side, where Klietos was already preparing for an outdoor meal. His surprised gasp when the meat appeared in the preparation areas brought a wider smile to Erinn's face, and the Kitchen Master expressed his thanks.

"My Lord! Ye have sent us an entire Auroch! We will have meat for days!"

"Good, I like my Army well fed," Erinn answered, turning back to Lillith and Calla. "Daughters? The portal will take ye directly home, if ye chose to use it."

"I want to use it," Lillith declared. "I am dirty and sweaty, I want to bathe and dress comfortably. It looks like 'tis hot at the House."

"Me too! Thank ye Father, for providing our way home!" the two young women said together. Taking their horses' reins in hand, they said their farewells and led them through the aperture. They were followed by the rest of the Army, until it was just Erinn and Deborah remaining.

"I am glad ye are finally home, and ready to assume yer former duties," the High Lord said in parting. "Farewell, Master Balor, and Madam Cethlenn. I hope to see ye again soon."

"Farewell, My Lord and Lady," Balor spoke for all. "Thank ye for allowing us to return to our home. We also look forward to seeing the both of ye again."

With that, Erinn nodded to show respect, then a portal opened suddenly right in front of them all. Erinn walked Deborah through, then it closed behind them, leaving the Giants to return to their work of returning their home to good working order.

When the two of them appeared just outside of the huge, rustic house in Dragon Valley, Erinn put Deborah on her feet, then put her hand on his arm to escort her inside. Once they were within, Deborah wanted to sleep and so Erinn helped her up the stairs into the room they used while there. Putting her to bed, he closed the curtains, leaving the windows ajar to provide a bit of cool air to help her sleep.

"Sleep well, love. I shall attend to supper, ye need not worry. We are here to relax, which is precisely what I want ye to do. Ye have accomplished a great task, the ridding of one of the worst of the Nagas from the Land. I am grateful that ye are still with me after that."

"I am glad to still be with ye as well, Erinn," he heard her say. "I love ye."

"I love ye too," he replied softly, closing the door, leaving it ajar, just a bit.

While he went downstairs to the cold room to choose their supper, Calla and Lillith bathed quickly, then returned to their rooms for clean clothing. The day was very hot, promising a very warm night, and they dressed sparsely, both of them choosing a brief outfit much like the Amazons generally wore. Such clothing exposed more than it covered, leaving them free to move about, and they braided each other's hair tight to the head, leaving long, neat braids running down their backs. Once they were dressed, they ran downstairs and through the kitchen, wanting to get to the party field as quickly as possible. Gwendolyn saw them dash through the busy room, heading for the garden door, which was the shortest path to the wide swath of green.

"I wish I still looked like that," she thought to herself as she observed their fine musculature, well-defined and lithe. "Ye two girls have a good time!" she called after them.

"Thank ye Madam Gwendolyn!" they responded as one, closing the door behind them before speeding down the path, racing to be the first to the cooking area. It did not take them long to arrive at the station where Klietos and his brothers were even now preparing the Auroch for cooking. They had cut it into quarters, which would help it cook faster, and Klietos was standing in front of a huge metal bowl, surrounded by jars of spices and herbs.

"Good afternoon, Master Klietos!" the two young women called out, and the older man turned, his face registering both surprise and pleasure to see them. He was also appreciative of the brief outfits they wore, which displayed their considerable charms very well, and it took a moment for him to regain his composure.

"Good afternoon, Daughters of the House," he called back. "Yer arrival is most fortuitous, as ye can save me a bit of work if ye would?"

"How can we be of service?"

Klietos smiled at their willing attitude. "Do ye remember how to make yer Grandfather's rub mix for meat?"

"Aye!" they both replied, grinning widely.

"Then may I impose upon the two of ye to fill these four bowls with enough rub to cover a quarter Auroch?" he asked.

"We would be happy to help ye with that!" they both replied, laughing at the unison of their responses. "We will get to work right now!"

"Thank ye," Klietos smiled, leaving them to it.

The two young women quickly sorted out the herbs and spices they needed, and using the huge mortar and pestle at hand, they began the process of grinding the ingredients together. While they were so occupied, a small crowd of men gathered around the cooking area, and when they spied the two young women working together, they could not help but wander over.

They were treated to quite the picture, for the first bowl of herbs and spices was now ground fully, and ready to be mixed. Without a thought, the two bent over the huge bowl and used their hands to begin stirring and turning the ingredients, as they had been taught to do. Such a thing provided a fine view of their well-tanned, well-defined bodies, and so the quiet comments began.

"Just look at that," one of them said. His name was Lux, and he had admired the two young women from afar for a long time, knowing full well they were out of his reach. Still, he could not help but notice that they were very well muscled, especially Lillith. Her muscles rippled like taut cords, and he felt inadequate next to her as he looked over his own body's definition, finding it wanting.

He was not the only man comparing himself to the two gorgeous young swordmaines, many of the other men, old and young, were doing the same as they watched the two young women work. The older men just walked away, each with a heavy sigh, but the oldest man among them expressed what they were all thinking.

"Ah, if only I were thirty years younger. Takin' one of them on at my age, it'd kill me, but what a way to go," he chuckled wryly. The others joined in his laughter as they all walked off, headed for the ale cask and the comfort of other men. The young men watching Lillith and Calla did not leave, instead, they began to find ways to be of service to them, just to have the chance to talk to them.

"My goodness, it certainly is hot out here," Calla said after they finished the second bowl of rub.

"Would ye like a cold ale?" Lux asked at once. "I would be happy to fetch one for each of ye, so ye do not have to leave yer work station."

"Thank ye!" both young women answered at once, for their mouths were dry and their throats a bit parched from their work. Lux was gone in a flash, then back just as fast with two brimming, cold cups of brown ale. Both women took the cups, nodded their thanks, then downed them like troopers, not stopping until they finished. Wiping their mouths then on a clean napkin, they handed the cups back to Lux with another thank you.

"Would you like another cup?" he asked.

"I would!" Lillith answered emphatically.

"I would too!" Calla put in.

The rest of that afternoon, all while the two young women made four huge bowls of the rub mix for the meat, Lux was their servitor, running back and forth to the ale cask for them. When they finally finished the task, they decided to take a swim, and Lux tailed along after them. In fact, he followed the both of them around all night, along with a few other hopeful young men. Calla and Lillith began to understand their power over men, and it both frightened and intrigued both of them. As the meat cooked, the party atmosphere continued to grow, Knights and Dames broke out their instruments and lively music sprang up. Dancing soon followed, and while both young women were asked by many, they refused all of them because they were now very tired.

"I want to go to bed now," Lillith whispered to Calla about an hour after they had eaten.

"I am too, let us return to the House for some peace and quiet."

They made ready to leave, only to have their group of young men try to persuade them to remain, one of them putting a hand on Lillith's arm. It was Lux, who had consumed far too much ale, so much so he thought he was owed payment for his volunteered service. Lillith, however, set him straight on the matter.

"Get…your…hand…off…me!" she said, enunciating each word clearly, in ever increasingly angry tones. "I did not give ye permission to touch me." Lux's face took on a series of expressions, finishing with realization, and he quickly unhanded Lillith, mumbling an apology. His friend beside him had consumed much more than ale, and his lusts were now fully engaged. His body was now doing the talking, rather than his mind as he now tried seduction, which had worked on other young women in the past.

"I'd like to do more touching," the young man, whose name was Daile, replied in a seductive tone. Lillith did not waste her time, she simply took his hand off her arm and twisted it at the wrist sharply. Daile yelped in pain and grabbed his wrist, feeling it quickly to make sure it was not broken.

"I told ye to let me go. Never touch me again, unless ye would like more of the same!" Lillith told him.

"You little bitch!" Daile growled, assuming an attack posture. "I'll teach ye!"

"Teach her what?" they heard a deep, resonant voice ask. All of them looked up to see Ishmael ben Cain standing there with his wife

Zameera. "I see ye standing here, bothering the Daughter of the House. I suggest that ye offer yer apology, now!" he went on.

Daile stood there, his heart now racing in fear to be confronted by the huge, black man, who inserted himself between the group of young men, and the two young women. "Well?" Ishmael insisted, his face tight with restrained anger.

"I am sorry I touched ye," Daile said quickly. "I meant no harm."

"Bullshit," Lillith answered in a depreciating tone. "I know full well what ye were thinking, I am a Natanleod. I can hear yer thoughts even now and they are not good ones. Ye are angry and frustrated, ye thought ye could persuade me to be with ye tonight, and are now publicly denied. Go away, and do not talk to either of us ever again."

Daile stood there his mouth gaping with shock, for she had expressed exactly what he had been thinking. He did not linger, simply walking away quickly, headed for his room in the Barracks, which now represented safety to him.

"Are ye well, Calla and Lillith?" Ishmael asked kindly.

"Aye, and we thank ye for yer timely arrival," Lillith answered, still angry. "I would have hurt him very badly if ye hadn't stepped in."

"He had no idea what ye could do to him, young one," Ishmael grinned. "But I did, having seen yer work in the arena. He would have posed no threat to yer skills, for certain."

"I hope he has the good sense to thank ye for what ye did," Calla spit out, her anger evident. "Goodnight, Ishmael ben Cain. Good night Zameera. Ye are looking wonderful!"

"Thank ye, I have finally shed all of that baby weight," she laughed a bit. "I am enjoying being back in the arena, even if on a restricted schedule for the moment."

"Have ye a name for the babies yet?"

"We do, but as always, we will wait until their Naming Day to reveal it. But they are growing and thriving, for which I am grateful. I am very old to be having babies after all. They are our little miracles."

"So they are," Ishmael beamed, the proud father. "Good night, Daughters of the House."

"Good night, both of ye," the young women answered in turn before Ishmael and Zameera walked away.

"Come on, before anyone else wants to start trouble," Calla urged. "I want to take another bath, then I want a pipe and a sikar."

"And some cordial!" Lillith put in, having developed a love for the drink similar to her mother's. Off the two of them went, leaving the rest of the Barracks to enjoy the warm, starry night.

At the family house in the valley, Erinn prepared a simple meal of salmon retrieved from the ice house section of the cold room. He baked the fish with lemon slices and dill, made a pot of wild rice, and cut up a salad, all while Deborah slept. When she finally came back downstairs, the meal was waiting for her, and she ate heartily until her appetite was sated.

"Thank ye Erinn, the meal was truly delicious!" she said. "I am ready for a sikar though, and some cordial."

"I am ready for the same, except I shall choose whiskey," Erinn grinned. "Come, I have everything already set out for us to enjoy."

They sat up until their sikars were finished, and then retired for the night. Deborah slept well, but Erinn tossed and turned until he finally sat up. He felt a presence he had never felt before in the Land, and while he felt no threat from the presence, his curiosity was roused. He got up and summoned his war armor, armed himself fully, then disappeared from the room. Reappearing outside of the house, he stood there and let his senses tell him where to go. Striking out at a good pace, Erinn followed his senses until he reached a thick grove of old trees, or at least that is what they appeared to be. The presence was here, Erinn thought to himself as he worked his way into the center of the grove, finding that the trees had grown up around a bare circle of grass. Erinn was intrigued, for the circle was perfectly round, which would be unusual in Nature. Finally, he strode to the center of the circle, drew his blade, and announced himself.

"I am Erinn Natanleod, the High Lord of the Land. Reveal yerself to me!" he called out to the nameless presence.

"I am here," he heard, a deep, cultured voice answer, and out of the midst of the trees stepped a tall, thin but wiry man. He wore a simple robe, long stained with moss and mulch, and his beard was long and braided into three strands. "I am the Entkeeper."

"Entkeeper?" Erinn repeated, trying to remember where he had heard the term. "Ye have not been seen in the Land for many decades, and no one has seen an Ent for at least that long."

"Ye have seen them today," the Entkeeper laughed merrily, making a gesture to the *trees* surrounding them. Erinn's eyes opened wide to see what he had perceived to be plants changed subtly. Eyes, noses and mouths appeared, as well as arms and legs, and Erinn realized that the Ents had been standing there all along.

"I am a blessed man," he said reverently, for the Ents were the very spirit of the Wildwood. "Our forests have missed yer presence."

"I can see that," the man chuckled. "I have my work laid out before me. I am called Toona."

"I am glad to meet ye," Erinn smiled, offering the Grip. He was astonished at the strength of Toona's grip, which seemed improbable due to his extreme thinness. "Where have ye been?"

"Such a story would require nourishment, and something to soothe my parched throat," Toona chuckled.

"I have drink at the house, and a small river runs right beside it, if yer friends are thirsty too," Erinn replied.

"Ye needn't worry over them," Toona laughed a little harder. "They can see to their own entertainments. Come My Lord, I should like to see if the house is still as I recall it."

Erinn led the way, and they soon found their way back to the rustic lodge-style home where the Natanleods found their rest and relaxation.

"The house has changed considerably," Toona remarked upon his first sight of it.

"Raad burned it, and my father rebuilt it to suit an ever-growing family," Erinn explained. He could see the lights were on inside the house, and when they opened the door, the scent of cooking sausage hit their noses. "Ah, I see my lady is up and about. Come, step over the threshold, my friend. I would imagine she has caffe ready to serve."

"Caffe?" Toona asked.

"Aye, a rich and bitter beverage, one I favor with a spoonful of honey and a shot of good whiskey," Erinn explained. "Such a thing was rare in the Land before, but we grow it now, so we have plenty."

"Excellent, I shall try this drink!" Toona announced grandly as they walked through the common room, seeing that Herb was laid out along with small sikars. "And...what are those?" Toona asked, pointing at the table with a curious expression.

"Those are called sikars, they are made from leaves of tabac, a plant from outside the Land that we also grow here now," Erinn explained again, happy to do so.

"And one would smoke those to enjoy them?"

"Indeed so, and I believe I would like to do that now," Erinn chuckled harder. "Let me go and speak to my wife about having a guest for first meal."

"Yer wife knows already!" he heard from the kitchen, and then Deborah appeared, dressed in comfortable clothing, slippers on her feet, her hair up in a loose bun. "And the Entkeeper is welcome in our home."

"My Lady!" Toona replied, his voice filled with respect. "Excuse me for being a bit bold in my words, but I have seen ye in my dreams of late!"

Turning to Erinn quickly, the man went on with his explanation. "I have a bit of a psychic gift of prophecy, My Lord. I meant to say that I have seen me meeting yer wife for a few weeks now, although I had no idea what I was seeing. I did not mean to offend."

"Of course not," Erinn replied genially, glad for the man's clarification. "But I find it interesting to know that the Lady has gone to such effort to pre-introduce ye to my wife."

"Yer wife is High Lady, she is the Goddess' direct representative in a different way than the High Priestess. How is Elanor?"

"My aunt passed on relatively recently. I miss her wise counsel a great deal," Erinn replied smoothly.

"I am sorry for yer loss, My Lord," Toona replied sincerely, a pair of tears falling from the corners of his old eyes. "She was a great, magnificent woman. May she be reborn in the Land, and very soon."

"Thank ye, my friend, for such a wish," Erinn smiled. "Now my wife, how long do we have before our meal is served?"

"How long do ye want it to take?" Deborah laughed a bit. "I have the sausage in the oven on a low temperature, along with cubed papas. They will wait for a long time, if necessary. I shall simply add two fried eggs to each plate to finish the meal, and I have biscuits already done."

"Ye are a marvel of organization, my dear," Erinn smiled broadly, and it hit Toona that these two were a love match, something a bit rare among nobles. "Come and join our conversation, if ye would?"

"Gladly, I have always wanted to meet the Entkeeper," Deborah smiled warmly. "Are they out there?"

"They are, at least some of them. The rest are a few days behind us."

"I see," Deborah nodded. "Are there many more now?"

"Aye, there are Ent children now too," Toona smiled. "Which is why we have returned. Are we still at war with the Nagas?"

"Aye, but we are slowly stamping them out now, since Secundus and Raad are dead."

"O my goodness, I have missed a great story, I think!" Toona exclaimed. "But, ye have brought me here so I could tell a story, aye?"

"Aye," Erinn smiled as he lit the pipe and passed it to the man. Toona took a great long dose, choking a bit at the end due to the length of time it had been since he had imbibed. Erinn offered him a cup of ale to help soothe his throat, noting that the drink disappeared quickly.

"The Herb in the Land has grown in strength and sweetness!" he exclaimed. "I am glad to see that!"

After they had all shared a pipe or two, Erinn clipped a sikar for Toona, then one for Deborah, and finally one for himself. He showed the man how to enjoy them, cautioning him not to inhale deeply, and demonstrating a few times. Toona seemed to learn quickly, Erinn noted, and soon was sitting back with the sikar, truly enjoying it.

"I am glad to be home," he finally said, drawing a heavy sigh. "Is there a chance I might talk to yer father?"

"Who knows?" Erinn chuckled. "As an Ascended one, he could be right here in the room and we would not know 'till he decided to reveal himself."

"I know ye would like to hear about where I have been," he finally said after a few moments. "But if ye would indulge a request, I would like to hear of how Secundus was slain and by whom, and who killed Raad?"

"I killed Secundus," Erinn replied, a trace of a smile playing at the corners of his mouth at the memory. "My Father killed Raad in a fair swordfight, with witnesses to tell the tale, myself included."

"O..." Toona said, a touch of wonder in his tone. "And ye are certain they are truly dead?"

"Secundus went to the Goddess without his head on his body, and Raad had a Mythrill sword thrust straight to the heart," Erinn replied seriously. "Their bodies were burned to ashes. They are most certainly dead. I can show ye if ye would like to see it."

"Ye can do that?"

"Aye," Erinn confirmed gravely. "As High Lord, I can do many things. Why I was not able to detect ye 'till ye entered the Valley, however, I do not understand."

"We were in one of the small, isolated worlds with a barrier around it," Toona answered at once. "The world of the Saurians provided a good screen for us, so that the Nagas could not follow or find us."

"I see," Erinn nodded, something falling into place for him. "So, now I understand why they were so set on removing the barrier from that world. 'Twas not the Saurians they were after, 'twas ye and yer Ents!"

"I was sorry to see that," Toona nodded.

"Ye saw Ulric's death?"

"I did, and the young man who was with him faced his death with great courage as well. I have never seen anything more beautiful than the courage of their passing. Surely, they will be re-born in the Land quickly!"

While they spoke, a small, tattered sail appeared on the horizon, just off the coast of the Land. By the will of the Goddess, it found its way into the current stream that led to the gates of the Port City, and it managed to evade the Kraken that guarded the gates. The small, battered ship floated up to one of the docks and nudged to a halt, bobbing against the wharf while the dock men tied it securely.

"Ahoy!" Decker, the man in charge of such things called out in a friendly tone. "Is there anyone aboard?"

Faint noises could be heard, and then footsteps up a ladder, and then more footsteps on the deck until a man appeared at the top of the ramp.

"Thank God the Father, we are safe at last!" he spoke out in a reverent tone.

"If ye are here in the Land, then no father god brought ye here," Decker chuckled. "Welcome in the name of the Goddess, who has saved yer life."

"There is no such thing as a goddess!" the man shouted at Decker in an angry, fanatical tone. "To think so is heresy!"

"Well, ye can call it that if ye want to," Decker chuckled harder, and the other men around him joined in. "We call it gratitude, those of us who have been brought here by Her mercy. Ye should be more mindful, if ye wish to stay."

"Who are ye to threaten ME?" the man clad all in black demanded. "I am the Lord's Prophet, and ye are naught but a damned heretic! Stand aside, and let us pass!"

It was at that moment that Decker mentally summoned the Lord of the city, Triton, who appeared suddenly at his side.

"What is amiss?"

"This *person* is recently arrived in the Land due to the Goddess' intervention, but he will not acknowledge Her gift. And he is being very rude as well, proclaiming us all damned," the Captain of the Day Guard told his Lord, a bit of laughter in his tone at the very suggestion of damnation for believing in the Goddess.

"Rudeness is not tolerated in the Land," Triton responded at once, turning to the man, observing him keenly. The first thing Triton noticed was the smell that hung around the man, he smelled abominable as if he had not bathed in years. Also, he was dressed in what looked like a long, black frock that was faded and patched in many places, sometimes with multiple patches. The hem of the garment was tattered and torn, and but the man's boots looked relatively new. He was grossly fat, and heavily unshaven as well, his hair was unruly, as if he had not brushed it that morning, or for many mornings as far as Triton could tell. "What is yer name?"

"And who are ye to demand my name?" the foreigner responded in hot tones. "I am a preacher of the Holy Word. I do not account to ye!"

"As to who I am, I am in charge of deciding whether ye stay or go," Triton told him matter-of-factly. "And right now, I am leaning towards ejecting ye from the Land. We will call the High Lord, such things are his province, after all," Triton continued. Taking a moment to compose himself, as his anger was kindled toward the rude man in front of him, he reached out with his mind, looking for Erinn's.

"What may I do for ye, Lord Triton?" he heard Erinn's soothing tones.

"I have someone new here in the Port City, My Lord. Perhaps ye should come and talk to him. He seems very confused."

"I shall come and help him then," Erinn replied, and Triton noted the tone was slightly amused.

All the while, Triton kept looking at the seven women with the dirty, filthy man, and to his eyes they appeared to be identical sisters. The eldest looked to be no more than thirty years of age to his eyes, and the rest of them younger in descending years. What would such women be doing with this lout, Triton asked himself in wonder as he felt the High Lord's presence, then saw him arrive in a flash.

"Where is this man? My wife is waiting for me to continue our short holiday," Erinn asked, very business-like.

"He is right here, My Lord."

"And does he have a name?" Erinn inquired coolly.

"I can speak for myself!" the man said in a hostile tone. "Ye needn't talk about me as if I were not standing right here!"

"Ah, but I would imagine ye talk about yer women that way," Erinn replied, his voice dropping a bit and taking on a very harsh tone. "Ye are one of those who profess to follow the ways of Jesus the Christ, or Yeshua as He would have been known to His people, am I correct?"

"There is no other path other than that of the Christ. *Ye* have read the Bible?"

"Of course I have, so I might be able to converse with such as ye upon necessity. I shall tell ye plainly that we follow the Goddess' way here. We do not have temples or shrines to other gods, of any kind, and I would imagine that ye would find yer message falling upon deaf ears, should ye choose to practice the usual way for such as yerself. I am the High Lord, Erinn Natanleod. If ye are to remain in the Land, 'tis best for ye to acquaint yerself with Her way."

"I shall not accept such heresy!" the man blustered, and Erinn watched the women cower in fear. So, he hits them when he is angry, the High Lord noted, and his face tightened with outrage as he mentally called for his wife's presence.

"My dear, could ye join me please? Ye will have seven new charges to welcome, if things go the way I think they will here in the Port City."

"I shall be there shortly," he heard her response, and from the terse tone, he guessed she was aware of the situation he faced. "Try not to kill him before I get there?" she laughed coldly. Erinn shared her humor in a similar vein as their connection severed and he turned back to the fuming man in front of him. "I have given ye my name, and here in the Land 'tis considered to be rudeness for ye not to do the same."

"Very well, my name is Virilitas. I come directly from the Mother Church in Rome, and I am empowered by the Pope himself!"

"Which means naught to me," Erinn grinned a bit at the man's pompous nature. "Yer Pope would have no voice in the Land, indeed, the Goddess might call for his head for his crimes against women, and those of other faiths. How big is his harem now?" he asked in a taunting tone. In his mind, the Goddess was with him, and he heard Her warning to step back a pace or two from the huge, fat, slovenly man.

"He is about to get exactly what he has earned by his words and deeds," She said softly. Erinn simply complied, knowing that Her warning would be a timely one as he continued his conversation.

"Also, I have been waiting to discuss your book with a learned man of yer faith. If ye are from Rome, ye must be well-learned, and able answer my few, simple questions."

"Of course I can," the man continued, his tone now taking on note of sarcasm.

"Very well then," Erinn smiled, and Triton noted that it was a feral expression. "In the very first book, Genesis, there are two stories of Creation. Which one is the true one, or are they both true?" he asked innocently.

"There are not two stories of Creation!" the man denied. Erinn simply called a copy of the book to him from the Library at the Capitol House and showed the man chapter, verse and line.

"There, ye see?" Erinn pressed. "First yer god made man and women equally, then when he was displeased with His Creation, He took a rib from Adam and remade them as copies of one another, male and female. I would imagine that Eve looked a great deal like Adam in such a case, aye? That would bother me, and most men in the Land, to have their wife look like their sister."

The itinerant preacher's face turned red, and he puffed as he answered, for his outrage had been kindled.

"What are ye trying to say?" he asked in hot tones, drawing himself up to his full height, which was still a full head beneath Erinn's chin.

"I am simply asking questions of a learned man, so that I might achieve understanding," Erinn answered plainly. "Also, is it yer god's plan to wipe out everyone on the planet that does not follow him? All of the genocide, rape and child murder described in the older part of the book seems a horrific thing to me. And then yer god called up a flood to wipe out His Creation. What benevolent god would slay his own for practicing the free will he gave to them?" Erinn pressed. "And one more thing," he went on as Virilitas' face turned redder and redder, until it was nearly purple. "If yer god created the Earth, along with everything and everyone, and if Adam and Eve were the only two creations of god on the planet, then where did Cain's wife come from? Yer book says he stumbles out of the desert to find a women, so where did she come from if yer god created the only people on the Earth?"

Virilitas stood there, shaking with rage and confusion. He had never been confronted by anyone like this before, and he did not know how to deal with it. His frustration led to anger, and as always, he attempted to vent his anger on one of the women behind him, only to have Erinn restrain him with a strong hand on his arm.

"If ye touch them in anger, I shall kill ye!" he said in a growling tone. "I shall not allow them to be abused by someone such as ye!"

"Ye cannot stop me, I am their husband. I own them, and 'tis naught ye can do about it!" Virilitas shouted back, now trembling with religious fervor. "I can see why God has led me here, ye are all godless heathens!" he shouted out, causing many of the citizens to turn and stare, most of them with simple curiosity.

"I am the High Lord here, and I rule. Women are not to be harmed here in the Land. I can and shall stop ye from doing so!" he returned, noting that Deborah had just arrived, as had Drake.

"Ye have naught to say about it!" Virilitas screamed back, his anger now fully aflame. "I can treat them as I please. They are women, cursed by God for their dealings with Satan! They deserve every beating they receive!" he continued on, still unable to move due to Erinn's restraining hand.

"Ye cannot treat them evilly, not here in the Land, not as long as I live to prevent it. The Goddess will simply not allow ye to do so, and if I cannot stop ye, She will."

"I shall simply take my women and go then. Ye cannot stop me!" Virilitas screamed in a high pitched tone. "As God is my witness, ye are all cursed! May God strike me down if I am lying!" he went on, raising his staff to the sky and looking up in an expectant manner. He did not receive what he was expecting however, for clouds had been gathering over the Port City while he had been arguing with Erinn. As soon as the words were out of his mouth, a huge bolt of lightning descended out of the clouds and struck the top of the staff, traveling down and through the body of the dirty preacher. The man instantly disappeared, his scream of pain cut off as his body was reduced to ashes, and a small spot of black on the ground. His boot prints remained on each side of the small black, oily spot, a testament of the man who had stood there. As soon as it happened, a gasp could be heard from the women, and they all fell to the ground as if released from puppet strings, released from whatever enslavement he had over them. Once the crowd calmed and business resumed in the Port City, Drake strode to stand beside Erinn, a grin on his face when he saw what remained of the vile man.

"Well done, my son," he said quietly.

"I did not do that," Erinn answered in a similar tone, and then they both turned at the same time, fixing Deborah with inquisitive glares.

"I had naught to do with that. Ye have seen the Goddess take a direct hand, something rare even here in the Land. Surely, a day to remember," she finished with a slight smile, walking to where the seven women now stood, each looking a little lost. "Sisters, do not fear. No one here will harm ye, or the others. Ye are free."

"F…Free?" the older woman stuttered a bit.

"Aye, he is no more. Our Goddess has found him wanting. Now he will enter the cycles of incarnation again, hopefully to learn his lessons this time. Would ye tell me yer names? I am Deborah Natanleod, I am the High Lady of the Land, and I would like to help ye."

"He…he is really dead and gone?" the older women asked in a quavering voice.

"Come and see for yerself," Deborah invited, extending her hand to assist the woman to her feet. Helping her to walk the short distance, Deborah showed her the small, oily black spot between two boot prints, the pile of ash quickly disappearing in the ocean breezes. "He is most certainly dead."

"Good!" the older woman hissed out, her anger apparent. She hawked up a huge blob of phlegm and spit it out on the spot in disgust. "There, 'tis all ye deserve, bastard!" she screamed at the spot, finding it a very purging experience. Afterwards, she turned to the others embracing each of them with joy and tears, glad to be rid of their tormentor.

"We would like to bathe if possible?" she asked. "My name is Martine. We have all been together so long, we feel as if we are truly sisters. May I introduce us?"

"Of course, we would like to be able to call ye all by name," Deborah smiled warmly, and Martine felt as if she were being embraced.

"My Lady, here is Christina and Marian, and these two are Rachael and Eve, and finally, our two youngest sisters, Esther and Hannah."

"Welcome to the Land, all of ye," Deborah greeted. "If ye will gather around me, I shall take ye to where ye can bathe and dress in clean clothing. Are ye hungry? If so, we will make sure to feed ye."

"I am hungry," Hannah's voice could barely be heard it was so soft. "We have not eaten for days, any of us."

"And yet he was fat enough," Deborah growled. "I am glad the Lady has brought ye here, so I can look after ye. Come now, let us depart. I shall take ye to our house in the Capitol City, and ye will be welcome there too. Husband, shall we go?"

"Indeed, I am ready for ale and a sikar. I have a bad taste in my mouth after dealing with such a fellow."

"Excuse me, My Lord?" Triton spoke up, still staring at the spot on the dock. "But what shall we do about that?" he asked, pointing.

"Leave it as a reminder to everyone about offending the Goddess," Erinn smiled. "Besides, I like it," he added fiercely.

"I do too," Drake chimed in, a grin on his face.

"My Lord?" Decker put in.

"Aye?"

"What would ye like me to do with that filthy, vermin-ridden ship they came in?"

Erinn's first thought was to simply have it burnt, but another thought occurred to him as he stood there.

"How long has it been since the Kraken that guards our port has fed?" he asked, loudly enough for the seven new arrivals to hear.

"Months, My Lord, and the pickings have been relatively slim of late," Decker grinned.

"Have the ship loaded with meat for the beast, and set the ship to sail past the beast's lair," Erinn ordered quietly.

"Very well," Decker nodded. "I happen to know the cold rooms all over the Land are being emptied in preparation for the coming harvest, and the house of the Port Lord is no exception. My Lord Triton, may I have yer permission to send a few stout Marines up to fetch what is unsuitable for people to eat?"

"Of course, I was wondering what to do with all of that meat that is ice-burnt," Triton nodded. "I shall send word for a wagon to be loaded for ye."

"Thank ye, My Lord!" Decker smiled wide, saluting in the way of the Land before calling to his mates and heading up to the huge house that overlooked the beautiful port.

While Erinn waited for the ship to be loaded, which did not take all that long in his mind, he conversed with the citizens passing by him. They all felt comfortable talking to him, as he never put on airs or talked down to them. He spoke to them in warm tones, using the words they used, never demeaning or being condescending towards them. Because he was so genial, people just talked to him as if they were talking to a neighbor, and so Erinn learned a great deal from each of them about how the mood in the Land was running. After speaking with them, he knew they were happy, well-fed and content, just as they should be, he thought to himself as he watched the last of the almost frozen meat be loaded on to the ship. Some of it was quite odiferous, having been frozen for almost a year and now nearly thawed, but Erinn knew that would make little difference to the Kraken. The High Lord was simply grateful that the food would not be wasted as he watched them lash the wheel and sails in the proper place to guide the ship to the Kraken's lair.

The entire complement of people standing about also turned to watch, including the seven women who had been recently freed. They watched the small ship enter the current outside the gate, which lead right past the lair of the beast. Their shock was complete when they saw the huge tentacles covered with huge suckers reach up out of the deep, curl themselves around the ship and then draw it beneath the waves.

"Such a beast is *real*?" Martine asked in fear.

"Aye," Erinn answered at once. "There are many things here in the Land which have become legendary in yer world due to the predation of men, and the lack of belief. The Kraken is only one of them, as ye will soon learn as ye continue to live here. Now, I am ready to return home," he said. "Come and gather round me, all of ye, and we shall go there without delay."

The women simply did as they were instructed, not knowing what to expect. When the portal opened, they all gasped in unison, as they had never seen such a thing before. They were all shivering due to the brief exposure to the biting cold, and then the heat of full noon hit them as they stood at the back door of the kitchen.

"Let us go in," Deborah encouraged with a smile. "A bath and fresh clothing will put ye to rights, and then a hot meal."

"A bath *and* a meal?" Esther and Hannah both said at the same time.

"Of course," Deborah smiled at their surprise. "Come now, before the baths get crowded. We will use the upstairs one, but we should still hurry, unless ye do not mind communal bathing."

"O!" they all said in shock, and Deborah understood they were still thinking as if they were in the outside world.

"Ye need not do so if it makes ye feel uncomfortable," Deborah replied. "But, we should go now, so ye can be finished before the first housework crew of the day gets there."

"Lead the way, please?" Martine asked. "I am ready to wash away my old life, and embrace a new one."

Finis

The adventure continues in Book 18...